Saxon Blo[illegible]

Book 4 in the
Wolf Brethren series
By
Griff Hosker

Published by Sword Books Ltd. 2013

A CIP catalogue record for this title is available from the British Library.
Cover image by Design for Writers

Dedication

Dedicated to those new readers who appear to like the Saxon series. I enjoy writing about the Warlord of Rheged and there may be more in this series.

Part 1

The rescue

Chapter 1

Mona 599 A.D

"What I know, Lord Lann, Warlord of Rheged and king killer, is that every Saxon in the land is coming to get you and we have your brothers surrounded. Prince Pasgen is a prisoner in Civitas Carvetiorum and Saxons come from all over the land to kill the Wolf Warrior. When King Aethelfrith comes he will dangle your brothers' heads before you. Is that enough?"

The words of the Saxon chief, who had died, emasculated but defiant, still rang in my ears. Men who have nothing to lose speak the truth and, despite the fact that Myrddyn did not believe him, I did. Had I abandoned all those I loved just to escape to Wales and were they now in danger of losing their own lives? The sanctuary I had created meant nothing if my brothers and their families were dead. I had given them the chance to accompany me and they had spurned the opportunity. They were my brothers and I had made an oath to my dead parents to protect them. You did not break an oath to the dead.

I am Lord Lann of Rheged. I am infamous for wielding Saxon Slayer and for the Saxon kings and champions I have slain. When the king I served was killed and his son became a Saxon vassal, I led those who wished to follow me to Wales where we found sanctuary on the island of Mona. Having won over the people of the island we defended it against the Irish, the Saxons and the Welsh raiders from the mainland but now, when we should be enjoying the fruits of that peace, I would have to consider going to war again. This time the war would be to save my brothers and their families.

Myrddyn, my wizard, had an ability to see beneath the skin, almost beneath the skull and he came to me one evening as I gazed out at the southern seas. Brother Oswald, the priest who organised our weapons and ensured that we had enough to eat, joined us. There were no secrets between the three of us.

"My lord, you are troubled by the words of the Saxon chief?"

"I am, Myrddyn. It is in my mind that he spoke the truth."

"Even if he did, there is little you can do about it. You gave Prince Pasgen and your brothers the chance to escape with you. Your responsibility ended with their decision to remain."

I looked at him trying to fathom the cold mind he had. "Was that how you were able to forget your family when they were killed by the Irish slavers and seek me? Or were you merely working to get me to conquer your home for you?"

I thought he would become angry but he was Myrddyn and he nodded. "A just statement, my lord. I may have used you for my own ends but it has suited you and the sensible men and women of Rheged has it not?"

"And so I should ignore those who tried to fight on and did not run away as I did?"

"I did not say that."

"No but I thought it when I abandoned Aelle and Raibeart."

Brother Oswald spoke for the first time, "You are hard on yourself my lord. You did what you did for the good of all of the people. They have prospered since they reached this golden isle. What would it have benefited them if you had stayed with them? Then you, too, would be in the trap and who would come to save you? "

I suddenly saw it all clearly and I knew what I had to do. "Oswald. Is the army ready to fight? Do we have enough food for the people?"

He hesitated and I saw the hint of a scowl on Myrddyn's face. "Er, yes my lord but if the army is away in Rheged then we would be at the mercy of the Irish and the Saxons."

I wagged my finger at him. "I did not ask that question. I merely asked if the army was ready and you answered yes. Good."

"What is in your mind lord?"

"Another good question, Myrddyn. I believe that Garth and Ridwyn can both command and defend the island as well as I do. Correct?"

"Perhaps."

"Don't play with words Myrddyn. We both know that, as generals, they are better than the Saxons. So if I left them here with my soldiers then the island would be safe and, Brother Oswald, they would be well fed as would the people?"

"Yes my lord."

I could see that I had perplexed Myrddyn. "Would you go to Rheged alone, Lord Lann?"

"No I would take you wizard." I paused for effect and enjoyed the widening of his eyes as I said something he had not expected. "And my horsemen and Miach's finest."

"You would attempt to save Rheged with less than one hundred men?"

I shook my head. "I cannot save Rheged; only an arrogant fool would believe that. I do not think that I am either arrogant or a fool. I can, however, save my family. And I have something the Saxons do not; I have a wizard." I rubbed my hands together. "Brother Oswald, I want as many arrows as can be made in the next week. I want every one of my equites with the best armour that my blacksmith's can make in the time available. I want fifty spare horses and I want you to organise and manage our land while I am away."

He smiled. So long as he knew what he was doing, he was happy. "And Hogan, my lord?"

"He stays here under Garth's tuition and Myfanwy's watchful eye."

Myrddyn smiled for the first time, "I look forwards to you telling her that."

In truth that would be the hard part. She was an intimidating woman and I suspected she would be the woman I would spend the rest of my life with; just not yet! I want sixty equites and forty mounted archers with ten of our scouts and a total of one hundred and fifty horses. So you had better start preparing, priest, and you, wizard, you will need all the spells and potions you can muster."

I left them both speechless and sought my son and Garth. I knew that Tuanthal and Miach would not object to some action but Hogan was a different matter. He had been my squire for some time and he would be offended that I was not taking him. I found Garth first and asked him to accompany me. Hogan was sparring with Pol, who had formerly been my squire. I could see the improvements in Hogan already. A month ago Pol was easily beating my son and barely breaking into a sweat but now he was having to use every trick he had.

I waited until a suitable break in the bout. "Well done; both of you. A word with you my son and then you can spar some more. Garth, come with us if you please." We wandered out of the gate to the cliff top where the sea birds screeched and cried in the sea breeze. Garth and Hogan waited. Everyone knew that I did not speak until ready.

"I am going to take a small party north to Rheged to see if I can aid my brothers."

Garth kept a stony expression on his face but Hogan exploded with joy. "We are going to war!"

"No, I am going to war and you will stay here with Garth to learn to rule this land when I am gone."

His face fell and it was as though I had plunged him into an icy bath. Garth hid his smile. He would sympathise with the boy. "Why leave me behind? Have I displeased you in some way?"

"No, Hogan, but you are the only child I have left and the journey I take will be the most dangerous I have ever undertaken."

"Even more dangerous than sneaking into Morcant Bulc's castle and killing him?" His anger made him indiscreet.

I put my fingers to my lips, "Ssh! We all know that was a ghost but this journey will be more hazardous. Every Saxon in the country will be hunting me and they will expect me to attempt something. I am only taking horsemen and archers. The rest will need to defend the island against our enemies. It is a responsible job I give you." I could see him fighting back tears. He knew that to cry would be to give me another argument and I felt sorry for him. "The skills that Garth and Oswald will teach you will make you a better ruler than I could ever be for I was ill educated and badly trained. I want you to be the one to wield Saxon Slayer when I am gone." He nodded. "Will you do it for me?" In answer he threw his arms around me. "And Garth, will you help to rule the island in my absence?"

"You know that you do not even need to ask my lord. I am, as I ever was, your oathsworn."

Tuanthal and Miach, as I had expected were more than content. The prospect of a ride of more than one hundred and fifty miles through hostile territory did not worry them. They were both consummate warriors; one as an archer and the other as an equite.

"We shall need plenty of arrows, my lord. There will be no re-supply."

"I know Miach, and Brother Oswald has the fletchers working every daylight hour to make as many arrows as he can."

"Aye well, when I tell the lads that we go hunting Saxons they'll be making their own."

"Captain Tuanthal, I want every man as fully armoured as we are. I am taking forty spare horses so that, when we do need them, most will be fresh. I am taking scouts to not only scout, but also to guard the herd. If we can acquire more, then so much the better but we have sufficient."

Tuanthal shook his head. "The Saxons do not use horses. We will have to be careful and husband them." His face creased into a frown. "Will we be taking wagons?"

"No for we will have to ford rivers sometimes."

"Then the horses will have to carry the armour. If we are able I would like to take some mules." He saw Miach's face and he shrugged. "I know, they are awkward and truculent beasts but they can carry great weight and we can eat them when we are hungry."

I nodded. "See the Brother and he will arrange it." I beckoned them closer. "We tell no-one where we are going. There may be Saxon or Irish spies nearby. Your men will need to know we are going to war but let them think it is with those who live across from the Narrows."

Micah picked some meat from his teeth with an arrow- it was most disconcerting. "Do you mind me asking how we are going to get by the Saxons at Deva?" The Saxons had captured Deva from my Strathclyde allies, who now held the fort at the Narrows.

"Simple, we travel further east first and avoid both Deva and Wilderspool." I saw the looks on their faces, "I know, it is unknown territory for us but think on this. We will be the most mobile we have ever been. There will be no shield wall to slow us down. We can move faster than any Saxon and we are strong enough to hold our own with any but the greatest army." I smiled. "This is not a suicide mission. This is not a hunt for glory. I wish to rescue my brothers as quickly and quietly as we can."

Miach burst out laughing. "The Wolf Warrior wants to do things quietly. I tell you Tuanthal, it will be worth going on this just to witness that!" Tuanthal joined in the laughter and, at that moment, I knew that they were with me.

Myrddyn was correct. The hardest one to persuade was Myfanwy. "You are the Warlord of Rheged. Surely one of these other men can trot across the Narrows and fight these animals. Why must it be the lord?"

I could see, behind her, Hogan, Garth and all the others with self-satisfied smiles upon their faces. I stood as tall as I could to muster all the dignity I could manage. "I am lord here and I make the decisions." I could see from her face that she was not convinced. My eyes pleaded with her as I took her hand. "Please, Myfanwy, watch over my son while I am away."

She threw my hand down and snorted, "Well that is the worst insult! As if I wouldn't care for that dear boy while his thoughtless and reckless father is off seeking more glory. Men!" She stormed off but I knew that she would do as I asked.

Everything was ready in the seven short days I had given them. Brother Oswald had copied all of Brother Osric's maps and given them to Myrddyn who guarded them as though they were gold. Pol carried my Wolf Banner and Aedh deputised for Hogan as my squire. As far as the men and the people were concerned we were heading for the mainland to punish the ones who raided our island. There were just the four of us who knew our true destination- Rheged!

Chapter 2

We carried our armour on our horses for the first part of the journey. Although we held our shields and our spears we did not wear our mail shirts. The armour gave us safety and security but they were a heavy weight for the horses. Our scouts, led by Aedh, would range far ahead of us and we would, hopefully, have an early warning of any attack or ambush. Miach and our archers gave us the edge we needed. They were ahead of us and others behind.

We travelled along the valley pausing briefly at the monastery of St. Kentigern. Bishop Asaph greeted us warmly as he always did. He liked the security our presence gave him. While our horses were fed and watered he took the four of us into his cell for some refreshment.

He was a polite man and we ate and drank before he spoke. "You have heard the news then?"

I wondered if he meant the news of my brothers but I had learned to listen more and speak less. It was Myrddyn's way. "What news my lord?"

"Beli ap Rhun has died. He was slain by the Saxons on the eastern borders."

I glanced at Myrddyn who shrugged. We were heading towards the east and might run into this same band of Saxons. "And his son, is he now king?"

"Yes, King Iago was not with his father." He smiled, "I suspect that was planned; that family was always careful."

I had had a working arrangement with King Beli, I would protect the west and he would not ask me to subjugate myself to him. It suited both of us. Some of my captains had suggested that I wrest the kingdom from him; his warriors were not a match for mine but they did provide a buffer from the Saxons. "And Iago, what kind of man is he? I never met him."

Bishop Asaph understood my question; he was a clever man. "He hates the Saxons and, I believe he will honour his father's wishes."

"Good. If you see him then tell him I sympathise with his loss and he has my support, should he need it."

He nodded and ate sparingly of the small cakes on the platter before us. "And this visit, Lord Lann, what is its purpose?"

"We go to the east. I would know how close the Saxons are to my lands." I spread my hands at my three companions. "It is a scouting expedition only. I did not bring my whole army. The island and the peninsula are well defended still."

I saw relief on his face. I hated lying to the old man for he was kind and he was honest but I did not know how discreet he was. The wrong word here and we might be ambushed long before we reached Rheged. "Good. My monks appreciate the security you provide. Since that nest of vipers from Wyddfa was destroyed we have had peace and pilgrims return to us."

After we left, to continue up the vale Myrddyn and I discussed how this would change our journey. "It means, my lord, that there are belligerent Saxons up ahead."

"Then we will need to be careful but it also means that they will be recovering from the battle and in no position to fight a swift and well-armed force such as us."

"The Romans had a fort at Mamucium."

Myrddyn knew the maps of Rome well. "I know and we could use it if needed but I would avoid anywhere which is occupied if possible."

By keeping to the vale, we hoped to avoid detection and we camped just on the edge of the border between Gwynedd and the lands of the Saxons, the land of Mercia. We built a camp in the Roman style and Aedh had his scouts beyond the perimeter. I was awoken by a shake from Myrddyn. I opened my eyes and saw that it was still dark. "My lord, Aedh is here. There are Saxons around."

I became alert instantly. Aedh bowed, "A mile away, Lord Lann, there is a band of Saxons. They too are camped. It was our horses which alerted us. They are directly in our path. If we wish to avoid them we have to either go north or south. East is blocked."

We could not afford either deviation as time was of the essence. "How many of them are there?" The numbers would dictate our actions.

"Less than a hundred." he hesitated. "They appear to be some of those who defeated the Welsh king. They have some of the arms and shields of those people. I also think they have some prisoners. There were four bound warriors although one looked to be little more than a child."

I sighed. "So we must destroy them. Wake the men." Aedh went to rouse the camp and I looked at Myrddyn. "Any magic from you wizard?"

He shrugged. "I think not, Lord Lann. I suspect this is one of those situations where brute force and Miach's archers will do as well as magic."

When my captains joined me I outlined my plan. "Tuanthal, take half the men with Aedh and get to the other side of their camp. We will use the archers and the rest of the equites to drive them towards you." I turned to Pol and Myrddyn. "I want you two to release those prisoners. They may prove useful."

My men were experienced and confident. They left without another word. Miach's men approached on foot as did half of my equites. We needed accuracy this night and horses made a poor platform for archers. The equites might pass for a shield wall in the dark.

The Saxons only had four men on guard and they had their throats slit quickly and quietly. We had silent killers in our ranks. I led the equites who were on foot. We were fully armoured and all wore the full-face mask helmet favoured by the Saxons. I knew that it gave us extra protection and it frightened the enemy who could not see the face beneath. When they saw us in the dark we would have an instant impact. As we strode into the camp I knew that this was not a glorious venture. This was akin to murder. The enemy had no warning as we raced amongst them, killing them where they lay. The archers behind watched for any movements. Inevitably one of the Saxons awoke; he probably had to pee and his shout woke the camp. It made no difference. A man awoken from a deep, and probably drunken sleep, is no match for a wide awake and fully armed warrior. They fled. Our line was wide and it was like hunters driving animals into a net. Tuanthal and his men slaughtered all who escaped us.

"Take anything of value from the bodies and be swift."

"Lord Lann?" Myrddyn and Pol stood with the four released prisoners. The youth was about Hogan's age. They looked both surprised and relieved to have been rescued. "This is Cadfan ap Iago, the son of the King of Gwynedd."

The young man nodded, "Thank you, Lord Lann. My grandfather often spoke of you and your brave horsemen. I am glad that you happened along this way." There was an unspoken question in his words.

I did not like to lie and so I gave him a half truth. "We did not happen along this way. We were heading east. I spoke with Bishop Asaph and he said that your grandfather had been killed. I wanted to make sure that there were no roving bands of Saxons to threaten the monastery." I spread my arms. "If these were some of the men who did that then they have been brought to account."

The youth seemed relieved by my answer. "Then I thank you, Lord Lann."

Tuanthal rode in with his men. "We found half a dozen horses my lord."

"Good. Give four of them to the prince here. "Will you and your companions be able to get home without assistance?" I pointed at the dead, "We have some work to do here."

"No we can manage that." He turned to his men and spoke with some authority. "Get our weapons and armour and we will leave the filth here for Lord Lann." They hurried to do his bidding. "I am in your debt, Lord Lann. Should you ever need it repaying then speak the word and it will be done."

"And you Cadfan ap Iago, if you ever need a friend then I am close by."

Cadfan was an honest prince and he later made a good ruler. After they had left and we had piled the bodies on a pyre we ate the food left by the Saxons. Our horses now had extra weight from the arms and armour of the dead. Our journey north would be even slower from now on although we had gained two horses.

We were travelling through land new to all of us, Myrddyn included. It was flat, undulating land and made us, ironically, safer. You can see long distances from the back of a horse and any danger is seen when it is far away. We moved as swiftly north as our horses would allow us. The rivers we crossed were shallow and easily fordable. By the second night we were camped to the north of Mamucium. The land appeared to be without settlements. We knew that there was a Saxon presence at the bridge of Witherspool but, when we had travelled south to settle Mona, we had seen few signs of the Saxons.

The next day I sent out some of the younger equites, the former scouts, to aid Aedh in his exploration of the land ahead of us. We were just building our camp when Aedh himself rode in. "My lord there is a Saxon settlement on the Ribble." He pointed to the north. "It is but three miles in that direction." When we had come south the Ribble had posed us few problems in crossing. We had not seen any Saxons nearby. If there was a Saxon settlement there then it could be disastrous.

"Are there many people there?"

"It looks well defended my lord."

This was our first real set back. We could travel to the north east and approach Aelle's lands from that direction but it would add to the time the journey would take. The quickest way was north and west. "Let me go my lord."

I turned to my wizard. "You Myrddyn? You would make it disappear?"

Tuanthal laughed. "No, my lord, I would visit the town as a healer and ask questions. I can go now and be back at dawn."

Miach nodded as did Tuanthal. Myrddyn had spied for us before and could easily pass for a Saxon. He was a born dissembler and actor. "Very well. Take Pol with you. He can wait outside the settlement in case we have to come and get you."

Myrddyn snorted, "The day I cannot outwit a few Saxons will be the day I become a farmer but Pol can come with me. He is pleasant company and wittier than most others." Pol grinned at the compliment and, I think, at the pleasure of an adventure.

Pol returned in the middle of the night and I was awoken.

"Myrddyn has stayed in the settlement, it is called Prestune." He saw the worried look on my face. "He is safe enough. He will join us on the road tomorrow. There is a ford to the east and he has drawn me a map. I can lead us there. He said that it will not look strange if he travels tomorrow northwards but leaving in the night might have aroused suspicion."

I nodded, "You have done well. Now get some sleep." Myrddyn was the consummate spy. The Saxons would have taken him for one of their own; their king, Aella, had done so and we had reaped the rewards. I slept easier, knowing that, the last obstacle before Rheged was out of the way.

The land we were now travelling through was more like the land of Rheged. There were hills rising on both sides of us and we had to have scouts spread in a wide area to avoid being ambushed. The ford identified by Pol was wide and shallow. We all breathed a sigh of relief once we had crossed it. The Ribble was the last barrier before we reached Rheged. I sent Aedh to find a camp area south of the borders with Rheged. We would need to ascertain where the enemy was. I knew that my brothers had fortified the Wide Water fort but there were many places for the Saxons to besiege that tiny enclave of freedom.

Unencumbered by pack animals Myrddyn joined us at mid morning. He had not had to ford the river and he was remarkably cheerful.

"The good news, Lord Lann, is that your brothers hold out still." He saw the relief on my face. "However the bad news is that every Saxon, from miles around, has joined the siege. There are rumours of much gold in the treasure of the Wolf Warrior."

"But that is not true!"

He spread his arms. "We know that but the rumours are there. It does not help that King Ywain, before he died, told of the treasure of Rheged. He made it sound greater than it was and, when Aethelric and Aethelfrith took over the treasury they were disappointed and assumed that your brothers had purloined the rest."

"And Prince Pasgen? What of him?"

"He and his remaining equites harry the Saxons from the hills to the west of Wide Water but," he added ominously, "they have been silent since their settlement was destroyed."

"You have done well and we will talk more this evening when we hold our council of war."

We camped in the lee of a hill overlooking the sea. From Aedh we learned that the nearest Saxon settlement was on the coast, some way from Prestune. With scouts ahead of us and far away from the camp we should remain invisible and undetected.

"As from tomorrow I want us all fully armed and armoured. I do not want to come upon some Saxons without protection. I know it will tire the horses but that is better than losing warriors. Aedh, you need to find us a safe way in to the fort." He looked appalled. I smiled, "I know that it is a tall order but we do have some advantages. We know the area. There is a thick forest on the western side of the lake. If you can get there then you might be able to get a man into the stronghold."

Myrddyn shook his head. "That is risky. The scouts have grown since Raibeart and Aelle knew them. The messenger might be killed by a frightened sentry."

"Very well then but Aedh can still use that forest to scout out the lake. From there a scout can see directly up the water towards the stronghold."

Miach ate constantly during these discussions. Myrddyn was certain that he had a tapeworm! "What about the eastern side of the lake?"

I shook my head. "Too open for us to approach unseen and that, I suspect, will be where they have their main force."

"I could go."

I turned to look at Pol. "You?"

"They know me and I can swim. They are less likely to kill a swimmer out of hand; it is less threatening."

"He is right Lord Lann. I would go but I cannot swim."

I laughed, "Something that Myrddyn cannot do. That is a first. Very well then. The only thing we need to do is to work out where we will hide the army."

Tuanthal laughed, "This handful of men an army?"

"It is the only army we have."

"If Aedh is scouting to the east of the lake then we should be approach from the north east. We can then use that flat area north of the fort to make the most use of the equites' horses and skills."

Miach's plan was accepted and, early next morning we all set off. Pol and Aedh, along with the scouts left first. We took the longer route west, north and then east. I used Miach's archers as scouts for there were many places we could be ambushed. Suddenly two of them rode in waving their arms.

"Saxons! Up ahead. We think it is a camp of those besieging the fort."

We had passed a small lake, the locals called them tarns, a hundred paces or so back. It was hidden from the track by a stand of trees and was not overlooked. "Miach, take charge of the men. Tuanthal and Myrddyn, you two come with me. Show me these Saxons."

We rode through the thick forests to evade detection. I vaguely recognised where we were. There was a range of hills to the north with two small lakes and, as I recalled, a huge cave up there. That could prove useful. I also had an idea where the Saxons would be; there was a young but vigorous river which emptied into the lake and there was a stone bridge across it. The site made a perfect barrier to stop any escaping from the stronghold.

The two men held up their hands for silence and dismounted. The three of us did the same. While one of the archers held our horses, we followed the other one to a rock above the bridge. We could see without being seen. It was indeed a Saxon warband. There were few of them, probably fifty or so in total, although we could not see the whole of their camp. They had a barrier across the bridge and it was, as I suspected, to keep men in rather than preventing reinforcements. They were not worried by the thought of a relief force. Prince Pasgen must not be considered a threat. We retreated to the horses where we could talk.

"You two archers stay here and keep watch. We need to know if they are reinforced."

As we rode back Myrddyn spoke what was in all of our minds. "We have to get rid of them before we do anything else."

"True but if any escape then we will have every Saxon for miles around attacking us and this is not an easy place for horsemen to defend."

"You are right Tuanthal. I want you to take our men to the two small lakes just north of here. If you remember there is a cave there where they can hide."

Myrddyn could see my mind working. "You have a plan, Lord Lann?"

"Tuanthal is right we need somewhere to fight where we can use our horsemen. North of the fort there is a large flat area, just after the small lake. If we could make the Saxons form up there then Tuanthal could attack from their rear."

He grinned, "We use the buccina!"

"Exactly! When you hear that call then you attack. We will get rid of the men at the bridge. If there is a problem then we too will head for the cave. It is an easy place to defend but, hopefully, it will not come to that."

As we walked I asked a question which had been on my mind for some time. The Saxons did not appear worried by Prince Pasgen. "I wonder if Prince Pasgen lives? It would help me to know that he did. I feel I owe his father still."

"Oh he lives but you owe his father nothing. You have repaid that debt many times over." With that the enigmatic wizard shut up! He could be most annoying.

We returned to Miach and explained the plan. We designated ten of his archers to remain with the horses while the rest would follow us to the bridge. We had the dozen boy slingers who could care for the mounts but we needed guards who could fight if we were surprised. Tuanthal left and suddenly it felt lonely with just the handful of archers remaining. We had decided to use the river. It was a bubbling and lively stream, cascading over rocks and small falls. Its noise would disguise our approach. Four of Miach's most skilful cut throats would descend the torrent and emerge on the other side to deal with any Saxon who fled. The rest of Miach's men would be in the trees and they would use their arrows from concealment.

Despite Miach's concerns Myrddyn and I intended to walk down the road towards the Saxons. We would be attacking after dark and we could both speak Saxon. They would hear our voices and, I hoped, it would allay any fears they might have. We would distract them by approaching from what they would consider their safe side. With my helmet down and carrying my shield I would, indeed, look Saxon. If the plan went awry then Miach and his men would kill as many Saxons as they could and we would have to fight our way out. I was not worried. No Saxon yet had bested me and Myrddyn the wizard was as slippery as an eel.

Miach and his men left to take their positions. Myrddyn and I walked down the road; horses would have aroused suspicion. Myrddyn carried no shield but he had his sword and a dagger. I held a dagger in my shield hand and Saxon Slayer was in its greased scabbard.

We began talking in Saxon as we descended towards the bridge. Myrddyn did most of the talking; he was a born actor and story teller.

"So I said, what are you talking about, Ida? The bitch was already dead so what was the point of being kind to her."

I laughed, "That is Ida all over."

"He is the biggest fool I have ever known this side of the water."

There was a brazier by the bridge and I could see the Saxons there. That was good for it would spoil their ability to see into the dark. They had their weapons levelled at us but they appeared relaxed.

"Who are you two?"

"We are from the camp at Prestune we have been sent with a message."

"Who for?"

"Why Aethelric of course."

One of them laughed. "Then you have wasted your time for King Aethelfrith has sent him to watch Elmet. He was fed up of waiting for him to take this piss pot little place."

Myrddyn shrugged. "Then the message is for King Aethelfrith."

"Who is it from?"

I stepped forwards with Saxon Slayer half out. "I have had enough of your questions. Let us through and we will talk to some real warriors."

I am a big man and others have told me how intimidating I look. The guard on the bridge must have been worried by my tone for he backed off. "Don't get so high and mighty. We are just asking questions. You could be anyone."

"What do we look like? Rheged scum?"

One of the others gave a little laugh, "No but you are big enough to be the Wolf Warrior."

The first guard who had spoken must have recognised my shield for he suddenly shouted, "Shit! It…"

He got no further as Saxon Slayer pierced his throat. Myrddyn slew the warrior next to him and I killed the third. The fourth man turned to run and warn the camp and an arrow thudded into his back and pitched him into the river. There was an eerie silence. The rest of the guards had to have been asleep. I strode across the bridge and into their camp. Then Miach and his men began loosing into the sleeping forms on the ground. This time the screams of the dying woke up the camp. I stood at the bridge. "Myrddyn, get behind me and protect my back."

Although the bridge was wide enough for eight men, by standing in the middle Saxon Slayer could keep all from me. The Saxons could not see the archers who were slowly whittling down the opposition but they could see me, framed in the light of the brazier and they rushed at me. Most had not bothered with armour and charged towards me with whatever weapon they could grab. The most dangerous weapons were the spears for they could out range me but they came at me piecemeal. I deflected the first spear and gutted the man holding it. My backhand slash took the right arm from a second and then my shield punched the axe man who was trying to swing at my head. Myrddyn's blade darted out to stab any flesh which came within range and others suddenly sprouted flights as the arrows from the trees struck them.

Soon there were just the sounds of the groans from the dying. Miach's four cutthroats walked from the other side despatching those who still lived. Miach came from behind me. "My lord, you have the luck of the Hibernians! I thought for certain they had you."

"If they had had their wits about them then I would be dead but they were not vigilant and they were not ready. I was!"

We had no chance to burn the corpses and so we collected them and piled them in a dell behind the stream. Some of the younger archers were in high spirits and boasting of how we would defeat the whole of the Saxon army single handed. Miach turned on them, he was, after all, their leader. "We were lucky! The Saxons are tough warriors. The moment you get over confident is the moment that you die! Remember that!" They immediately became subdued and hurried about finding tasks to do.

Three of the archers were dressed in the dead sentries' armour. It would not fool anyone for long but, hopefully, we would not have to wait long.

Myrddyn approached me. "Lord Lann, I will wander to the east and see if I can spy their lines and camp. It would be useful to know how close they are."

I knew that he would be careful and I let him go. We sent a couple of men back to the camp for the horses and, as dawn broke we were reunited. When Aedh and his scouts returned we had our small warband again.

Aedh's report was worrying. "There are many of them camped my lord. I counted at least five hundred. They have some boats too. It looks as though they have spent some time building them for they look and smell new. They seem to be ready for use and I think they will attack that way." I knew that Aelle and his defenders had the Roman ballistae but an assault from land and the lake would overwhelm them. "And Pol?"

He smiled, "He got away! That boy can swim like a fish! He made it safely into the water and we waited until we saw him land. So long as he has not been killed as a spy he should be safe."

"Good, you have done well and now you and the archers should rest. We wait for Myrddyn and his news."

I rested my back against the bridge and closed my eyes. I was asleep almost instantly. I had total confidence in my men to keep a watch and I knew that I would need to rest as the day promised to be a hard one.

I was shaken awake by Myrddyn himself. "The sleep of the innocent eh my lord?"

"What news?"

"There is a camp of about a thousand men but it is spread all the way from here to the other side of the lake. Their nearest outpost is about five hundred paces that way."

I told him of the ships and he frowned. "It means, Myrddyn, that we need to strike today, rather than wait. Pol will have told my brothers that we are close and they will be ready."

"Ready for what?"

"Whatever we manage to pull off. Fifteen hundred men is less than I thought they would have."

"I saw fires on the eastern shore. There are more there."

"It matters not. We deal with this one thousand first and we use Tuanthal and his men to do it." I waved over Miach and Aedh. "I want all but one of your scouts and ten of your archers to ride to the end of the small lake. You will approach the Saxon lines. Halt, loose a few flights and then let them pursue you; when they do then sound the buccina. You will lead them on to Tuanthal's spears. Miach, we will use the rest of your men to attack them in the rear when they follow Aedh. If they do not take the bait and they chase us then we will return here. Myrddyn, you will accompany the scout and get into the fort. Come with me and I will explain what I intend."

Myrddyn left with the scout. I said to Aedh. "I want your scouts and Tuanthal's men to get back here when your horses tire. This is a diversion only. I want them to think that we are Prince Pasgen and it is his men who are attacking from the north. When they see the equites they will think of Pasgen and not the Wolf Warrior. Today we do not unfurl the banner. Let us keep that surprise for them. I want as many of these northern Saxons killing as we can manage and I want no casualties on our side. If you retreat north west first it will add to the illusion and then you can cut through the pass and rejoin the rest of us."

"A tall order, my lord."

"If it was any other band of soldiers I would not even dream of giving the order but you are all my men and I know that you can do it."

Aedh and his men rode away and there were just thirty-two of us left. I slung my shield across my back and took out my bow. If I had to use Saxon Slayer then it meant that my plan had failed. We edged towards the Saxon camp. There were plenty of trees to hide us and there was much noise emanating from within. They were sure of themselves and had no fence at all. They relied on the guards at the bridge and, I assumed the same on the other side of the lake. I wondered what had become of Prince Pasgen. We could use his equites. They were the finest I had ever seen. My own were a pale copy. I edged as close as we could get without being seen and then we waited. The signal would be the buccina and, hopefully it would result in the Saxons hurtling north to meet the threat.

I was wondering if there had been a problem, when I saw the men at the far end begin to grab their weapons and stream towards the pass near the two lakes. I saw a chief yell something and the majority of the Saxons, this time fully armoured, lurched northwards. I turned to Miach. "We kill those left in the camp first." He nodded.

"Ready men. Pick your targets!"

I aimed at a chief who was busy organising the twenty or so men left in camp. The arrow struck him in the neck. I notched another and loosed again. Soon every Saxon left in camp was dead. I saw that they had tents. "You two. Burn the tents and then follow us!" The two archers dismounted and set to work.

I heard the buccina. We galloped towards its mournful wail. We would not fight on horseback but dismount and use our speed and our accuracy. There was yet another bubbling stream to our left as we rode along the trail. Its noise helped to mask the sound of our hooves. I suddenly saw a knobbly hill, topped by a few spindly trees and, close to it, the Saxons trying to form a shield wall. Tuanthal had arrived.

"Dismount!" We were a hundred and fifty paces from their rear and we were unseen. We could have been closer but I wanted time to escape when they did spot us. Each man tied his reins to his leg. It stopped the horses from fleeing and was easy to untie when it came time to escape. The eight hundred or so Saxons must have thought it would be easy as the sixty horsemen thundered towards them. Tuanthal's men had javelins which they would throw. The Saxons did not go in for missiles save for the odd throwing axe. They would be confident that their shields would bear the brunt of the attack.

"Loose!"

A trained archer can loose ten arrows in a very short time. After ten he becomes tired but Miach and I hoped that three hundred well aimed arrows would break their hearts as well as their spirits. The first to die did not cause a stir amongst the rest but when gaps appeared, their chiefs turned and saw us. They quickly raced across the grassy turf to get to grips with us.

"Mount!"

We had done enough. One of our archers had not tied his reins properly and the throwing axe thrown by the Saxon struck him in the middle of the back. He fell and his horse, in panic, raced after the rest of us, dragging the corpse behind it. We easily out distanced them but I knew they would continue to come. We halted in their own camp. The archer's horse followed us. Miach cut the corpse free and took the dead man's arrows. They were more valuable than gold. The dead bodies of the guards formed a rough barrier. We prepared to loose our arrows. The first Saxons to arrive were the fittest and the fastest and they quickly became the first dead. Someone was using his head because the individual attacks stopped and a shield wall appeared.

Miach grinned, "Three more flights and then let's get out of here. Aim for their rear ranks."

We aimed high so that the last arrows left before the first had struck and then we mounted. We galloped over the bridge through the burning smoke of their camp. I could hear their screaming rage as they saw what we had done. They would be even more annoyed when they discovered how few we had been. We had dented their defences and, more importantly increased their fear. They would no longer be safe in camp.

They would build a fence and they would patrol. They would wait for the next attack but that attack would come from an unexpected direction.

We rode hard for the meeting place which was well to the west of the road. We halted and the men tended to the wounds and injuries suffered by both men and horses. "Shame about Callan, my lord, he was a good archer."

"*Wyrd*! It was meant to be Miach. At least we did not lose his horse."

"True but I hate to think of his bow being in the hands of those barbarians."

"You know they can't use them and it takes years to train a man to become a true archer."

"Aye I know that but one day they will get a king who understands that and then may the Allfather help us!"

Chapter 3

Aedh and Tuanthal were at the meeting place before us. The slingers were already watering and feeding the tired beasts. They had only had to cross the ridge. We had lost one scout and two of the equites had slight wounds. As Tuanthal said, "We would have taken the loss before we left, my lord."

I nodded. He was right. "Any loss is irreplaceable. I just hope that they think that you were Pasgen and his men."

Aedh spoke up, "I will send a man to watch them. That way we will know for certain."

We fell upon the food we had left and devoured it like wolves. We were starving and we were tired. Miach shook his head. "We need fit men who are wide awake this night. We will sleep now and the boys can watch."

I looked at the ten horse guards we had brought with us. None of them was older than eleven summers. "They are young."

Miach said quietly, "No younger than you and your brothers when you fought King Aella. They will do the job. Trust them."

As I drifted off to sleep I hoped that Myrddyn had made the stronghold successfully. We benefited from the sleep. The boys, who had kept watch, looked as proud as though they had fought a battle. When Aedh's scout came in and said that the enemy had split his defenders then we knew that our plan was working. The hard part was to come. We moved the whole camp and slowly headed south along the lake. We were attempting to move over a hundred men and a hundred and fifty horses quietly through the forest and it was not easy. It was as though nature was on our side for the midges and biting insects were out in force. They would make life unpleasant for any Saxons on guard duty. Myrddyn had made us all eat garlic and they seemed not to bother us but I knew that the guards at the Saxon boats would be as close to the protective smoke of their fires as possible.

We halted two hundred paces from the ship which was on the end of the line. I could see that they had built five. They were not as big as the ones we had destroyed along the Dunum but they were big enough. When loaded with warriors they would easily be able to attack the stronghold from the water. We could see that there were lights higher up the hill, away from the water and the pernicious little biting bugs. That was their main camp. The firelight of ten fires showed the boat guards.

The first part seemed easy. The guards at the fires were silenced. There were only twenty of them and the forty archers did not miss. We left Tuanthal with half of his horsemen while the rest spread out in a skirmish line to warn of any Saxon attack. We slipped aboard the boats. It was as I had expected, they had not left a watch on board as they had no need. We tied the boats together stern to bow after having pulled in their anchors and then Miach and his men boarded the first one.

"Captain Tuanthal, you and the scouts must remain free. Harass the enemy but we cannot afford one casualty. Remember the signal will be three blasts on the buccina. Much depends upon you and your horsemen."

The two leaders grinned. "With respect my lord you sound more like Myfanwy each day. We will do as you order and later perhaps you can teach us how to suck eggs too!" They disappeared with the slingers into the night; their high spirits boosted me as well.

Miach and I had decided that the archers were best suited for the job of rowing as the mighty archers all had powerful arms. I took the helm and Miach stood on the prow. "Don't forget that small sail boat there. Tie it to the last ship."

"Be like a bloody anchor that will."

"Stop moaning and do it."

We used hand signals and the oars all dipped into the black waters of the huge lake. I wondered if we were anchored for we did not appear to move. Then slowly, inexorably, we began to edge away from the shore. I leaned on the tiller and the prow headed east into the middle of the lake. We began to move faster and then suddenly we were jerked back. I looked over my shoulder and then realised it was the first of the other ships, dragging like an anchor. We could expect this until they were all floating free.

I turned the helm so that we were heading north for the fort. I noticed that there was a slight current in the lake; had we not rowed then we would be drifting south. It meant hard work for us now but it would aid us eventually when we tried to escape the lake. Finally the tugs on the stern stopped and we began to make progress. It felt to me as though we were moving like a crab. This was where I needed Ridwyn. He could sail well and I was desperately trying to remember how we sailed from Din Guardi to the Dunum. The black waters seemed to blend into the shore and

I worried that we would hit rocks- that would have been a disaster. Suddenly I saw two lights appear and I headed towards them.

Miach's voice suddenly sounded from the prow. "Stop rowing!"

That was the signal that we had reached the stronghold. I saw faces behind the wall and I pushed the tiller hard over. Miach shouted, "Oars in!"

We bumped against the wooden wall of the outer defences and I knew that we had made it. Willing hands suddenly threw ropes and we tied up the ship and then clambered ashore. The first faces I saw, to my relief, were Aelle and Raibeart. It was dark and I could not see them clearly but, even so, I could see the strain upon their faces and then there was joy as they threw their arms around me. I knew that Miach and Myrddyn would sort out the other boats and I just enjoyed the reunion with my family.

"Your families?"

Raibeart nodded, "They are well."

"As are mine. Come let us get within the walls." Aelle led me through a maze of walls to the inner part of the stronghold. I looked at the emaciated warriors and animals moving lethargically around. "It has been hard. Had these ships come to attack us …?"

"Well I am here now. Did Myrddyn tell you my plan?"

"He did." Raibeart smiled, "He seems even more…"

"Strange? Mystical? Enigmatic? Perplexing?"

"Aye all of that."

"Well be grateful for it. He has used his powers to aid us on more than one occasion." I had made the plan with Myrddyn but I still didn't know if it would work. "Have you sailors who know the lake?"

Aelle nodded, "There are ten fishermen. They will crew the ships. They say there is a river at the far end. The ships may be able to travel a little way down that but there are shallows and rocks."

"The further we can travel on the water, the easier the journey will be. It will be harder now than when I travelled south. There are more Saxons and more Saxon settlements."

Raibeart began to bristle, "Do not blame us."

I held my hand up. "I do not blame you, brother. I am merely stating a fact. I understand why you did not come when I left but do not argue with every statement or the spring will find this land filled with all of our bleached bones!"

Aelle put his arm on my shoulder, "Forgive me. It has been hard. We are grateful and we will do whatever we must and whatever you demand."

"Then get your women and children on the ships. If there is space then put the animals in. The women will have to row but they have all the time they need for there are no other ships on the lake."

Raibeart shook his head, "I am sorry brother. I should have known you were not criticising."

Pol and Myrddyn ran up to me. I embraced them both. "Well done. Myrddyn, how many warriors do we have?"

He glanced at my brothers and said, "Forty archers, twenty slingers and a hundred warriors."

We both knew that was not enough but I could not let my two brothers see that. "Good. And how many horses?"

"Thirty."

Again it was not enough but it would have to do. "Brothers get your people on the boats. Miach, Myrddyn gather the warriors. We have little time." I was calculating. We had two hundred men inside the stronghold and sixty without. We were going to take on four hundred men. That was not counting the ones who had been at the boat camp. Events were now out of my hands. It was up to the Allfather and *wyrd.* The plan was the only one we had and the only way any of my brother's people would survive. I was not sure if we would.

I turned to Myrddyn, "You go with the ships and lead the people." He looked as though he would argue. "You are a leader and the others are better warriors. Don't argue, wizard, just do it."

"Very well my lord." He grinned. "It is good to hear the Wolf Warrior growl again."

I watched his back as he sped away. Raibeart, Aelle and Miach joined Pol and myself. My brothers were fully armed and armoured. "Miach, you take charge of the archers. Aelle, they are your slingers. Raibeart I want you to lead the shield wall."

They all looked at me. "And what of you?"

"We have two surprises. Three if you count the fact that they will not expect us to attack. The buccina will signal the attack of my horsemen. Half of the Saxons are waiting two miles up the road and so Tuanthal should be able to fall upon the backs of the enemy. By the time you reach them they will be becoming demoralised. Pol and I will then raise the Wolf Standard in the stronghold. That will enable all of you to slip away towards the west when they race towards the stronghold. We will then follow. Of course by then Pol will have barred the doors to slow down their pursuit."

Even Raibeart looked appalled. "That is suicide, I cannot allow it."

"You forget brother that you swore an oath to follow the Warlord of Rheged and obey all of his orders. Would you become foresworn?"

"No but…"

"Trust me. I will lead you to my island of Mona. You have my word on that. Besides Pol and I can handle four hundred Saxons; although the more you kill the better for Pol and me!"

We made sure that all of the food that was left was eaten and we piled brushwood and kindling near all of the walls and around the bolt throwers. It was vital that they did not fall into Saxon hands and they were too heavy to take. Aelle looked sad, "I never thought that I would burn my fort."

"Things change and we must change with them… or die!"

We waited until we saw the first glimmer of grey in the eastern sky and then the warriors, archers and slingers slipped out of the gate. Pol and I barred it and then stood at the top of the main gate. In the middle of the compound lay the five torches burning fiercely. They would ignite the inferno which would protect our backs and deny the Saxons Aelle's hard work.

Pol's eyes were slight with excitement. "Thank you for choosing me my lord."

"Who else would I choose? You are the standard bearer and besides, without Ridwyn or Garth, who else will watch my back?"

From my standpoint I could see the fires from the Saxon camp in the distance and the shapes of the Saxon guards as they moved around. The line of warriors led by my brothers moved slowly forwards, slightly hidden by the early morning mist. Behind them the line of archers stood, drawing their bows back. It was strange watching without any control in my hands. It would be Miach, Aelle and Raibeart who would begin the attack. I notched an arrow; it gave me something to do and I aimed at a shape moving to the right of the camp.

Suddenly I heard the noise of eighty bows releasing arrows and I released mine. I notched and released a second. Then the line of warriors hit the sleeping camp. When I heard the buccina call three times I knew that soon the camp would be filled with the sound of battle and death. The initial surprise of the attack would only last for a short time and then the weight of numbers of the enemy would take over. I heard the clash as the horsemen over ran the outer defences and then I heard Miach's orders, "Retreat!"

With the warriors in the front and the horsemen as a rear-guard my small army headed towards the western edge of the lake. Soon the remnants of the Saxons and the men they had left to the north would arrive and it would be up to me to attract and hold their attention. I wondered how the ships were progressing as they edged south. As soon as the Saxons on the eastern shore saw them then it would be as though a wasp's nest had been disturbed. Now that the sun had risen I could see the dead and dying, both Rheged and Saxon, although there appeared to be more dead Saxons than our own warriors. I heard a roar and saw a warband emerge from the north.

"Stand by Pol. As soon as the banner is unfurled then go and light the first fires. I will follow soon."

He hesitated, "Should I not wait a while my lord?"

"No. They will only have eyes for me anyway." I took off my helmet and held it in my right hand. I had my wolf shield in my left and my wolf cloak around my shoulders. I was ready. I saw a chief organising his men. There were some wounded Rheged warriors for I saw them have their throats slit. "Now Pol!" He unfurled the banner and gave it to me and, as he leapt down the steps I shouted, "I am Lord Lann, Warlord of Rheged, the Wolf Warrior and I have returned to punish you for your treachery. Behold the Wolf Standard!" It was *wyrd*, but a sudden breeze made the banner flutter and stand erect. The effect was instantaneous. The Saxons hurled themselves at the walls. They were desperate to get their hands on me, their enemy. I barely managed to deflect the axe thrown at me and then, as smoke and flames began to lick at the walls, I fled the battlements.

Pol had two torches left in his blackened hands. His face was alight with excitement. "There is just the last wall my lord."

"Good, then light the fires." I went through the gate which had been left open by Myrddyn when he had left and threw the standard into the bottom of the small boat we had stolen from the Saxons. The flames from the front wall of the fort rose high into the sky as Pol jumped into the boat, threatening to capsize it. "Steady Pol. It would not do to drown here in plain sight of the Saxons."

He gripped the thwarts tightly, "Sorry my lord."

"Now let us row! "

We were gambling that their desire to get their hands on me would allow the soldiers of my small army to escape unseen south towards the ships. We seemed to move slowly across the water although with the sunlight shining from the east it was quite pleasant. I kept glancing to my left. Aedh would, hopefully appear with our horses. Until I saw him we had to keep rowing down the lake to fix the Saxon's attention on us.

"How many men do you think were killed back there my lord?"

"It looked to me as though more than a hundred had fallen." I shook my head. "I could not count them all but the important part is that it has weakened them. We have a long way to go and this time the Saxons know where we are going." When my people had made the exodus we had done so in secret. It was now obvious, from the dead Saxon chief, that they knew where we were and King Aethelfrith had shown himself to be as cunning as Aella had been. I would have to use more cunning; the cunning of the wolf!

The stronghold of Aelle was now a blazing pyre. The Saxons had warriors on both sides of the conflagration and they pointed towards our lonely little boat in the middle of the lake. They began to head south along the shore in pursuit. There was still no sign of Aedh. I peered to my right and saw that the ships were a dot on the far horizon. The families, at least, would soon be beyond the Saxon's grasp; at least for the time being. "Pull harder Pol. Now that they have seen us they will be able to move quicker than we. We began to move faster but I could see the Saxons were still gaining. We appeared to have moved some distance and I began to worry that something had happened to Aedh. Perhaps the other band of Saxons had ambushed my whole force. That would be a disaster not to be countenanced.

"Lord Lann! Over here!"

I looked to my left and saw Aedh and three of the scouts with two horses. "You keep rowing. It will edge us closer in to the shore." I stopped rowing and the boat headed directly west. There were Saxons less than six hundred paces from us and the shore was still twenty paces away. Boats were so slow. I began to row and breathed a sigh of relief as the bottom ground on the gravel. "Thank the Allfather."

We leapt out and Pol grabbed the precious standard. The Saxons were now a hundred and fifty paces away. The scouts took out their slings and began to hurl shot at the approaching warriors. By the time we had mounted the slings had slowed down their advance.

"Captain Miach is over there." Aedh pointed to the south east.

"And the other Saxons, the ones from the ridge?"

He grinned, "They are following the boats."

That was a relief. I knew, as we all did, that we would need to fight them but this way we would be surprising them some way down the lake from their main army. "Did we lose many?"

"Tuanthal said there were fifteen. The captain is with the rearguard, watching the main band."

"Good. You find the southern band and I will join Tuanthal." We headed south and soon reached Tuanthal. I saw four empty saddles. Equites were our most valuable resource and we could ill afford any losses. I knew that my captain of horse would have done all that he could to mitigate the losses but the sixty of us were all that stood between a couple of hundred Saxons and our army.

He smiled with relief when he saw me. "The southern band is just three hundred strong. Miach and Lord Raibeart think they can defeat them."

"Good, but we must discourage these Saxons and slow them down." Fortunately the chase and hunt to capture the Wolf Warrior had meant that they had not reached us in large numbers. The fastest and the fittest had arrived first. We waited. The rest would help the horses in the long run. We needed then to be as fresh as possible. It would be a long chase. And then the Saxons began to appear from the lakeside. They had followed our trail. As soon as they saw our serried ranks they halted and formed a shield wall. They expected us to attack. There were just thirty of them and we could have sent them packing but there was no need, as yet. We needed to halt the whole of their warband. Every moment spent here gave the rest of the refugees time to get beyond their grasp.

I unslung my bow. "I think I can discourage them a little."

Although loosing arrows from the back of a horse was not as accurate as from the ground, my horse was still and the Saxons were just a hundred paces away. I drew back and sighted on the middle of their line. My arrow soared upwards and I loosed a second and a third. I could see that some of the men had fought against archers before as they held their shields up but others made the mistake of looking upwards. Two men fell, one wounded and one, from the arrow in his head, dead. I loosed three more and wounded a second man. They began to pull back, northwards.

"Edge north." The whole line moved forwards and the Saxons began to move quicker. Suddenly they stopped as they ran into their main band.

"Good. At least we know where they are!" I glanced down the line. The equites looked confident. "Pol. The standard!"

He unfurled the banner and the whole line of my warriors saw it and roared their cheers. They began to bang their shields with their javelins chanting, "Wolf Warrior!" over and over. I slung my bow.

"How many javelins do your men have left?"

"Most have two but some only have one."

"Then on my command we charge and hurl one javelin and then retreat a mile down the road."

"Right my lord. Equites! Ready with a javelin!"

He glanced at me, "Charge!" I drew my sword, "Saxon Slayer!" The sun from the east glinted off its blade and the jewels on the handles. I knew from the Saxon prisoners we had captured the effect the blade had. They thought it made me invincible and, much as they wanted it they all believed that they would die if they tried to take it from my living hand. When we were thirty paces from them the men hurled their javelins. Two axes flew back in return but most of the shields rose up. However three warriors burst from the line and raced towards me. A javelin from Tuanthal took one in the throat and hurled him back to the line. Pol was still moving forwards and he jabbed the end of the standard, like a lance and it punched a warrior in the eye knocking him unconscious. From the mess I suspect he had lost the orb. The last man had a helmet like mine and he ran at my horse with his axe raised. I jerked my horse's head around and the axe swung into empty air. I slashed down with the blade and it ripped his neck at the shoulders. The Saxons deigned to wear mail coifs beneath their helmets and this brave warrior had paid the price.

"Back" We wheeled into a column of twos and galloped along the track. I heard the roar as the Saxons lurched after us but they had no chance of making up the ground between us. We were mounted and they were on foot. They only succeeded in making their warriors more tired.

The trail rose above the trees and Pol pointed to the western shore. "My lord. The warband to the west is moving south."

I looked and saw that the other Saxon army was also moving south to cut us off. I had expected it. If they did reach us then it would have meant the plan, Myrddyn and I had concocted, had failed. "Keep an eye on them."

After a mile we halted and turned to face the Saxons we knew would be following. We waited longer than I thought and I wondered if they were trying to outflank us. The thick woods to the east did not favour large numbers and so I was not particularly worried. They must have been more tired than I had expected. When they did arrive they came in a wedge formation with shields bristling with spears. They had learned their lesson. "I want them to think we are charging. On my command ride ten paces, wheel and retreat a mile down the trail." The Saxons pulled their shields up as we charged. They would have anticipated the thud of javelins on shields but there were none. By the time they peered from behind their defences we had disappeared.

Tuanthal pointed to the south. "The end of the lake is just a mile away."

"Then it is time to rejoin my brothers." We now had the most difficult aspect of the fight. We had to destroy one Saxon band before the second struck us. The second warband would be fresher and would not have suffered any casualties. I hoped that the men of Raibeart and Aelle still had fight left in them.

We found the army just a half mile along the lake. Aedh took us to them. When we arrived he pointed to the distant masts of the ships. "The Saxons have moved swiftly," he grinned, "and they are tired. They are a mile from the boats but Myrddyn still has them moving, somehow, down the river." I knew not how he had done that as the river was neither wide nor deep. Perhaps the recent rains had swollen it or perhaps it was *wyrd*! "Their attention is on the boats and they have no men facing north. They are not expecting us. They must think we are all on board their boats."

"Tuanthal, get more javelins from the pack animals. Miach, Raibeart, Aelle, this is the plan. Five flights from the archers and the equites charge under the arrows."

Aelle said, "Isn't that dangerous?"

Miach snorted, "If the archers are under my command then no!"

I waved an irritated hand to silence them. We had no time for this. "Raibeart you and Aelle will follow up. I want the Saxons split so that Raibeart and Aelle can get to the boats, along with the scouts and the pack animals, and form a defensive position around them."

"Where will you be brother?"

"I will be with Tuanthal and Pol. We will be the arrow head!"

I took two javelins. I would not need any more. We moved forwards. Aedh had brought us to a small hill which overlooked the rear of the marching warband. They were Saxons and there was no order. I nodded at Miach. "Ready! Loose!"

The rest of his commands were lost as I led the sixty riders at the rear of the line. I watched as each successive flight thumped home. Some struck helmets, knocking their owners to the ground, some struck shields, making them unwieldy but most struck flesh and the Saxons fell. Someone took charge and turned just when we were forty paces away. We all hurled our javelins. Most of Tuanthal's men had three but I wanted Saxon Slayer unsheathed ready to inflict even more damage.

"Saxon Slayer!" With the banner bravely flying we struck the disordered and disorganised line. I hacked down to the left and right of my horse's head. The only way to stand up to a charge of horse is to have an unbroken line of shields. They had not formed such a line and they paid the price. We struck individual men and they fell or they fled. The arrows and the javelins had accounted for half of their number and we were cleaving our way through the rest. Tuanthal pushed to the right and I pushed to the left towards the lake. Pol was laying about him with his sword, the standard still showing those behind the way to go. The Saxons before us fled into the water. We had the advantage of height and it was a slaughter. Some attempted to escape in the lake but the weight of their armour and their exhaustion did our work for us. The mud at the bottom of the lake sucked them to their death. Soon we were facing an empty lake, save for the bodies.

"Turn and form line."

The thirty warriors with me turned and straightened our rank. I could see Tuanthal and his men pursuing the last remnants up the hillside. "Raibeart, Aelle, get to the boats. We will watch the enemy. Miach join them." Miach and his men, being mounted would reach the boats first and they would provide a defence until the rest of us reached them. We waited until Tuanthal and Aedh had rejoined us. "Aedh, send a rider across the lake. I need to know how far the other Saxon band is away from the boats." He whipped his horse round to find a rider with the freshest horse.

"The horses cannot charge again, Lord Lann. They have done too much already."

"I know Tuanthal. We are here to watch only. When we leave here we walk to the boats." I held my hand up to shield my eyes. It looked to be well into the afternoon. If we could hold them until dark then we stood a chance. The Saxon line marched along the track. This band still outnumbered us and we were tired. The next few hours would determine if we lived or died.

Chapter 4

Myrddyn was waiting for me some way from the boats. "We have got as far as we can, my lord. There are rocks which will tear out the bottoms. I have those skilled in such things making wagons from the wood of the last ship." We had brought the few wheels left from the stronghold with us. The horses we had taken from Aelle's home could pull the wagons with the old and the infirm. "I have put kindling in the others."

"Do not fire them yet. There is still an army yonder." I pointed to the western shore.

"We have been watching them. There are over three hundred in the band."

"And with about the same number on this side we do not want to be caught between those two rocks. I peered to the north. We must defeat these before the others join them."

"That, my lord, is out of our hands. They know you lead us and there is nought else to draw them on."

"Then we shall have to defend as best we can."

My two brothers' wives had organised hot food and the men greedily devoured the hot sustenance. Raibeart and Aelle had begun to build defences from masts and trees. We would ensure that the Saxons could not use their preciously built ships again! I chewed on some mutton. I stood on the deck of the last ship and I began to count the n we had left. There were, give or take, sixty horsemen, not counting the scouts. There were over seventy archers. The slingers remained untouched and there were twenty of them but there were but seventy warriors. If we used every horse we had then there would just be the slingers and warriors afoot but that would not aid us. We would still have the lumbering mass that was the people of Rheged. We had to fight and win.

I jumped down from the boat and gathered my leaders and Pol around me. "Until Aedh reaches us with news of the western army we will concentrate upon defeating this one." I pointed up the lake where the Saxons were forming a shield wall in preparation for an attack. "Pol, make sure the Wolf Banner flies. I want them hungry for my blood. Myrddyn, as soon as the wagons are ready then begin to move the families south and get as far as we can before dark. Take half of the warriors, the ones who are weakest, with you for protection." He threw me a questioning look. "The families have had the day to rest. They do not need to march far.

The land flattens out four miles to the south and we can make a camp there. Tuanthal and his horsemen can escort you."

"Is that wise brother? The equites are feared by the Saxons. And you leave yourself with few men for the shield wall."

"True Raibeart, but the horses are exhausted and need rest. We will need the equites ere long. We rely on arrows and the shield wall. I know it is a small shield wall but the gap they defend is narrow. When we defeat this band," I saw the looks of doubt on their faces, "oh we will defeat these but the others, I am not so sure. When we defeat this band we will fire the ships and get away in the confusion. The western band will have to cross the river and that will give us time to reach Tuanthal and the families. The Saxons are as tired as we are and they will need to rest. On the morrow our equites will be in a position to charge again. In a perfect world we would travel down the other bank of the river as that is the most direct route but there are Saxons there. We will have to try to cross further south and hope that the Allfather is with us." I paused and they looked at me.

Then they banged their shields with their swords and shouted, "Wolf Warrior!" They were still confident and that could win a battle for you.

I smiled and gave a slight bow. "Myrddyn, Tuanthal, go! Aelle take charge of the boats. Your slingers can use them, as can Miach's archers. Fire them when you deem it right."

There was a sudden scrambling as the slingers and archers clambered aboard the ships. Miach had the remaining scouts lead his horses further south; away from the fighting. I looked at the shield wall we were making. With Pol, Raibeart and myself there were forty of us. It was a pathetic number but I wanted to induce the Saxons into attacking. The archers and the slingers were our secret weapon. Just then Aedh's rider galloped in. "My lord! The other warband is just two miles away!"

"Then we have less than an hour to defeat this band! Aedh follow the wagons and aid Tuanthal."

We locked shields. Pol was behind me and Raibeart to my right. It was like old times. The Saxons had decided to attack and their wedge, three hundred strong, came lurching towards us. We were aided by the uneven ground which stopped them being as tightly packed as we were and Aelle and Miach took advantage of it. Their shot and their arrows rained down finding the gaps in the Saxon lines. As soon as a man fell an arrow or stone would take the one behind. This created bigger gaps than their leader would have liked. I could see the wedge shrinking and loosing unity as it neared us.

"Lock shields and ready yourselves!" We only had two ranks but the rear rank was pressed against the last Saxon ship. They would not push us back!

I was already swinging Saxon Slayer before they struck our line. My height and reach meant that I could strike an enemy before he reached me. The edge of the blade sliced across and through the cheek of the first man. It ripped through the bottom half of his jaw, tearing open his throat. Raibeart's sword hacked down and through the skull of the chief next to him who tried to spear me. Pol punched through from the second rank to strike another of their warriors and then we were face to face and none of us could swing our weapons. My left had held my dagger and I stabbed upwards into the stomach of the surprised warrior who looked down to see his guts spilling out. There were so many men pressing that his body stayed there. The slingers and the archers behind us had a clear field and were choosing their targets. The warriors pressing to get to the front were the ones to fall. The pressure began to ease and the body before me slipped to the ground.

Suddenly Pol shouted, "Equites!" and pointed to the hillside.

He was right. Had Tuanthal disobeyed me? It was too late to do anything about it now for the line of equites suddenly charged down the hill towards the Saxons who had no idea of their fate. My shield wall was not moving and the archers were still killing. When the horses, spears and equites struck the rear of the line it sounded like the crack of thunder! And then it was over. The Saxons fell like a field of wheat. It was not combat, it was slaughter. As we rushed forwards to despatch the wounded I prepared the tongue lashing for Tuanthal. Despite the success he had disobeyed my orders and we would have won anyway. It might have taken a little longer but we would have prevailed.

The first of the equites pushed forwards and I saw the nearest one raise his helmet. "Well met Lord Lann. I thought I had served the Warlord of Rheged for the last time!"

"Prince Pasgen! By all that is... You are a sight for sore eyes." I looked down his men. There were only sixty of them. He had commanded five hundred when I had left.

Aelle's voice came from above me. "Lann. The other band is coming. I am firing the ships."

I turned to Raibeart. "Take the men south. Pol, watch the western band. Prince Pasgen, will you join with us?"

His face suddenly looked ten years older. "I might as well. I have failed to retake Rheged and this is all that remains?"

"Your families."

"Slaughtered!"

I could think of no words and I merely grasped his arm. Behind me the flames started to lick around the hulls of the Saxon ships and palls of thick black smoke erupted from them. "Then let us head for the rest of the remnants and refugees of Rheged."

Pol had our horses and we rode with Prince Pasgen as the rearguard of our forces. I could see that the warriors or Rheged had stripped the Saxon bodies already, taking anything of value and the better mail shirts and helmets would help us in the days to come.

"What happened my prince?"

He snorted, "Prince of what? My brother gave the kingdom away and my people are in thrall. It was he who sanctioned the attack on my town and the slaughter of the innocents. I wish that it had been me who had slain the treacherous snake."

"No, Prince Pasgen. Your parents would not have wished you to soil your hands." I turned to look at the few who were still equites of Rheged. "We wondered what had become of you."

"Aye well, we found high places to hide and we raided them when they ventured on the roads but they learned to hide behind walls and we no longer had the archers you have." He shrugged it made the difference. "With the harsh winters our horses died and we had none to replace them. We had no Myrddyn to heal our sick and wounded. More died after battle than during."

I nodded. I knew the worth of a healer, especially one as good as Myrddyn. "You will come with us then?"

He looked at me curiously. "I am surprised to see you here. Did your journey to Wales fail?"

"No. We have a secure island and we are beholden to no man. I rule the land as Lord Lann, Warlord of Rheged."

"Then why are you here?"

"The Saxons raided me and I found out, from a prisoner, that my brothers were besieged. I brought my archers and horsemen to help them."

His jaw dropped open. "You came north with just two hundred men?"

"No I came north with one hundred men. Ridwyn and Garth guard my son with my army until I return."

"Riderch?"

"No, he died in battle. We still have the men from Strathclyde although they are fewer in number but we are as safe as anywhere. We taught the Irish a lesson or two and they do not bother us. We have an arrangement with the Welsh and they leave us alone."

He laughed, "This is well done then. We just need to trot on down to Wales eh?"

"Slightly more than a trot. There are many Saxon settlements between here and Mona but this was the highest hurdle." I hesitated. "How did your brother die?"

He laughed, "It was not a glorious death. It was not a death that people will talk of and write songs about. He had a feast and all of the Saxon nobles and lords were invited. One of them became drunk and began to mock Ywain as the king who let a shepherd do his fighting for him. Ywain became outraged and insulted the Saxon. The Saxon stabbed him. Of course King Aethelfrith feigned horror and shock. The Saxon lord was executed but many believed he was put up to it. It ensured the Kingdom of Rheged became Saxon, finally and completely. It was about that time he spread the rumour that I had been captured but I had not. We lived in the fly and midge ridden forests where other men could not live and even we just existed. We survived on the scree side where even mountain goats struggled to live. We ate lichen and insects. We did all that we could so that one day we would tell our story or perhaps conquer Rheged again." He looked wistfully to the north.

"You know that can never be."

"Aye, I know it now but we can build another Civitas perhaps on Mona and learn the lessons of Rheged. Then we will have a story that they will tell for years to come."

I clapped him about the shoulders. "Together we will write that story! It will be a story of glory and men fighting as brothers in arms to defend the poor and defeat the invaders."

He nodded and then shook his head as though to clear a memory. "Gildas is dead too. Ywain captured the youth and had him tortured to death. He lured him to the castle with promise of peace and then he tortured him to find out my whereabouts. I wished I had killed him for just that one act of cruelty. Gildas worshipped his cousin."

That too saddened me. We had all three fought together for Ywain's father, Urien and had been as close as brothers. I too wanted revenge upon Ywain but now I would have to wait until I faced him in the afterlife.

We had reached the camp. Myrddyn had built a barricade of the wagons and trees. There were fires going and he had men on watch. He did not seem surprised to see Prince Pasgen. "Good to see you again."

I threw him a questioning look. "You knew?"

He shrugged, "I dreamed he was not dead. That is all." I wished that, sometimes, Myrddyn would share more of his information with me!

Raibeart and Aelle were surprised to see Prince Pasgen. "We had heard rumours that you were in the cells of Civitas Carvetiorum?"

The prince, who had aged considerably since the last time we had seen him, shook his head, "No they tried with traps and ruses but your brother taught me well and I did not trust Ywain."

"You knew him better than any. What made him change?"

"He thought he was invincible and when he was wounded it cast doubt into his mind and then he relied on the likes of Bladud too much. He forgot the basic rule that a warrior must be true to himself first." I saw, for the first time, the armour and weapons of Pasgen and his men. It showed the lack of maintenance. "Aelle, do you have a blacksmith?"

"There is Alan. He is good with metal."

"Have him take a look at the armour and weapons of Prince Pasgen. We will all need better protection if we are to traverse this next part of Saxon England." Pasgen looked to be embarrassed by their state. I went to him and spoke quietly. "It will take time, my friend, but soon you will command the finest equites in the land again. We have many fine horses on my island and we have begun to breed excellent mounts."

Pasgen knelt and offered me the hilt of his sword. "As always, Lord Lann, I serve the Warlord of Rheged. Command me as you will."

I raised him up. "Let us get to Mona first and then work out our allegiances."

As my captains went to see to their own men Myrddyn put his arm around my shoulder. "And before you collapse Warlord; get some sleep. You have made many good decisions today but if you do not sleep then you may make foolish ones in the morning. I can watch for you and besides," he waved his hand at the rest," if you do not sleep then your men will not either."

"Very well, Myrddyn, but wake me at the first sign of trouble!"

I dreamed again that night, perhaps it was Pasgen who stirred the old memories or the reuniting with my brothers but she came to me again, the lady in white, the incarnation of my mother.

'*The dragon must be fought and its child nurtured. Use your brothers wisely and your son will be a great leader.' She seemed to walk across water and reach her hand out to me and then, just as suddenly, she was gone.*

I awoke and saw that it was Myrddyn. "Aedh's scouts are in. There are Saxons heading down the river. Miach and his archers are in position." I opened my mouth and he said, "We will talk of the dream later, when we have more time."

I shook my head. It was hard living with a man who knew your very thoughts. "Raibeart and Aelle?"

"They are rousing the men."

I watched as the four leaders walked over to me. "Tuanthal and Prince Pasgen, take the horsemen and secure a camp close to the place we used when travelling north. Raibeart and Aelle get your people moving. Aedh, get one of your scouts to lead them you will need to go around the estuary and then follow the coast. The equites should have built a camp by then. It is not a short journey, brothers but we need to put distance between us and then we can try to work out how to get across the Ribble, unseen."

Raibeart asked, "And you brother?"

"I will be with my archers slowing down the Saxons." I flicked a glance at Myrddyn. "And my wizard will be with me."

The people moved urgently when the word spread that the Saxons were close. The women and children had had the comfort of the boats the previous day but now the lucky ones were riding the crudely constructed wagons while most walked and looked fearfully over their shoulders. Pol and I joined Miach and his eighty archers. We had mounted Raibeart's men too, on the spare horses. The rear-guard had to be mobile.

"They are coming down the western bank of the river." Aedh's report was the worst news. The Saxon leader knew that we had to cross soon. Had we ported the Saxon boats over the rocks then we could have sailed all the way back to Mona but the shallows three miles back and the proximity of the Saxons had meant that we had to do it the hard way.

"Then let us wait for them on the western bank. Mount your men and we will ride south, catch up with the column and then cross over. We will ambush them instead of waiting for them to strike."

"There are three hundred of them."

"We will fight from a distance and make them pay for every piece of Rheged that they tread."

When we reached the rearguard, with Raibeart in command, there was a little panic from some of the warriors; they had not had the success against the Saxons that Miach and my warriors had. "Are they close behind you?"

"No Raibeart but they plan to attack you when you cross and are vulnerable. We will wait in that wood, yonder and ambush them. Keep your men in a line across the river and wait for them there."I pointed to a wide section of the river.

"Will they manage?"

"Let us see." I plunged in and the water came up to the horse's hocks. "It you put a rope up then they can hold that if they are fearful." Miach had crossed the river higher up and he waved to me as he led his men over the small field next to the river and climbed to the small wooded area. "We will hold them Raibeart, but you and Aelle must push them hard. I have done this and know that there will be complaints. Harden your heart. It will save lives in the long run."

"I will and stay safe brother."

The woods were not much higher than the river but when the Saxons came they would be forced closer to the water. Once we were behind the trees and the small rise we dismounted and tied our horses to the branches. The ground to the north was hidden from us and, equally, the Saxons would not know where we crossed. They would be counting on the women slowing us down. I peered anxiously through the trees as the column slowly crossed the river. There were fifty men in a thin line across the river with Raibeart in the middle. They would slow down any Saxon charge but they could not hold them.

We had one scout on the low ridge to the east and he suddenly galloped down. "They are just over the rise, my lord."

"Well done. Ride down and tell Lord Raibeart and then return here." I turned to the archers. "We have to wait until they are level with us before we loose and that means we release our arrows quickly. We loose five and then Captain Miach and my archers will retreat two hundred yards along the ridge. Lord Raibeart's archers will stay with me and loose another five before we join them." I could see pride mixed with apprehension amongst Raibeart's men but Miach would ensure that his men covered us when we retreated. I saw Raibeart wave and the column moved quicker when the word was spread.

The scout returned to me. "He said to say thank you my lord."

"Good. Now you stay with me and Pol. We may need you."

His eyes widened. "Yes, my lord!"

Suddenly the line of Saxons erupted over the ridgeline. Their attention was gripped by the column, the tail end of which was just entering the water. They must have thought that, with so few warriors guarding the river, they had the column cold for they spent time forming a wedge and then they began to lumber down the rock littered slope. I could see a chief at the front and the warriors were banging their shields as they descended. It was intended to intimidate the men in the river but they stood calmly as the last few women and children crossed. Raibeart took his men and formed a shield wall two men deep. The Saxon chief would have been hoping that his enemy would do that. He would destroy the warriors and then capture the column at his leisure.

The Saxons were coming obliquely down the slope and they were treading carefully. Their leader did not want to risk his men losing cohesion. He did not need to run hard; the slope and the sheer weight of numbers would ensure his success. He outnumbered Raibeart by almost seven to one. It was impossible for him to lose.

When the wedge was before us, just a hundred paces away, I shouted, "Loose!" The archers needed no more orders. Their five flights flew effortlessly into the air and into the wedge. The Saxons were confused and looked for the source of the death which rained upon them. Even as they saw our hiding place and began to turn Miach and my men mounted their horses and galloped from cover. Raibeart's men still loosed their next five flights. In that time the wedge half turned and tried to lumber towards us. It could not complete the manoeuvre quickly. "Right lads. Well done and to horse! Let us get out of here!"

We mounted and set off after Miach. The Saxon chief urged his men towards us. One of them hurled his throwing axe and it struck the scout's horse a lucky blow on the hind leg. It suddenly bucked and then slipped, throwing the unfortunate youth to the ground. "Pol, grab him." As Pol reached down to help him up I notched another arrow and aimed it at the warrior who was but thirty paces from me. The arrow went through his helmet and out of the back of his skull. I wheeled my mount around and followed the others as the cheers of Raibeart's men and the archers rang in my ears.

Raibeart and his men were trotting down the valley after the column and I saw the line of archers awaiting us to join them. There was no hurry; our horses could out run the Saxons and Miach waited until the Saxons were a hundred paces away and then he loosed his five flights. The Saxons were ready and held up their shields. They had to stop to do so and even then some of the arrows found gaps and I heard the shouts as Saxons were hit.

Raibeart's men formed a line behind Miach's. "Dismount. Now breathe slowly and ready yourselves." As soon as Miach's men had finished they led their horses to a spot ten paces behind us. "Loose!" Again they held up their shields and the effect was the same. We were buying time for the column and the price was our precious arrows. I could see the stiffening corpses which showed our success. "Pol, take the scout to Raibeart and then rejoin me."

The Saxons were wary now and had taken many casualties. I led my men to join Miach and the wedge changed to a shield wall and continued down the valley. Miach looked at his rapidly emptying quiver. "We only have twenty left my lord."

"I know. We cannot afford them to hit shields only. We will watch them. Follow me."

My brother was now leading the column due east. From our vantage point I could see the estuary. Had the Saxons had a better leader then they could have headed due south from their camp and cut us off but, instead, they had tried to catch us and that gave us the lifeline we needed. The ridge we were on headed south east. By keeping to its top we prevented the Saxons from using it and every moment took the column further away from danger.

Pol galloped up. I could see excitement all over his face. "The head of the column has reached the estuary. We have seen the equites on the other side!"

Once we lost the ridge then the Saxons could use their weight of numbers to their advantage. They could not know how few arrows we had left but our lack of aggression would give them a clue. "Are there any more obstacles twixt here and there?"

"There is a small stream and then a hill and some woods."

I made up my mind. "Good. We will use the stream. Take me to it." I could see the ridge dropping down to the sea and I yelled. "Captain Miach, follow me. We ride swiftly." We galloped away, taking the Saxons by surprise. We dropped over the ridge line and I saw how close the estuary was. The stream was no obstacle but any body of men crossing it would become disordered. Behind it lay the woods. Once again we disappeared from the view of the Saxons.

"Captain Miach, take your men and prepare an ambush behind those trees on that hill. I will lead them to the sea and you can attack their unprotected backs."

"That is just ten arrows each Warlord!"

"Then make every one count." Shaking his head he rode off. We crossed the stream and halted just forty paces away. I looked over my shoulder and saw that Miach was already hidden from sight. "We are not going to release our arrows together. You are Lord Raibeart's men, and I know that you can hit the dick on a fly if you want to!" They laughed. "When the Saxons come," just then the first of them appeared three hundred paces away over the ridge, "then we make them pay. Spread out and your task is to kill as many Saxons as you can. When your quiver is empty then mount and ride to Pol. I will join you." As they began to align themselves I turned to Pol. "Place yourself below the hill. If I fall then lead the men along the estuary. Miach will do the rest."

"If you fall I will rescue you!"

"You will obey my orders, young Pol, or I will be looking for another standard bearer!"

"Yes, my lord." He rode off. he was a good warrior but he needed to learn discipline.

The Saxons were now approaching the stream. As I had thought they could not keep a shield wall together as they stepped down and across its rocky bottom. I saw one warrior slip without the aid of an arrow and then Raibeart's men began to kill them. There were many warriors who did not have a full-face helmet, and they were the first to die. I killed one who had had his shield up but when he slipped it dropped a little, I saw his face and he died. As they formed up, just forty paces away, we changed targets to hit the legs of those warriors who did not have long mail shirts. The wounds were not life threatening but they stopped pursuit. Finally, when they were thirty paces away we aimed at their heads and their chests. Unless they had expensive armour, the arrows would penetrate. Had we had full quivers it might have ended there but we did not. I glanced around and saw that most of the archer's quivers were empty. "Ride!" I loosed my last two arrows and then I joined them. The Saxons roared in anger and frustration as they hurtled after us.

I could see that most of the archers had reached Pol and I shouted. "Lead them along the estuary Pol." I was annoyed, he should have obeyed orders and I would have to speak with him later; if there was a later.

The horses were now tiring. They had been ridden all day with little food and virtually no rest. I had to hope that the Saxons were tiring even more. My spirits rose as I saw that they were spread out more than they had been before and we had certainly whittled down the numbers. "Pol, keep riding. Make them think we are fleeing." I was counting on the fact that they would not have counted our men and would not be expecting the ambush. I deliberately slowed down to encourage those at the front to hurry after me. It also saved my horse a little because I had my armour on and, although he was a powerful beast, he could not run all day with me on his back. I glanced over my shoulder. The leading twenty warriors were just fifty paces behind. These were fit men. I hoped that Miach would allow them to pass before he loosed at the main band of a hundred men who trailed further behind. Looking back, at the stream, I could see the last twenty Saxons limping along, gamely trying to keep up.

Suddenly I heard the whoosh of the arrows followed by screams as Miach's archers struck. Five flights were enough to halt the main band who held their shields up and then he changed his target and the twenty who were closest to me died to a man. My archers joined me and I could tell that the Saxons had had enough. If the equites had been with me we could have slaughtered them all but I was happy with the victory we had had. We had escaped their trap and now just had the long journey home.

Chapter 5

We caught up with the column sooner than we had expected. Myrddyn had chosen to camp on the estuary. In fact we could see, if we went from the dell he had chosen to the river, the Saxons limping northwards on the other side.

"I took the decision Warlord, not Tuanthal. If you wish to blame someone and to berate one of us then it ought to be me."

"Why would I do that?" I was as mystified as any by my wizard's reaction. Although, to be honest, they all seemed equally afraid of me. Was I so bad tempered and intolerant these days? "I can see nothing wrong with the site but I am interested in knowing why you chose this one."

"Here we have fresh water. However the main reason is that everyone is tired; you and your warriors especially. We need to rest and, when I saw how few Saxons remained after your valiant efforts I knew that we were in no immediate danger. You had sucked the spirit from the Saxons."

"Do not flatter me wizard!"

"I speak the truth. But the real reason is that I think we can avoid the Saxon settlement at Prestune. We can use the road we did the last time when we travelled south."

It was such an obvious answer that I berated myself for not thinking of it. "Excellent. Then we camp here."

Tuanthal and Pasgen had had time to scout for miles in every direction and there were no Saxons to be seen. We put out pickets and slaughtered some more of the animals. While the food was cooking I walked the camp with Tuanthal and Myrddyn. "We need more horses."

"That is easier said than done, Myrddyn. They are as rare as hen's teeth in these parts."

"Let me take some of my men and range further ahead of the column. Now that we have Pasgen we can spare six or seven of us."

"He is right, Warlord. If we have more horses then we can move faster. It took four days for us to reach here from Wales. It will take at least twice that moving at the speed we are and the longer we are on the road the ore chance the enemy has of seeing us."

""Like me, do you think they will follow us when we venture further south? Perhaps we have broken their will."

Myrddyn shook his head. "Aethelfrith has to follow us. He lost you and now he has lost your brothers. He was outwitted and beaten by you on too many occasions. There are others who seek his throne and, until he defeats you he is under threat from within."

"Very well. Tuanthal, you had better choose your men and leave first thing."

"I will my lord!" Tuanthal, was still a young man at heart and loved adventure. I envied him the freedom to ride without anyone giving him orders. I would be tied to the slow-moving column and all would be looking to me to make decisions. He raced back to the camp to choose his men and begin his quest.

I turned to Myrddyn. "And now the dream!"

"Ah yes the dream. Your mother came to me and told me that Pasgen was alive and then she told me to beware those who pretend to be friends."

"She warned me of dragons. That makes no sense at all."

"Of course it does."

"The Welsh are the dragon. I can see that but they are our allies and there is no reason for betrayal."

"There doesn't need to be. Remember Morcant Bulc."

I remembered the king who was so jealous of King Urien's success that he had had him killed. Myrddyn was right. "Let us keep this suspicion to ourselves eh? It may not be true and I would not like to lose the only friend and ally we have over a misplaced word."

"As you wish, but the spirits have yet to be wrong."

When we reached the camp Myrddyn sat with my brothers, Pasgen and Miach to pore over his maps. To me they were truly magical. They showed land we had never seen before. They were the result of Brother Osric's long life. Each time some returned to Civitas he asked them of the land through which they had travelled and he had carefully drawn his maps. As he received more information the maps were refined and what Myrddyn held were the culmination of that life's work. The wizard pointed to the road painted red on the map. It ran straight and true. "That is the main Roman road. We have travelled it before and know its course." He waved a finger at the area to the west. "This is where we are. As you can see there are neither roads nor settlements but there are valleys and passes. By heading towards the south east we can, effectively, disappear."

Miach sniffed. "But we can be tracked. There are hundreds of people and animals. Ort perhaps you have some magic to hide us?" Miach, of all of us, was sceptical of Myrddyn's powers although he was happy to take any advantage the young healer gave us.

Myrddyn pointed at the sky and smiled. "We have all lived in this land to know of the rains. When we cross towards the road we will be travelling on rocky parts of the land. When the rains come they will wash away all evidence of our passing. If that is magic then," he waved his hands around like a village conjuror, "so be it. However we can spread our tracks by putting our horsemen further away from the main column. I estimate that we will be at the road by early afternoon tomorrow and then we will not have to worry about tracks."

Raibeart and Aelle both understood maps. "You have travelled this road before brother. How long to reach our destination?"

I shook my head, "I am not sure Aelle. We went more directly the last time. Since then Deva has been occupied by Saxons and we will have to travel further east. There are also Saxons who are now attacking Gwynedd. It could take ten days, it could take eight days. Much of it depends upon what Tuanthal discovers."

Myrddyn, Miach and Pasgen could see that my brothers had many questions for me and they took their leave. With Tuanthal gone Pasgen would have to get to know the equites better and Miach had the rest of the warriors to organise.

When alone with me, my brothers relaxed. They could speak to me without thinking about their words. They could be honest. "Will we get there Lann?"

"Yes Raibeart, and I know that you fear for your family."

He started, "Are you becoming a wizard too that you can read my mind so easily?"

I laughed and began to relax myself, "No but I was as worried as you were when I travelled with Hogan. I had just one to worry about but you have a wife and children and you have had to flee before." Raibeart's face hardened at the memory. He had had to be rescued by my warriors when he had fled Elmet with his father in law, the King of Elmet. He had lost many men and almost lost his family. "The difference this time is that we are not being closely pursued." I pointed across the estuary. "Our pursuers have been beaten. They will return but by then we will have along lead and their speed will weaken them. I am more worried by what we do not know. Who lives along our route? Will we have enough food?

Those and many other questions, questions we do not yet know. We three will have to find answers to these unknown questions."

Aelle nodded. "You have become a thinker as well as a warrior brother."

"You were always the thinker Aelle. I have learned from you."

"No Lann, you have vision such as Myrddyn has. You are good for each other. It is as though the two of you are more powerful because of the other. It is *wyrd*!"

Freja and Maiwen brought us food. I smiled when I saw the subtle look my brothers gave to their wives; they left us alone. I knew that it meant some more questions and the two brothers did not want their wives to hear the answers. I had been married and I knew why men kept such secrets from their women.

We ate for a while and then Raibeart asked, "And what of the island? What happens when we reach it?"

I could not quite understand where he was going with these questions and I frowned as I said, "You will be home, of course."

Aelle said, "No Lann, Raibeart asks where, on the island, we will go? Mona is your home and your people live there. It is not like Wide Water where no one lived. There are the people of Mona and your people who followed you from Rheged. Will they be happy about being displaced?"

I smiled, now I understood. "No-on will be displaced. The island is large and there are many fertile places as yet, without people. The Irish had been raiding the island for years and using it for slaves. It is only since I arrived that the practice has ceased and then there is the mainland. The King of Gwynedd, Beli, was happy for us to occupy it as the ones who lived there were brigands and thieves. You need not worry about your destination. It is the journey which vexes me the most." I looked at the two of them. "Where do you wish to be?" I could see they did not understand me. I suppose we had been absent from each other's lives for some time and lost each other's ways. "You have lived in close proximity and harmony for some time. Would you continue as such or would you wish to have your own towns which were separate from each other?"

"We will have to think on that and then there is Prince Pasgen."

"I know Aelle and I am worried. He and his men have lost all family. We all know that family is important. I will ask Myrddyn on our journey south but, for the moment, just watch him for me."

We struck the road towards early afternoon and I sent Aedh and his scouts in a ring, two miles ahead. Prince Pasgen split his horsemen so that half were a rearguard a mile behind us and the rest a vanguard a mile ahead. Finally Miach and his archers lined the two sides of the column, ready to react in case of danger. The first part of the road was devoid of all life, human and animal and, when we camped I asked Miach to send out a couple of hunters. "We will begin to run short of food soon and we know that those who are not warriors can cope with tiredness and they can cope with hunger, but not both at the same time."

"We have seen precious little so far, my lord."

"I know but even squirrels or rabbits would provide some sustenance."

Tuanthal returned at noon the next day. He had eight horses, of varying quality with him. "Five were wild but three we liberated from their Saxon owners."

I immediately became alert to danger. "Saxons? Where? To the south?"

"No Lord Lann." He pointed to the west. "North of Prestune. We led them north to make them believe that was our direction of travel. It is why we have taken so long to reach you."

I hated this veiled, unknown area into which we travelled. I felt blind and helpless. I trusted my scouts and I trusted my men but I needed to judge myself. "Tomorrow I will lead your scouts and you can remain with the column."

His face fell. "Have I displeased you Warlord?"

"No Tuanthal but I must share the riding and the responsibility. I will just be gone for one day."

At camp that evening the others also tried to gainsay me. The only one who remained silent was Myrddyn. Raibeart asked, "Why do you not add your opinion wizard? You know that my brother values your opinion."

"It matters not. I have not see his death yet. Besides it is good if he can see the road."

Miach snorted and pointed to the nearby cobbled way. "We can all see the road wizard!"

Myrddyn shook his head, "I mean the way ahead rather than this Roman Road we travel. He has decisions to make which he can only make if he knows what lies ahead."

Myrddyn was hard to fathom. Sometimes he would argue with you and you couldn't see why and at others he agreed with you for no good reason. *Wyrd*!

Tuanthal ensured that I had his five best warriors with me. Tadgh, Rafe, Gwillim, Adair and Rowan would one day each lead ten men. They were not only accomplished equites but they were all good scouts. Three of them had been with me since I first went to Castle Perilous and I knew them well. None of us wore armour or carried shields. I had Saxon Slayer and my bow. Arrow numbers were now becoming critical and I would have to husband my supply.

I knew that we were coming close to the land of the Ribble. Although we would have no difficulty crossing it I knew that the Saxons were not far away at Prestune and we had not investigated the land to the east. I spied a forest and led my scouts towards it. I knew that we could hide within its trees and we might manage to get some game. As soon as we entered we saw animal tracks, which we followed, and then human tracks. I held up my hand and dismounted. The hunters were on foot and were tracking the animals. It meant they were probably Saxon although there were still pockets of people whom the Saxons had ignored. We would find soon enough. I sent Tadgh and Gwillim to the east; Adair and Rowan to the west and I kept Rafe with me. Their orders were simple. Follow the hunters. If they were Saxon we would kill them and if not then we would talk.

We rode our horses for a while and then we dismounted and tied the animals to a tree. I notched my bow as did Rafe. The last spoor had been fresh which meant the hunters were closing on their prey. Suddenly there was a crash in the brush ahead and then the death squeal of at least one animal. We both went even more cautiously then. I saw a lighter area ahead and I began to creep, one step at a time. I saw the hunters, there were five of them and they had killed two deer. They were clearly Saxons.

I did not know where the others were but I trusted their ears. They would have heard the noise in the silent forest and they would be close. If Rafe and I could kill two with arrows then I knew that we could finish the other three off with swords if needs be. I pointed to the man on the right and then at Rafe. He nodded. I drew back. At twenty yards there was no way that I could miss. The arrow took him in the back a heartbeat before his companion died. I loosed my second which struck a third man and then a flurry of arrows killed the last two.

When we reached them one was still alive and Rafe reached for his dagger. I shook my head. I spoke in Saxon to the dying man. "Where are you from?"

He looked at me uncomprehendingly. "Who is your chief?"

"Where are you from?"

He pointed to the south. "The Roman fort." He still looked puzzled as he died.

As the others arrived we stripped the dead and prepared the animals. I also wracked my brains. I remembered that the map Myrddyn had shown us had a major fort at a place marked as Bremetennacum. It was situated where five roads met. We had not seen it when we came south but it was close and now it was occupied.

"Rafe you and Rowan ride back with the deer to the column. Tell Myrddyn and Tuanthal that we are heading for the Roman fort called Bremetennacum and we will return before dark. Tell them that there are Saxons there!"

We left the woods and headed south. Soon we found their tracks. We saw the main road to the west. It headed towards the river and what had once been a Roman fort although now most of the stones had been taken. There was a small stream which ran parallel to the road and it entered a wood. We took advantage of the shelter of the small valley and rode in the middle of the stream to confuse any trackers. When we reached the woods we dismounted and made our way to the edge. We could see the fort some forty paces from the bridge. The fort had had most of its stones removed and looked to be a ruin which explains why we had not noticed it on our way south but now I saw a new stockade and wooden wall much closer to the bridge and there were Saxons there now. It seems the Saxons had seen the potential of the site and were exploiting it. Leaving our horses in the trees we made our way cautiously down the stream. There were bushes and trees lining it and we would be invisible to all but someone in the stream as well. I had an arrow ready in case of that eventuality.

We met no one. The cover ended just thirty paces from the wooden ramparts of the Saxon settlement. I could see a couple of men at the gate but they were not heavily armed; they looked to have a spear and an old and somewhat rusted sword. There looked to be twenty huts which put the number of people at a hundred or more. There were no horses and so we left. After we had mounted our horses I led us directly south to the river. It was less than twenty yards wide at this point. I had Tadgh keep watch while I urged my horse into the current. It was shallow, apart from the middle three paces, where we had to swim. I made my way back and we explored the river further downstream. It was the same the whole way. We had a problem. I led us back to the column.

"And so we have two solutions," I smiled as I glanced over to Myrddyn, "unless our wizard has a third, to this thorny problem. We can attempt a crossing at night of a narrow river but our people may have to swim a few paces or…"

"Or?" asked Aelle, fearful of my tone.

"Or we massacre a Saxon village!"

Aelle shook his head, "As much as I hate the Saxons that is a step too far."

I nodded. Aelle was half Saxon himself and had Saxon blood in his veins and I agreed with him. However I also knew that ruthless decisions had to be made.

"I for one would happily slaughter the Saxons." I nodded at Prince Pasgen to acknowledge his views. I could have predicted his reply.

There was silence. "And the rest of you?"

Myrddyn gave an apologetic smile. "I think most of us would baulk at slaughtering villagers just to keep them silent but I know that a night crossing would cause great risk and danger to our people without the guarantee that the Saxons would not discover us the next day."

Again there was silence. "So the Warlord makes the decision?"

"You are Warlord, brother and we support whatever you decide for the best of us all."

"However," interrupted Myrddyn with an apologetic wave of the hand to Raibeart. "I do not think that you heard me correctly. I was saying that all of us thought that the river crossing was the only solution but it does, perhaps, need refining."

He had everyone's attention now. "Explain wizard!"

"The river is less than twenty paces wide?" I nodded. "Then we create a bridge."

Everyone gasped but it was Miach who spoke for all of us. "Build a bridge! At night! You have taken too many of your own potions wizard!"

"Firstly I do not take potions either mine or others but we do not build a bridge. I said create. We have a bridge already. Much like the one we used at the Narrows."

I suddenly saw it! Of course! The wagons and two ropes!"

"Well done Warlord. Except that it will not be hard to get the ropes over as it is so narrow."

"I am sorry, "said Prince Pasgen. "What am I missing? Bridge? Wagon? Rope?"

Myrddyn explained by drawing in the soil around the fire. "Here is the river. Two men cross with two or more heavy ropes. They secure the ropes to solid objects; perhaps a tree or a rock. We put people in a wagon and men pull the wagon across. The people stay dry and they could be across in less than an hour."

Aelle almost shouted for joy. He jumped up. "That is an amazing idea. It will work." One by one they all nodded. Even Miach, with a wry grin and nod to Myrddyn were in favour.

"Tuanthal, we will need you men to form a skirmish line to prevent us being seen and your men and Aedh's scouts will need to be in place by tomorrow afternoon."

As we rode south we refined the plan. We had six wagons which meant that each one would just need to make two trips. This would speed things up as we could load one wagon whilst another was crossing. Aedh met us when we reached the river just after dark. "I have two men at the village. If anyone leaves they will tell Captain Tuanthal who is just a mile from the walls. We will have ample warning.

As I watched I reflected that this would also cause some confusion for the Saxons. They would see where we had crossed but not see how we had managed to do so. It would add to the myth of Myrddyn's magic. We still had the problem of game as the two deer had soon been devoured and I knew that there were few forests to the south. We would be travelling through the open land where game was scarce and farms more likely. We had to rely on the fact that farmers bothered themselves with their own business. We now had a mere five days to reach the vicinity of the Dee. Although that would bring its own problems, one we were beyond that barrier then the Saxons could chase all they liked; we would be within reach of my army. The next few days would be critical.

Chapter 6

We reached the land close to the Dee estuary without further incident. Having lost no-one in the crossing of the Ribble, the spirits of the people were high. The bridge at Wilderspool was still guarded by a Saxon warband and as there were also Saxons at Deva we could not risk being halted and trapped north of the river. Aedh and Myrddyn had scouted to the east and found a small settlement and an easy ford. Myrddyn would, once again, play a Saxon if it was needed. When he returned, his face told me that it was not.

"They are of our people Warlord. It is called Caedwalestate and was built by an ancient lord called Caedwal. They too fear the Saxons. I gave them some coins but they would have helped us anyway. They say that there are over five hundred Saxons at Wilderspool. They are not bothered by them but they fear that when more come then their homes will be taken." He hesitated. "I promised them sanctuary on Mona if they needed it in the future."

"You did right. Well done." I turned to my brothers and Pasgen. "We are now on the last part of our journey. The danger is not over but we are now within three or four days of home; your new home."

Once we crossed the Maeresea I felt happier. The Dee was now our next obstacle and, so long as there were no Saxons nearby we should make it to Bishop Asaph's vale and safety. We kept the river to our right as we headed through the low lying land. We needed as easy a route as possible; our hastily constructed wagons and wheels were beginning to show signs of wear and tear. Rather than risking the Saxons who were threatening Iago's borders we would skirt Deva and hope that the Saxons were not scouting far from their castle.

We had travelled about twenty miles since crossing the river and we were tired. As we were making camp Aedh rode in fast and his face told the story before he had opened his mouth. "There are Saxons on the ridge and they have a fort."

We had gambled and it looked as though we had lost. Our choices were: to backtrack and find a route to the east of this place and risk passing the castle or head to Deva. None of them was particularly appealing. I summoned our leaders for a counsel of war. I gave them the three options and watched their faces. None of us could agree on a satisfactory plan of action.

Myrddyn came up with a solution, or at least the beginnings of one. "We had intended on passing the Saxons close to the east of Deva. The maps show flat land to the east of this place. If we sent out a scout we might find a route to the other side of this ridge. Aedh tells me that he thinks it is to control the land between here and the sea."

"Very well. Aedh see to it but the rest of us had better prepare for war. Unless we get a miracle then we will be fighting tomorrow." A sudden thought occurred to me. "How far to the monastery?"

Myrddyn checked his maps and his journal in which he had noted, as we had travelled, the distances. "As near as I can work it out about forty miles."

My shoulders sagged in disappointment. "That is too far to get in one day. We need somewhere to camp tomorrow which is safe." As everyone busied themselves preparing for the next day I looked north. Would Aethelfrith be following us? We had been lucky and avoided detection but, even on foot, his men could travel faster than we could with the families and the old. If we were held up by this fort then that might give the Saxon the time he needed to catch up.

Myrddyn found me. "There is a place here." He pointed at the map. I recall we passed it when travelling south. I believe it is called Haordine and there were people there but they had been our people then. When the men of Strathclyde joined us they too spoke warmly of the welcome they received. It is but twenty miles from here."

"And from there to the monastery?"

"Another twenty miles."

"In two days then we should be safe."

"I think so."

"Tuanthal!"

The tall equite was at my side almost instantly. "I want your best rider to get to the Narrows. I want a hundred of our warriors to be sent to the monastery. They have to be there in two days. Give your man a spare horse. He has to get through!"

"Yes Warlord."

Aedh brought some good news. "There is a good track to the east of the ridge and it will not damage the wagons too much."

"Good you have done well." I waved over Pasgen, Raibeart and Aelle. "We leave before dawn tomorrow and in silence." We had journeyed south in relatively high spirits with the children singing and playing as we lumbered through the land but we would need to hide on the morrow. There might be no one looking at night time but there would during the day. I wanted to be away from this potential death trap while we were still hidden from prying eyes. I watched the rider as he left with his spare horse. All our hopes now rested on one man and he was moving through a countryside riddled with danger.

The track was almost as good as a Roman road and that should have been a warning as it meant it was well used. We had our usual formation and the scouts could warn us quickly of danger. We had travelled about four miles when one of Tuanthal's men rode in. "Warlord, Captain Tuanthal sent me. There is a Saxon settlement yonder. There is a small warband heading this way."

"Have you been seen?"

The man looked worried, "I do not know Warlord. They may have seen me as I saw them."

I forced a smile. "It matters not. Ask the captain to watch them." I rode to the front of the column where Raibeart was leading. "Saxons are heading this way we need to hurry them up. It may be nothing. It is a small warband but I do not like it."

"I will do as you ask." He smiled, "There is not far to go. Look here comes the scout."

The scout reined in. "Have you found the place Myrddyn seeks?"

"Yes Warlord. There are the remains of a Roman fort but of the people there is nothing save some bones and burnt out huts."

My heart fell. The Saxons had been there and my hopes for a safe night were dashed. "You have done well. Scout two miles behind us. I would know if we are pursued."

I saw Miach on the left of the column and I approached him. "Pol, come with me." When we reached Miach I told him of the dilemma. "Ride with half of your archers and prepare the fort for defence. Pol, go with him and report back to me. I need to know if it is defensible. We may need it."

As the two riders left me I felt alone. I knew Aelle and Raibeart were good leaders but they had fought a defensive war hidden behind sound and safe defences. In the battle which was to come they needed quick minds and the courage to take risks. Would they take such risks with their families watching? I remembered how Ywain had changed when he married. Prince Pasgen would take risks and I sought him out. I trusted my brothers but I needed someone who would not be worrying about his family when he fought. He was riding ahead of the column and on the right.

The prince and his men all had grim determination written all over their faces. "Prince Pasgen. There is a warband to the east. It is not large but I like it not. I have sent Miach to fortify our camp for tonight but I need you and your men, should the need arise, to discourage them from following us."

"That would be a pleasure." He began to tug on his reins.

"Not yet, my prince, I await Captain Tuanthal. They may not be heading here after all and I do not wish to poke a wasp's nest until I have to. No matter how small the nest may be."

Tuanthal's rider returned. His face showed that he was happier. "They have continued west. Even if they have seen us we do not appear to interest them. The captain is watching them as you asked."

As he rode back I turned my horse to follow the column. Myrddyn had seen my comings and goings and he rode his mare next to mine. "Problems Warlord?"

"There is a small Saxon band. We think they have seen us but they appear to be heading west. I have asked Miach to fortify our camp for tonight." I pointed in the distance. "The Saxons have destroyed the people who lived there. There will be a cold welcome for us."

"Still, Roman walls are always welcome. They always choose a good position and will give us shelter." He looked across to the ridge. "They will either be going to Deva or that hill fort. If it is the hill fort then we may be in trouble; they could reach us tomorrow."

"I know. I contemplated attacking the warband but we would have had to destroy it completely and this close to the hill fort we couldn't guarantee it."

Pol galloped up and wheeled his horse around. "Captain Miach has fortified the hill. He says there is a good place for the wagons to the south and they will be out of sight of the Saxons."

As the afternoon drifted towards dusk I was relieved to see Miach and his men standing guard at the hill side Roman fort. Raibeart and Aelle put their wagons into a defensive formation on the Welsh side of the fort and away from any Saxon eyes. We ate our cold meal watching for the return of Tuanthal's men.

His news was the worst we could have expected. "They went directly to the hill fort. I left a couple of men watching them but I fear they are reporting our presence."

I knew that we could not leave early again; the people would not be able to manage two forced marches. "It looks like we may have to fight our way out of this. Keep all the horses on the other side of the fort. If they do come, and they may not, then they will come from the north. We can disguise our numbers and the secret weapon of the equites." I had no idea how many Saxons were at the occupied hill fort but we were in no condition to fight our way through a large number.

"We are down to thirty flights each Warlord. We have plenty of stones for the slingers but…."

"I know."

He shrugged and went off to organise his men. He would fight as hard for me no matter how many mistakes I made. It's just that he would let me know of my errors too! "Raibeart and Aelle you will need to be with the warriors tomorrow."

"There is a plan then?"

"Of course, Prince Pasgen."

Myrddyn stepped forwards and I nodded at him to explain. "If we assume the worst and that the Saxons will attack us tomorrow then we just firstly ensure that they do not see any horsemen, just the handful of warriors who will be standing here with Captain Miach's dismounted archers behind. We want them over confident and to make a shield wall." The wagons will already be rolling south with an escort of a few equites and half of the warriors. When the archers have loosed all of their flights then they will mount their horses and flee because they are afraid of the mighty Saxons." Miach snorted but I could see that he enjoyed the humour. The warriors will also rush through the fort after their comrades. The Saxons cannot climb the walls and the defences in a line and they will race over piece meal. On the other side they will see the fleeing warriors and they will race after them and then, Prince Pasgen, you and Captain Tuanthal will attack from two sides and slaughter the Saxons."

"It sounds good when you say it wizard but the Saxons may not dance to your particular tune."

I stepped forwards. "And that does not matter so long as the wagons get away and head towards the monastery. By now I hope that there will be at least a hundred men of my shield wall marching to our aid. All we need to do is slow down the Saxons until we can reach our men."

"And if they do not come?"

"Then little brother, the gods will not be smiling upon us but we will have a glorious end!"

When the equite woke me then I knew that the gods were not with us. "Warlord. The small band entered the hill fort and they left again an hour ago." He pointed to the distant ridge. "They were joined by five hundred Saxons. My companion is watching them and he will tell us when they are a mile away."

"You have done well. Pol, rouse the camp!"

Aelle led the wagons away with forty warriors while thirty of Tuanthal's equites escorted them. It made our numbers seem quite small. Raibeart and his men threw caltrops in front of the hill and spread themselves in an invitingly shallow line. Pasgen and Tuanthal each took half of the horsemen and they rode to two spots half a mile away where they would be hidden from view by folds in the land and bushes. Their signal to attack would be the buccina, held proudly by Pol. Finally the archers of Miach and the slingers were hidden behind the crumbling walls of the fort. The horses of the archers were tethered to logs at the bottom of the southern side of the hill. Pol and I stood, with the Wolf Banner in the centre of the line next to Raibeart. "Like old times!"

We clasped hands and chewed on some dried venison. It gave us something to do and stopped us filling the silence with useless chatter. I suppose the warriors of Glanibanta who stood with us would have taken our behaviour as bravely stoical but we were as worried and nervous as they were. We just hid it better.

The equite whipped his horse out of the lightening early morning sky and reined in next to me. "They are a mile away, Warlord!"

"Good. Follow the wagons and join the escort." I saw the disappointment on his face. "You have done well but you have been awake all night. I need warriors who are fresh. Your turn will come again, fear not."

The Saxons formed two confident wedges and came at us at an easy pace. It was light enough to see each other but no more than that. I was confident that the archers behind the walls were well hidden. Miach did not need superfluous orders and, just before the Saxons reached the bed of caltrops we had laid, he loosed his first arrows. Many of the warriors were taken unawares and they halted while their chiefs organised the shield wall. Miach continued to rain arrows on the stationary target then they ordered a charge, faster this time. When they struck the caltrops their line became totally disordered and Miach's arrows found more victims. My archer captain shouted down. "I have left the last three flights, Warlord."

"Hold them until we run."

I glanced at Raibeart and grinned. "Let us show them we have filled our breeks eh?"

The Saxons were less than thirty paces away and Raibeart shouted. "Run!" The men had been awaiting the order and they ran back towards the walls and the defences. Pol and I galloped to the east. The Saxons were momentarily confused and they reformed, ready for another attack. Raibeart and his men were now almost at the top of the hill and the Saxons decided it was not a trap and they ran towards the walls. As they climbed the slope Miach's last arrows struck them. Pol and I had ridden around the hill and watched as Raibeart and his grinning men trotted down the other side. Miach and his archers were already mounted and I waved them away. We would need them later on. Pol and I joined the 'fleeing' warriors. It took some time for the Saxons to emerge. The sun was now shining- it would be a glorious day- and they saw the pathetic handful of warriors running away. They surged down the hill in pursuit. All order had gone and they were just running to be the ones to slaughter these strangers who had dared to camp in their land.

Pol and I found it easy to both watch the Saxons and keep pace with the last of the warriors. Until the Saxons entered the killing zone then we were their only frail protection. Raibeart's men had not marched for hours, nor had they had to fight their way through the fort and, as a consequence they were finding it easy. I could see that some of the eager Saxons were already blowing hard.

"Warlord! The trees!"

I glanced in the direction Pol had pointed. It was the ambush site. "Almost there Raibeart!"

"About time! It is all right for you, you are on a horse!"

I laughed. The fact that he could talk while running in armour told me that he was not in danger. "Another hundred paces and you can stop and kill some Saxons!"

We had marked the place where they would halt with two piles of whitish stones. When I saw them I wheeled my horse around, as did Pol. "Raise the standard!"

Pol unfurled the banner and shouted, "Behold, the Warlord of Rheged and the Wolf Standard!"

Raibeart and his men turned and formed a wedge and the two parties of equites launched their attack. The Saxons saw the banner and kept on coming, seemingly oblivious to the danger from their flanks. The first warrior actually reached me and raised his axe to hack at my horse's head.

He was tired and he badly misjudged his swing. As I jinked my mount's head around his axe struck just air. Saxon Slayer did not and hacked down between his shoulder and his head. The equites struck the Saxons when the enemy had no order while the equites were a solid line of metal and horseflesh. None made the shield wall. It was as though someone had squeezed an over ripe apple and it just disintegrated into nothing. The warriors to the rear just fled the field and the equites despatched the wounded.

Raibeart shook his head. "Perhaps we should have stayed in Rheged, brother. How could the Saxons stand against us?"

"Remember, Aethelfrith has fought us for some years and knows our ways. He would not have fallen for such an obvious trap. Our problem now is that there were survivors and they will tell of the Wolf Warrior and word will get back to Aethelfrith and he will know that I survived." I saw that the riders were now stripping the bodies. "Raibeart get your men to dig a pit. There." I gestured to Pasgen and Tuanthal and they rode over. "Have your men only carry what they can comfortably. All the rest will be buried in a pit which Raibeart is digging. When the soil is down we will burn the bodies on the top." I grimaced. "It should make it easy to find when we need the iron and the armour!"

The burning pyre marked the site of the battle for all to see. I do not doubt that those in Deva saw it and wondered what it meant. I was not worried any longer. We were beyond the Dee and now we could push on to Bishop Asaph's monastery and safety- if Garth had received my message. Myrddyn had pushed hard and we only caught up with the column five miles from the monastery. The rider we had sent to bring help was riding along the track. He spurred his horse on when he saw us.

He leapt from the saddle and bowed, "My lord. I did as you asked and Captain Garth is almost at the monastery with two hundred men!"

So my captain had doubled the number. I hoped it would not return to haunt us. "Good, you have done well. You may rejoin your comrades."

Aedh had been off scouting with his indispensable men. He rode in. "Warlord, the Saxons of Deva have sallied forth. There are a thousand of them heading in this direction."

"How long?"

"They should reach the monastery or the coast by morning. It depends on us I think."

Garth had arrived just in time. "Have some men watch them and their movements."

I rode, with Pol to the monastery. I was now feeling guilty. The peaceful monks had, so far, avoided the attentions of the predatory Saxons. This might be the undoing of the community and I had to speak with Bishop Asaph himself. I passed the head of the column and waved at a bemused Myrddyn.

When I saw the bishop again I realised how old he had grown. He was resting on the arm of a younger monk. It made my news even more important. I feared it might cause him distress if his precious monastery and its peaceful inmates came under threat.

He smiled as he greeted me. "I take it your efforts were not in vain? You have your family?"

The bishop was like Myrddyn; he knew things no other man did. The secrecy of the mission did not matter now. "Yes thank you bishop but I fear it may be bringing trouble your way."

"Trouble has a way of finding all men sooner or later. What is it you pagans say? *Wyrd*? Perhaps this is *wyrd* too."

"An army has left Deva to pursue us."

"And you fear that, when they discover us they will want our treasures?"

Once again he had read my mind. "Yes Bishop Asaph. Are you not afraid?"

"When you reach my age then the fears are different ones such as how many times will I need to get up in the night? Is the food soft enough for my teeth to chew? Besides I assume you will fight them?"

I nodded, "Of course."

"Then I have nothing to fear." I frowned; I did not understand. "The Wolf Warrior does not lose and certainly not to Saxons. Besides if you do lose," he shook his head rapidly and I thought it might fall off, "a highly unlikely occurrence I must confess. But if you do then they will ignore us and take Mona. However I will send a message to King Iago asking for aid against the Saxons. He is not happy about their incursions and the death of his father. I think that he is spoiling for a fight."

I struggled for a reply, "I just didn't want you or your people hurt."

"And that alone marks you as a Christian. I thank you for your thoughts now I had better prepare for I assume you have the families of your people?" I nodded. "Then their needs will be seen to." He turned to the monk, "Come Brother Stephen let us seek shelter and say some prayers for our friends."

By the time the column had entered the monastery, Garth and my warriors reached us too. They showed the effects of the forced march but they tripled my shield wall and I knew then that we had a chance. The women especially were pleased to be in buildings with clean water and hot food. The monks smiled as they tended to the children. For Myrddyn, myself and my leaders it was far from peaceful. We had plans to make.

"While the men eat and drink we will plan. Aedh will let us know of the approach of the Saxons. We have some time. As we sat in one of the quiet places in the monastery I patted Garth on the back. "Thank you for bringing my men. It might just save us all."

"I did as I was asked and I also brought five thousand arrows." He shrugged, "I was at the Narrows anyway anticipating your return. We did not have far to come. Brother Oswald continued to make them after you had left. He thought they might come in handy."

"That priest might be the one to make me a Christian," said Miach with an uncharacteristic smile upon his grizzled face.

"They will have reports which tell them we have only a hundred warriors. Your men, Captain Garth, will be our secret weapon. They know about the arrows and they know about the equites. I suspect their leader will have planned accordingly and that may be his downfall."

All of them, the ones who had marched from Rheged and those who had trudged from Mona, were exhausted. The tension of the chase and the lack of food as well as sleep had taken much from them. Their men would be just as tired but we had one more battle to fight and I needed every man to fight as though it was his first. "Make sure your men have enough food and sleep tonight. We will use the scouts and the boys to keep watch." I saw them exchange looks. "I know what you are thinking, they are all just boys, but we will need neither scouts nor horse guards tomorrow. We will need warriors and the boys have shown that they can be men when called upon." I pointed to the valley a mile away, now darkened and empty in the east. "We will hold them there where they cannot flank us. The equites will be on the flanks to stop them gaining the high ground. The archers will be behind Raibeart's men and behind them will be Garth and the shield wall, lying down." There was an audible gasp. "They will be a hundred paces behind Raibeart's men. Raibeart, you and I will retreat slowly before the Saxons drawing them onto Miach's arrows and destroying their finest warriors and, when we are close only then Garth and his men will stand. They will march forwards to destroy the enemy.

Myrddyn will remain at the monastery and we can send any wounded to him."

Aelle was not convinced, "Is that not the plan we used before? At the Roman fort? They will expect it."

"No brother, they will see the horsemen and not know that we have the extra men. They will not expect two hundred of the finest warriors in the world to be attacking them. They will think we are road weary warriors who have fled their comrades in the north!"

Myrddyn nodded. "The Warlord is correct and, tomorrow, we will end this pursuit." He paused. "I have dreamed it."

Miach looked sceptically at the wizard but the others took it as though it was already done. They would pass that confidence on to their men on the morrow.

Chapter 7

The Saxons who came down the valley did not look like Saxons we had fought before. Firstly they had long spears and secondly they had archers. They intended to fight our two powerful weapons with their own versions. They outnumbered us, as usual. We were used to that. They would be fresher; they had only come from Deva and they knew how we fought. These Saxons from Deva had ousted my men of Strathclyde who had held the fort for me. It would not do to underestimate them.

When the Saxon horde saw the forces arrayed on the ridges and in the middle, they halted. The warriors with the spears formed a wedge which preceded half of the main warband as they advanced towards Tuanthal on the ridge. Between the spears and the warband were fifty or so archers. They were doing something the Saxons had never done before; they were attacking horses! I was confident that my young captain would be able to deal with the advancing men. The second wedge turned to climb the ridge towards Prince Pasgen and his equites. There were fewer spears on that flank but they prevented Pasgen from charging. Already our well laid plans had faltered.

"Raibeart, let us advance towards Prince Pasgen." He nodded, like me, he worried about Prince Pasgen's state of mind. While Tuanthal would handle his own situation calmly, Prince Pasgen might just order a reckless and potentially suicidal charge. There was little point in hiding Garth and his men now. "Captain Garth, follow Lord Raibeart."

Our small army echeloned to the right and suddenly one of our scouts galloped in. "Warlord! There is another army approaching from the north and they are attacking Captain Tuanthal!"

Even as I wondered who it might be I was calculating how best to minimise our losses. "Ride back to the captain and tell him to withdraw down the valley and guard our left flank."

It was about this time that I wished I was mounted. "Pol, get to Garth and explain that we have another army to contend with. We have to destroy this warband and then try to hold the rest off!"

He ran to Garth while I hurried to join Raibeart at the front of his wedge. "Captain Miach, I want you to attack the warband and then retire behind the shield wall. Aelle, order the slingers forward to take out the handful of archers they have with them." The only factor in our favour was that they had counted on destroying Tuanthal and the majority of their spears and their archers were on that flank.

I glanced to the left and sighed with relief. Tuanthal had disengaged, although I saw empty saddles as he galloped across the front of the warband. Prince Pasgen and his men were still on top of the ridge as the wall of spears advanced. I hoped that he would withdraw a little but he did not. Pol returned and said, "The captain is taking the men at a run!"

Although it would tire them a little I knew that they were the fittest warriors I had. They ate up the ground and soon were arrayed next to Raibeart's men.

"Pol, signal the Prince to withdraw to our right."

The front of the wedge was now less than forty paces from the top of the ridge and their archers were sending sporadic arrows at the equites. I was relieved to see that their bows were not of the same quality as ours. They did not penetrate the armour. Pasgen seemed to take an age but, eventually his men retired towards our right flank. He had followed orders! As Tuanthal and his men rode alongside us to our left, we had cohesion again but we were well outnumbered. Aided by the slope the two warbands had merged and were coming swiftly towards us.

Pol pointed, "Sir, it is King Aethelfrith himself. There is his Raven Banner."

At least that problem had been solved. It did not change what we had to do but it made it more urgent that we defeat this smaller warband first. "Double wedge!"

Garth and my men formed one huge wedge while Raibeart and I led the smaller wedge of the men from Glanibanta. Miach and Aelle were now raining death upon the warband. Like a wounded and angry beast the leader tried to turn it to face its tormentors. We were forty paces away and I roared, "Charge!"

The two wedges picked up speed. Although we were slightly down hill we were tightly packed and I led with the Wolf Standard fluttering behind me. The archers and slingers were still firing over us and the lead warrior of the Saxon wedge suddenly fell with an arrow in his shoulder. I threw Saxon Slayer into the gap and smashed it into the shoulder of the next man just as Raibeart killed his companion. Their wedge disintegrated as Garth and his men charged into the weakened side of the wedge. "Pol, order Pasgen to charge them!"

I trusted that my standard bearer would be able to wave the flag and signal Pasgen although I suspected he was itching to do so anyway. Just when I thought we might have a chance of winning. Tuanthal shouted. "Warlord look to the left!"

I turned and saw the second warband, with a wedge formed hurtling towards us. "Left face!" We would have to let Garth and Pasgen deal with the first warband while our hundred warriors bore the brunt of this attack. "Tuanthal, take your men and harry their flanks!"

I saw that Miach and Aelle had switched targets in an attempt to slow down the behemoth which approached but they were taking casualties from the Saxon archers too.

We had barely changed our front when a huge war axe slammed into my shield. The blow numbed my arm but the metal on my shield stopped it penetrating. I twisted the shield to one side and exposed the warrior's chest. I thrust Saxon Slayer as hard as I could manage and felt it crack and break some of the mail links and penetrate his body. I twisted his dying corpse from the blade just as a sword tried to cleave my head in two. I just managed to block the blow and then Raibeart slid his sword under the warrior's arm into his chest. Pol was using the standard like a spear as he jabbed forwards but we were being slowly forced backwards down the valley. I could see nothing of Pasgen and Tuanthal and I hoped that they were still attacking. I saw arrows still flying overhead and knew that Miach and his men fought on but I could see our men falling to the superior numbers.

"Shield wall!" It was a desperate command in the middle of a battle but we needed a solid wall of shields. The wedge would serve us no longer. I punched with my shield and hacked with my sword as the line began to stabilise around me.

I knew that we had achieved the formation when I heard the voice of one of my warriors from my stronghold behind me. "Don't worry Warlord, your oathsworn are here now! We will protect your back."

That made me feel much better. I knew that, if we had to then we could rotate our men at the front but, even so, there were still many more Saxons before us. I heard a cry from Raibeart and saw the gush of blood from his shield arm. "Raibeart step back!" He shook his head. "I order you to step back!" He reluctantly did so and one of my oathsworn stepped into the breach but we were still moving backwards. All that I could see, ahead of me was a wall of Saxons as far as the eye could see. We appeared to be completely enveloped. I could see the Raven Banner waving less than fifty paces from me. Their king was eager for revenge.

Then suddenly the banner began to move backwards and the pressure lessened and then stopped altogether. I looked around and saw that my men, horse and foot alike were exhausted. We should have all been killed but the Saxons had stopped. Then a bloody Aedh galloped up. "It is King Iago, Warlord. He is a mile up the valley with his army and the Saxons are retreating before he can outflank them."

I said a silent prayer to the Allfather for delivering us. I was about to order my equites to pursue but, when I looked, I saw that the horses could not move another step and the riders, too were both wounded and exhausted. We could not aid Iago any further. If he was to defeat the Saxons it would be without our help. We had drawn the sting but Iago had to fell the beast.

The field was littered with the wounded, dying and the dead but my priority was Raibeart. I found him being tended to by Adair, the chief of his bodyguards. He looked up at me and said, "I am sorry, Warlord. I know not how the blow struck him."

"Do not blame yourself, my brother was watching out for me. Let us see what the damage is and then get you to the wizard eh?" Raibeart was pale but awake and alert both of which were good signs. The sword had cracked through the mail links and sliced across the top of the shoulder. As far as I could see it had missed the major arteries. I tore the hem from the shift Raibeart wore beneath his mail shirt and gave it Adair. "Hold this tightly to the wound and stem the flow of blood. Take him to Myrddyn quickly." I glanced down at my brother and took his hand. "You will live and I must see to the others."

"I know for you are still the Warlord."

I stood and scanned the field. Aelle, Tuanthal, Garth, Miach, Pasgen, Aedh and Pol; all walked and they were alive! This was a ritual which occurred after every battle. I checked on my key warriors; if they lived then, no matter what the outcome, the battle had been a success. The field was covered in far too many of our warriors. We had managed to cover a great distance without losses and now, so close to home, it was hard to bear. Many of the families now with the monks would search the field and find that their loved one was dead.

Further away I saw Aethelfrith retreating in good order. The men of Gwynedd were half a mile behind. I was under no illusions; had King Iago not appeared we would have lost. I believe that the Saxons would have lost many men but they would have retained the field and Rheged would have died. I thanked the Allfather that it had not been so. Once again I wondered about Myrddyn; had he seen the allies appearing, apparently magically? He had seemed convinced that we would not be beaten and I would not die.

Prince Pasgen rode up and dismounted. I could see that their mail and their helmets were scarred and damaged. A tendril of blood ran from Tuanthal's brow. "They almost had us there Warlord. Had the scouts not been alert we would have been caught between the two warbands with nowhere to go. As soon as I saw the Raven Banner I knew we faced a mighty foe."

"How man did you lose?"

"We have forty riders left uninjured." That was a terrible loss.

"And you Prince Pasgen?"

"I did not suffer as badly but we lost ten equites. They can never be replaced."

I shook my head. "They can, Prince Pasgen. We have many young men from Rheged who live in our land and they would wish to be equites." Garth, Aella and Miach approached having seen to their own wounded first. "How many?"

"We lost thirty from the shield wall. They were all good men."

"Six archers," Miach shrugged. "We were lucky."

"Five of my slingers but Raibeart lost half of his men." He looked to the monastery from which streamed monks as well as the families of the warriors. "It will be a hard blow to take."

"Had we not made it as far as here then how many more would have died at Glanibanta? The pot is half full brother not half empty. We have enough families to begin to build up the men of Rheged once more. Now collect all the weapons and the armour. It will be needed even more urgently from now on. That I know for certain. Aedh, send riders to Caergybi and ask Brother Oswald for some wagons. We will need them for the wounded and for the iron."

Aelle shook his head, "You are always the Warlord. Do you never think of yourself brother?"

"When King Urien made me Warlord I took an oath. Even though he is dead, until Rheged ceases to be because all of its peoples are dead, then I will continue to be single minded. I cannot change what is in here." I patted my heart.

"And none of us would want that, least of all Raibeart and me."

The monks helped Myrddyn to save many men's lives that day. Limbs which would normally be taken off to save a life were, themselves, saved. The food that the monks gave to the living helped to heal the body and the mind. For me the saddest part was when I saw the wives and children find a loved one on the battlefield. It was pitiful to see the tears flowing and knowing that they would have to start a new life without the rock upon which they had depended. It had happened to me and my brothers and I could understand their grief and the emptiness they all felt.

We kept guards and sentries patrolling but I was sure that King Iago would not halt in his pursuit of the Saxons. He would want revenge for the death of his father. However, I did not know if there were any other bands who might try to attack us whilst we lay like a wounded beast.

The next morning, we sent the wagons with the families and half of the warriors and riders who were fit. I wanted them on my island as soon as possible. We were safe at the moment but I knew that that could change. As Garth and I watched the last wagon leave I said, "Did Hogan not wish to accompany you?"

He grinned, "He did indeed but he has heeded my word since you gave that talk to him. He sulked and he stormed but I left him as commander of your castle, under the watchful eyes of Brother Oswald and Myfanwy."

"Thank you for looking after my son."

"Warlord it is an honour besides we all like Hogan. In him we see you and that is a good thing."

"How is he coming along?"

"He is a fine warrior but a better rider than an archer. I think he would be like you and excel in all things." I waved away the unwanted compliment. "Brother Oswald says he is becoming a good reader and is now devouring all the books on strategy. He loves to read Brother Osric's journals."

I was pleased. Reading of the mistakes of the past helped to prevent repeating them in the future. I then told Garth of our adventures beginning with the rescue of Cadfan and ending at the monastery.

"It seems you have had your fair share of luck."

"Yes, Garth, and that worries me for luck can always run out. Yesterday was a good example." I saw, in the distance, the first of our wagons sent by Oswald, arriving. "Let us take our leave of the good bishop. I fear we have exhausted his hospitality."

"I think, my lord, that he appreciates what you do and has enjoyed repaying you."

Garth may have been correct for there was no sign that the bishop and monks wanted us to go quickly and they would have been happy for us to stay longer. We left the most badly injured with a wagon and four guards whilst we packed the rest with iron, shields, armour, swords and, of course, our wounded. As I waved goodbye I never dreamed that I would never see him again for he died a month later. He died peacefully, in his sleep, and his monks said that he appeared ready for death. I am not a Christian but when they made him a saint I applauded for he was the kindest man I have ever met and I miss him still for his wisdom and thoughtfulness.

The journey home was uneventful. We did not have to hurry. Even if King Iago was defeated it would take the Saxons many days to catch up with us and I had the feeling that Iago was a better general than his father. Aelle travelled with me and we accompanied the wagon containing Raibeart. Myrddyn sat in the open wagon with him in case his wound needed attention. When they saw Wyddfa they were awestruck.

"The mountains we have at home are molehills compared with this mighty rock."

"It is said that a dragon sleeps beneath its rocky walls and the white clouds you see about its peak is its fiery breath." Myrddyn shrugged at the incredulous looks of my brothers. "All I can say, my lords, is that there is a power within and when I am close to it then my dreams become increasingly accurate."

When we reached the Narrows and they saw my pontoon bridge they both laughed. "Now I see where you came up with the idea of the bridge over the Ribble but this is a dangerous looking sea. Which fool did you get to swim it?"

Myrddyn laughed, "Why the biggest fool of all, the Warlord of Rheged!"

Aelle too laughed, "I can see it now! Lord Lann who must do everything himself, swimming this cauldron of water and foam! Now I know that you are indeed indestructible."

I sniffed, "Is there no dignity attached to my position?"

Aelle smiled, "Not from those who know you as well as we do brother." He walked up to the bridge and the ropes and examined them all. "This is clever. It is like a boat but it is not subject to the vagaries of the sea. You pull it over then?"

"Aye. For a speedy crossing we use the men from the fort and the bridge almost flies across the water. It can take five wagons or fifty men.

We did consider building a second such but this single one is easier to defend."

I thoroughly enjoyed the journey across the island, my island. Both of my brothers were entranced by its beauty and its bounty. The waves and cheers from the people we passed also confirmed that this would be a good place to settle. "You can see, brothers, that there are many places for homes and farms. The coast is also fertile and affords many opportunities for dwelling. You can, for as long as you wish, stay in my castle or nearby Caergybi but when you are ready I will take you on a tour of the island and you can find, for yourself, somewhere you would choose to live."

I grew as excited as a child as we approached the Holy Island and the fort which guarded its entrance. We had worked hard to build both the bridge and the two forts. Even as we approached I could see men at work using the plans drawn up by Oswald and Myrddyn replacing wood with stone. It was a statement that we were here to stay. Once we had passed through the two portals which led to my stronghold I could feel all the tension of the past days leave my body. Here we were safe and here we were protected.

As I stepped down, Hogan ran up to me, his face alight with joy. "Father, Warlord, I am glad that you are safe." We embraced and I held him just a little longer that I would have done a while ago. I had thought I would never see him again and I wanted to make the most of every moment.

"Brother who is the giant who towers over me? Surely that cannot be my little nephew Hogan Lann?"

Hogan laughed and picked Aelle up. He looked like a child in my son's mighty arms. From the wagon I heard Raibeart say. "Pray do not try that with me nephew or you will burst my wounds."

Hogan's face fell when he saw his Uncle Raibeart's pale face. "Uncle, what happened?"

"I forgot to move!" We all laughed.

I looked across to the main hall and saw Myfanwy with her hands on her hips. Aelle saw her at the same time and saw my look. He turned to Myrddyn. "And who is that?"

"Ah that is Myfanwy, the tamer of Warlords. Your brother can face down a warband and fight a pack of wolves but he quakes beneath the glare of Myfanwy."

I threw Myrddyn the most aggressive look I could muster but he smiled and shrugged. Hogan helped me out. "Myfanwy looks after the hall." He turned to me. "She has put my aunts in the guest chambers Brother Oswald had built." He leaned in and said quietly, "She would have appreciated more than one day's notice of the arrival but I think she was happy to be the hostess really."

"Thanks son."

Freja and Maiwen rushed from the doorway to greet their fathers. Raibeart was carried on a litter by six of his bodyguards. I strolled behind and reached the doorway just after they had entered. Myfanwy had a surprisingly happy smile upon her face. "I am pleased to see the Warlord return." She reached up to kiss me, chastely, on the cheek. She stepped back and seemed to search me for signs of war. A slight frown appeared on her face. "I heard that, once again you were taking chances and putting yourself in danger."

"No more than others, Myfanwy."

"I would have expected his wizard to keep him safe."

"He has no wounds has he? Besides," he sniffed, "I did not dream his death!"

"Pah, if that is the extent of your care then perhaps I will accompany him next time he goes to war." She stared at me. "You do not need to be a wizard to know that you will go to war again, Warlord!"

It was too late in the day and there was too much to do to organise a feast for the guests but Myfanwy and Brother Oswald organised one for the next day. I took the opportunity of riding to the port to see how the markets and the trade had fared. War kept us safe but trade would ensure we survived. I met with Gareth and Gwynfor. Gareth looked after the market and the taxes on the ships coming in while Gwynfor, who was a sailor, ensured that the port worked well. They were a good team and they were both glad to see me.

In answer to my question Gareth beamed, "We now have a ship coming from the Empire every seven days. ,, what was Roman Gaul seeking trade."

Since we had made the island safe the farmers had been able to grow the wheat which was in such demand in the rest of the world. We grew more than we could use although with the extra mouths we had brought that might not be so in the future.

"Good. We will have more settlers and I want to make sure that our weekly market is a success. That is up to you Gareth."

"Do not worry, Warlord. You will see more people on market days than you think live on the whole of Mona!"

I felt much better as Hogan and Pol rode with me back to the stronghold. "Do you think we have won now?" asked my son.

"I am not sure but we will continue as though we are still in danger. We train warriors, we make weapons and we remain vigilant. The new farmers and workers we have brought can continue to make us prosperous but the likes of Pol and you, Hogan, will need to protect what we have. I have learned that if you have something which someone else wants they will try to take it from you. The Saxons heard how prosperous our land was and decide to reap the benefit of our work. The Hibernians would rather steal than work themselves. People from other lands will always try to take what is ours and we must protect our land from such raiders."

"Excellent! I was worried that, when I became a warrior, there would be no wars to fight."

I shook my head, as did Pol. "Wait until you have fought your first battle before you become so bellicose. For myself I hope and wish that I never have to fight another war and another battle as long as I live. I have buried too many of my friends already."

The feast was a huge success. With Myfanwy and Brother Oswald as the organisers it was hard to see how it could have been otherwise but even the best food needs guests who get on with each other. The fact that all of the warriors knew each other helped but Myfanwy went out of her way to make the two wives, Freja and Maiwen, welcome. She knew that Maiwen had been the Princess of Elmet but she made her feel like a sister and I was grateful to the kind-hearted woman who seemed to have her sights set on me.

Myrddyn saw me watching her. "There is little point in fighting Sucellos my lord. You need a woman to run things here and she is good woman. She cannot replace Aideen and she never will. That part of you, along with your dead daughter, is protected and cannot be harmed. Myfanwy can see to your physical needs. Besides, Hogan likes her and he needs a mother still. He may be a man or almost a man but there is a still a boy within that body."

"So Myrddyn, you would be a matchmaker too?"

"I think of this land of Mona and what is best for it. You will never be King of Mona but you have no need to be. You will rule this land as long as you choose and I am merely trying to make that rule pass to your son. Myfanwy will help that succession."

I sat in the solar, long after the rest had retired, running Myrddyn's words over in my head. He was right and I knew it.

Part 2
Wales

Chapter 8

It was a week before Raibeart was up to riding and even them Maiwen and Myfanwy tried to prevent it. They only gave their permission when Myrddyn agreed to travel with us and because Aelle was also riding. We planned on travelling along the northern coast and then staying at the fort at the Narrows, Mungo's Burgh. We could then return along the southern coast and they would have a picture of the whole island. Pasgen and some of his equites escorted us although we did not need such a heavily armed presence with the Narrows so well-guarded. I think they wanted, still, to be seen as needed and as they had no families the stronghold brought back too many unpleasant memories of lost wives and children.

I could tell that both my brothers liked what they saw. I remembered my first view of this golden isle and I understood it. "But brother, what of the people who are here?"

"Look around you, Aelle. Can you see hundreds of huts and farms? No. Are there people living close to each other? No. We pass one clutch of huts and then see no more for many miles. There is room enough. We just have to be careful. Your people will want to be close together and I wish to avoid displacing anyone. We will sit with Oswald and use pen and parchment to make sense of this. But we have only seen one third of the isle as yet."

We reached Mungo's Burgh at the Narrows. Mungo was the leader of the men of Strathclyde who had tried to hold Deva for me. They had built and now defended the fort which guarded the main entrance to the island. The bridge was a vital link as well as being a crucial point of defence. Normally Tuanthal kept his horsemen there to patrol but since the rescue that warrior hall remained empty.

Mungo had briefly seen us when we returned but now he made us really welcome. He and his brethren brewed a lethal alcoholic drink which we had used before to start fires. We drank well that night. The following day, with thick heads aplenty we discussed the state of the fort.

"The problem is, Warlord, that we do get raids on the mainland from those animals you scoured when you first came. By the time my men get over there they are gone and we have lost three families of settlers already this year."

Aelle smiled, "Part of the answer is simple brother. Build a fort on the other side of the Narrows. It will provide shelter when there is a raid and the men from there can patrol the mainland."

"I do not have enough men for that and we are still not swift enough. I need some of Tuanthal's men."

I suddenly saw Prince Pasgen smile and I realised that it was the first time since we had been reunited that I had seen him happy. "I have a solution. If some of Mungo's men guard this new fort I can base my equites there and we can patrol the mainland side of the Narrows." We looked at each other, wondering about the wisdom of that. His eyes pleaded with me. "We would love to do this and Wyddfa reminds me of Rheged. No offence to Mona but it is flat after the mountains of Rheged and I know that my equites would like it too."

Raibeart coughed and said, "And I know that many of my people are mountain people and they would like to settle there too."

I looked at my brother. I had hoped that he would be closer to my home. "And you Raibeart where would you choose to live?"

"I am happy to live here or closer to you although I suspect my wife may prefer the security of your stronghold brother. She gets on well with Myfanwy." He shrugged. "I was, as you were Lann, a shepherd. Pasgen can be the shepherd of my people too. I would trust him with my life so why not that of my people."

Everyone looked at me for an answer. Myrddyn shifted in his seat. "I cannot see a flaw in it Warlord. Except, perhaps, that the King of Gwynedd, may object to more settlers in his land."

"Then I will have to speak with him. We can go ahead with this. Myrddyn and Raibeart can go back to bring any of Raibeart's people who wish to come and we will begin to build the fort. We will also need Brother Oswald the builder too!"

The next day I left with Aelle, Pasgen and Myrddyn to scout the land on the other side of the Narrows. Although I had camped, fought and killed there, I had never looked at the place as a defensive site. It was perfect. The mountain crashed steeply down to the sea and, in places was a bare one hundred paces wide. We chose one of the narrowest sites on the strip of land which was still close to the pontoon bridge. It was a mile or so to the north. We chose it because it meant the smallest amount of building while still protecting the precious bridge. Although Myrddyn had his own ideas about building he respected the engineer enough to await his arrival. Instead we went to find a source of stone. There was little point in building in wood when we had the scree from Wyddfa to take. We found more than enough and Myrddyn could see that we could quarry the larger stones from a site quite close to the new fort.

Prince Pasgen seemed to have become a different person since the idea had been broached. He was full of ideas, enthusiasm and humour. It was as though he had been reborn once he had crossed to the island. When we returned to Mungo's Burgh we began to plan how the arrangement would work. We decided that Mungo would control the Mona side and the mainland would be under the control of Prince Pasgen. For the first time since he had been ousted by his brother he had purpose and he had his own lands.

When Raibeart, Oswald and his people returned I was taken aback. There were thirty families who wished to risk the mainland. Prince Pasgen, too, was touched. "I promise you that I will defend you and your homes as my father, King Urien, The Great, protected Rheged."

As much as the people adored Raibeart the fact that a son of the king of Rheged was so passionate about their welfare made them his people. There were not many of them, but he now had his retainers and he never let them down. I stayed for a few days to help the process of building. The fort came first and then the homes. Brother Oswald suggested a wall which went to the sea and to the cliff making a barrier through which no man could travel without the permission of Prince Pasgen. It was similar in concept to the Roman Wall in Rheged. We almost had the plans for it already. I approved for it made Mona that little bit safer.

I left with Aelle, Pol and Hogan to complete our circuit of the island. Raibeart wanted to bed his people in and he had made his choice. When he returned he would have a safe home built within my mighty walls.

Aelle, too was taken with the beauty of the place, "This is truly an island like the Christian one of Eden. I can not find fault with any of it."

"You have yet to experience a raid from the Hibernians but you are right brother. I think that *Wyrd* had a hand in this. It is almost as though it was made for us." I nodded to Myrddyn. "Myrddyn's arrival was determined by forces beyond our world brother."

"I think I will do as Raibeart did and let my people choose where they wish to live. With your permission I will do as you did and take them on a tour of the island. Do I have your approval?"

"Of course you do and to confirm that approval then my son Hogan Lann will accompany you. It is time he became my heir." I swear that I saw Hogan grow inches when I said that.

I spent a week back at my stronghold with Garth, Tuanthal and Miach. We had new warriors to recruit to fill the gaps left by the dead. Tuanthal was happy that he could now roam the island with his men. As he said it meant that should we be invaded by either Saxon or Hibernian then he would be close to them and able to respond quicker. Miach wanted the arrow production increased as it was easier to produce more arrows than train the archers which he needed. Garth was just pleased with the arms and armour we had captured. The Saxon bodyguards had been particularly well armed and any new warriors would be impressively arrayed.

Myfanwy haunted me. Wherever I was she was close to hand; watching and observing. If she thought I was working too hard then she would show her displeasure with a look, or a tut or a beaker banged on a table. My men all cast me wry grins when she did so. Eventually I had had enough. If Myrddyn had been there then I would have sought his advice but he was busy building Pasgen Fort.

I plucked up the courage to corner her close to my chambers where we could not be disturbed. It took me some days to do so. I, who could face odds of ten to one, could not beard a woman in my own den! And they say that women are the weaker of the sexes!

"Myfanwy you are belittling me in front of my men and I want it to stop now!"

If I expected a storm in response to my attack I was wrong. Instead she became demure. She became a fireside kitten and not the vicious mother cat defending her young. "How, my lord? All I desire is to serve you."

"And you do this by scowling at me! You almost break beakers when you put them down on the table and you show your displeasure in many other different ways."

"My lord. I care for you. Surely you know that? And I want you to look after yourself."

Her pleading eyes made my resolve weaken. I was confused. "What is it you wish of me?"

She came closer to me her hair smelling of rosemary and she said, with a twinkle in her eye, "I would be your wife." I was so taken aback I had no answer and I mutely nodded my agreement. I am not certain it would have made any difference if I had objected.

We were married a week later. Apparently, everyone in the stronghold, Hogan included, expected it. I had been the only one oblivious to what was going on. To be truthful it was one of the best things I ever did. She was a good wife, a wild bed mate and a good housekeeper; added to that she was as good a mother to Hogan as one could have wished. If there was a bargain then I came out with the better half. We spent a day alone and then she sent me off to do my work. "Go and see to the new fort. It will soon be autumn and we will have long nights to get to know each other better. Now is the time to prepare the defences of your land." She was a very practical woman.

When Pol, Hogan and I reached the fort I was impressed with the progress. The wall leading to the sea and the cliff had been finished as had the main wall and the gate. Men were busily digging the first ditch. Brother Oswald greeted me joyfully. "The stone here is magnificent. It fractures exactly where you want it to and the sand makes for perfect mortar. We are building a wall with towers to the south of the bridge. It will be much like a smaller version of the one in Rheged but it will allow us to defend the bridge from any attacks from the south."

Hogan was particularly interested in seeing how the fort would be built. He had been but a child when we had left Rheged and the massive stone structures of the Romans were a mystery to him. Brother Oswald loved nothing more than to explain, to anyone who would listen, how the buildings worked and why he did what he did.

"You see, Hogan Lann, we have to dig deep foundations and provide a wide base upon which to build the walls. There we will put more stone supports to carry the tower that we shall build there."

"Why build a tower there?"

"That is a good question which shows that you are developing an enquiring mind. The tower can protect the section of the wall leading to the sea as well as protecting this corner of the fort. There will be two more towers around the gatehouse."

"And the ditch?"

"This is the first of our two ditches. The second will be deeper and we will have a wooden bridge which can be placed over the ditch to allow ingress and egress but be raised during conflict. The two walls will be well apart to protect both sides of the bridge."

I had heard it all before and I left the two of them to it. Pol and I headed south towards the land which had been dominated by the wild tribe who terrorised the area before out arrival. Already there were one or two families there. Raibeart's warriors had helped them to build their simple huts and we stopped to speak with them. "Is the land to your liking?"

"Aye Warlord. Lord Raibeart has promised that he will get us some sheep and then we will be truly happy." The man, a veteran by the scars on his face, nodded towards the fort. "We are mighty glad to have that so close by, Warlord."

His wife nodded and gripped her husband's arm. "We will be protected should the Saxons come again."

"I doubt that it will be Saxons who trouble us. We are as far from Saxon land as it is possible to get. I hope you prosper here and you have Prince Pasgen to watch over you."

The veteran shook his head. "It should have been him who was king and then we would still be living in Rheged." Many of the refugees from Rheged felt the same way about the anointed king who had failed them.

As we continued our ride I knew that he was right about Pasgen making a better king but not so sure that he would have halted the Saxon incursion. They were like the fleas on a dog and more were still coming from their lands across the sea. We were lucky to be so far to the west and away from their immediate threat. I did not doubt that one day they would threaten our borders but it would probably not be in my lifetime and by then our defences would make those of Rheged seem like wooden huts.

By the end of the week the fort was almost habitable. Pol, Hogan and I had ridden patrols with Prince Pasgen and I was impressed by how quickly he had come to know the land he now controlled. "There are many small passes where we can build small towers to control them. We will need more warriors of course but every woman for miles around is with child."

"And your men? How are they?"

He smiled. "Two have found widows from the wars and they are happy now. Soon, I hope that more of my men will take wives for their children will be mighty warriors."

"And do not forget to think of yourself Pasgen."

"I will. Perhaps there will be a Myfanwy who takes me in hand too!" Pol and Hogan laughed. Would I forever be singled out for ridicule? And then I smiled; I could live with them laughing about my love life so long as they took me seriously as a leader.

When we returned to the camp at the fort there was a messenger awaiting us. It was a monk from the monastery. He bowed his head. "I have some sad news to impart Warlord. Bishop Asaph has died. He did not suffer and he remembered you at the last." He gave a smile as he inclined his head, "He asked me to bring you the news."

"He knew he was dying?"

"Aye, my lord, and he was prepared for the end of his life. He put everything in order and just smiled as he made his peace with God."

"He was a good man and I shall miss him."

"He liked you too Warlord and always said that you were the most Christian man who was not a Christian!"

"I think that is a compliment. Will you stay and eat with us?"

"No Warlord, I have to get back to the monastery but I have more news. King Iago is coming too. He should be here tomorrow. He stayed at the monastery for the funeral of the bishop."

"Thank you for that news." We raced back to Prince Pasgen. "We had better prepare for visitors. We have the King of Gwynedd arriving tomorrow. The fort is not ready we had better take them to Mungo's Burgh and they can stay in the warrior hall."

"I will go and prepare it."

I looked at Pol and Hogan, "And we will see what we can hunt for the feast. Bring three spare pack horses in case we are lucky."

We headed up into the forests which lined the base of Wyddfa. As there were so few people living nearby, the wooded heights teemed with game. My son and my former squire were both skilled hunters. While Hogan's skills with a bow could not match mine or Pol's he was a silent stalker and could get so close that any inaccuracy was not a problem. We bagged six deer of varying sizes and rode back to the bridge. Once we reached it we could see frenetic activity amongst the men of Strathclyde and the Rheged horsemen. The two leaders were both taking the arrival of the king very seriously.

They had, indeed, made the warrior hall fit for a king. There was fresh hay on the floors and pitchers of water spread around. The doors had been opened to let the breeze make it smell fresher. The fireplace was ready with logs and the whole hall had been decked with fragrant herbs. It might not be a palace but it was better than a tent or a field.

We awaited the arrival of King Iago on the rocks by the Narrows. Oswald and Myrddyn still had men working hard on the fort but the wizard waited with me and Prince Pasgen. Pol had the banner unfurled and Hogan had polished my armour until it shone like silver. I could see that the king had brought many men with him as they snaked along the narrow coastal road. We could see them many miles before they reached us and I was glad that we had prepared the warrior hall. We would need all the accommodation we could manage. We had counted them before they arrived and knew that there were two hundred men with King Iago. Only a handful of men rode and the rest were doughty looking warriors who marched in mail shirts with shields across their backs..

King Iago was about the same age as I was. He had a chestnut or red tinge to his beard and I later heard that as a young warrior he had been called Red Beard but now he preferred the name Red Dragon. His standard was a red dragon on a green field and looked impressive. Behind him rode Cadfan who smiled and nodded at us when he came closer.

I bowed. "Welcome King Iago. We have prepared accommodation on the island if that suits you."

He smiled, "I look forward to travelling on your contraption but some of my men are a little fearful and think it is the work of a wizard."

Myrddyn did not take offence but merely smiled, "A wizard did help to build it majesty but I can assure you and your men that it is as safe a way to cross as any."

We did not overload the bridge and only a few of the bodyguards accompanied us. Mungo's men ensured that the crossing was both speedy and smooth. They had operated the bridge for so long that it was an easy task for them.

As we stepped ashore King Iago laughed. "The last time I crossed to Mona, as a young man, I landed in the surf and was soaked to the skin. This is by far a better way to travel. You have some good engineers." He looked at the fort and then waved to the mainland and Brother Oswald. "You are building powerful forts Lord Lann. Are you expecting trouble?"

I detected an edge to his question. "No your majesty, but the Hibernians and the Saxons have both attacked us recently and we have found that solid walls are the best protection and deterrent."

He seemed satisfied and we entered the hall. By the time his men had all been ferried across and settled into the hall it was almost time for food but the king asked for a meeting with Myrddyn and our sons. I think Pol and Pasgen were a little put out to be ignored but Iago was a king and they had certain privileges. As I told them quietly as we left the hall, "You will find out all eventually. Keep your ears open and listen to his bodyguards."

Mungo had allowed us to use his chambers which looked towards Wyddfa. "This is a good view Lord Lann. You know that Wyddfa is special to us?"

I nodded, "Myrddyn had told me."

"Ah your wizard, who was one of my people, before he chose to serve the Wolf Warrior." Once again I sensed an edge to the king's words but I just smiled. "You have a great reputation Myrddyn. They say you can see the future. Can you?"

"I dream your majesty and the closer I am to Wyddfa then the more accurate are my dreams."

"Can you dream for me?"

"I do not choose my own dreams. The spirits who control Wyddfa choose what I see. It is a little unpredictable."

A flash of annoyance crossed the king's face and then he smiled. "I understand. I suppose that makes it a little more believable then and, of course, gives you scope for creativity." Those who did not know Myrddyn would not have seen the glint in his eyes which told me that he was annoyed for his face was as impassive as the rocks of Wyddfa. "One of the reasons I came here was to tell you of my great victory. We pursued Aethelfrith and all of his Saxons back to their fort at Deva. We routed them and sent them back north. Deva is now mine. Gwynedd now has its old borders and I have avenged my father and his defeat."

I was genuinely pleased. "That was mightily done, King Iago, for the Saxons do not give up what they have captured easily."

"Aye we lost many men but I am grateful that you and your army managed to hold them until I was in position to spring my trap."

I was suddenly on the alert. "You knew of the presence of Aethelfrith?"

"Of course. My scouts in the borderlands tracked your army and the Saxon warbands. It allowed us to get into position and attack once they were committed to an assault upon you and your men. It worked well."

I could feel the anger rising within me. We had been used and many good men had died. Myrddyn sensed my rising temper. "And will you invest the Saxon forts?"

"You are a wise wizard Myrddyn. I have already garrisoned them. And now on to the second reason for my visit. You saved my son's life and for that I am grateful. In return for that kindness I will allow you and your people to live on Mona." He smiled at me as though he was doing me a favour. If he thought he could drive me from my land as he had the Saxons then he was in for a rude surprise.

Cadfan stood and took a pendant from his leather pouch. "I would like to give you this Warlord of Rheged. It was given to me by my grandfather and I know that he held you in special regard. It seems right that I give it to you."

I shook my head. "No Prince Cadfan, I cannot take a gift from your grandfather for doing something I would do again in an instant."

King Iago took the pendant and placed it around my neck. "No Lord Lann, it is the way of our people. We repay kindness with gifts and treachery with death as the Saxons discovered." Was there an implied threat in his words? I would need to speak with Myrddyn later. "And now my stomach tells me that it is time to eat and my nose tells me that the venison from our forests is ready to be devoured."

I had no time to talk to either Hogan or Myrddyn about what had transpired and the food, well-cooked though it was, tasted to me of sawdust. I smiled during the feast and, fortunately, my lords made witty banter and told tales of the Wolf Warrior. It allowed me to listen to stories about myself and wave my hand in embarrassment during the telling. I was able to half listen and think back on the king's words. His son had seemed genuine but what were Iago's motives? When I thought about the meeting I could see that my position had not changed but there had been an underlying theme to the king's philosophy, that I was his vassal. Had he stated that I would have refuted it but now I was annoyed with myself for keeping silent.

The next day I had little chance to voice my opinion as we were in the public view when the king and his entourage said their goodbyes as they stepped onto the mainland once more. "Farewell Lord Lann. Between us we will tame this Saxon beast eh?" We waved our goodbyes.

When he was out of sight Mungo and Pasgen both beamed, "That went well Warlord. It seems we are secure again."

Pasgen must have seen my black look. "What is the matter Warlord? Did I miss something?"

"Come with me and we will ride up yonder hill where we can talk without being overheard." I could see that both of my leaders were confused as well as intrigued. Once we reached the top of the hillock which overlooked the building site I told them of what had transpired. "Myrddyn, was I being over sensitive? Pray tell me."

I hoped that he would nod but instead he shook his head. "No Warlord, you were right. He sees you as his vassal." I saw Hogan nodding. "He also said nothing about our settlements on the mainland. I think our Iago is a cunning king. He allowed us to bleed for him and he will let us build a mighty fort for him. This building," he pointed to the work below us, "is a hostage to fortune. Whilst it protects our island if it belonged to Iago he would, effectively, control the island."

Pasgen almost exploded with anger. "I have not exchanged a Saxon ruler for a jumped up Welsh one!" I smiled and said, "Calm down Prince. I have no intention of being a vassal for King Iago. He can desire your fort all he likes but I would like to see him take it."

"The Warlord is right. The king will do nothing until the fort is built and besides he still has to fortify his borders. I believe we have a period of grace but it makes this castle even more vital."

Mungo stroked his red beard. "I think we will recruit more men."

"We are already seeking new men."

"I am sorry Warlord I did not make myself clear. I would recruit more men from Strathclyde. Just as there were warriors of Rheged in hiding I am sure that there are warriors in Strathclyde who yearn for freedom. I could sail north with a couple of men. Any recruits would be more than we have and we would only be away from here for a month." He gestured at Prince Pasgen. "I am sure the prince could manage to control both forts."

"Of course."

"I think that is a wonderful idea and I am annoyed that we did not think of it sooner."

"Amazing! Myrddyn confesses he is not perfect."

The all laughed and Myrddyn smiled, "Not yet anyway!"

Chapter 9

My brothers were less worried than I had been. Aelle was particularly philosophical about it all. "Why are you surprised? We come and take over the most fertile part of his land and you do not think he wants some of it."

"He will not get it."

"Of course he won't but we now have another potential problem apart from the Saxons and the Hibernians."

"I think the Saxons will lick their wounds for a while and one good aspect to King Iago's belligerence is that the Saxons will have to come through him first. Mungo will return to Strathclyde to gather more warriors. It is warriors that we need. He is already speaking with Gwynfor to arrange passage. Until then we need to see if there are any volunteers for the new fort."

Aelle nodded. "Some of my warriors wished to stay together and, with all due respect brother, they wanted to be a little independent of Garth and Ridwyn. I think that they would be good for the garrison. I mean no offence."

I smiled, "I know that my two captains tend to be a little harsh with newcomers and are both inordinately proud of my shield wall. But I take no offence."

"That is an understatement. It is as though no-one but they have ever fought before."

Aelle was right. I had overlooked their arrogance because it had not caused a problem until now. I would have to speak with them. "Then can I leave it to you to organise? You will need to speak with Prince Pasgen. I am allowing him to be lord of the Narrows. It must be hard for the man who could have been king to lose it all. We must be careful with his feelings. Your senior man can command the fort until Mungo returns and then we can make decisions."

Mungo sailed two days later with four trusted men. They planned on spreading out once they landed to avoid detection and to increase the number of warriors they might be able to recruit. Gwynfor and the ship would sail further north to establish trade links with the free peoples of the north. It looked like we would soon need even more friends.

I spent a precious week with my new bride. Since we had married she had become less critical of me, warmer and more loving. She listened more and spoke less. I found that I could tell her my inner fears and thoughts in a way that I could only do with Myrddyn. The problem with talking to Myrddyn was that you never knew if he had read your mind already. With Myfanwy you got a real opinion.

"I agree with your brothers. It changes nothing. You will not bend the knee to any man and I cannot see any man besting you. We stay on this fortress island and our people will grow stronger. You will build a kingdom for your son to rule."

I shook my head, "Not a kingdom my love, people envy and covet kingdoms. I will rule as Warlord and if my son is ready to be the next Warlord then he can do so."

She kissed me. "That is another reason why I love you so. You are the most sensible man I have ever met. Any more sensible and you would either be a wizard or a woman!" Her giggling laughter was infectious and we spent the next hour just enjoying ourselves. I came out feeling ten years younger.

I rode with Pol, Aelle and the new garrison for Pasgen's fort. I was not worried about the prince's reaction but I knew that my presence would ease any tension. Myrddyn and Oswald had finished their labours and the fort and its defences were almost complete. Mungo's men were busy deepening the two ditches while Oswald and Myrddyn supervised the building of the bolt throwers which would be mounted on the towers.

As I had expected Prince Pasgen was just grateful to have a garrison to man his walls. He also liked the fact that his garrison would be made up of men from Rheged. His equites needed to be beyond the walls controlling the countryside. Aelle's man, Calum was put in temporary command of the forty men that Aelle had brought. Calum was a sound warrior who had defended Glanibanta for years. He was a good choice. After my wizard and my priest had left to improve the stronghold I rode with Pol and Prince Pasgen on a patrol to see the land we now managed.

It was autumn and the winds from the west brought rain. I wondered why the snow only ever fell on Wyddfa? We never had any on the island. Even the waters around the island seemed quite warm in the depths of winter. I was beginning to see what Myrddyn meant about the magic and the power of the mountain. It was no wonder King Iago had chosen the dragon standard. The dragon that was Wyddfa was truly powerful. There was an irony in that the cavalry standard of Rheged, which Prince Pasgen still carried proudly, was an ancient dragon. It made an eerie and chilling wail when carried into battle. The fact that the mountain was also supposed to house a dragon was *wyrd*! Perhaps the prince was always intended to be here.

The prince showed me the passes where he intended to build towers. I could see that there were many places where a handful of men could hold up an army. We had chosen the perfect position for our fort. Already there were sheep dotted around the hillsides and the foothills of Wyddfa. The settlers waved at us, no doubt comforted by the sight of the mailed equites; they were a visible reminder of the power of Rheged.

When we returned to the fort we found that Tuanthal had sent four of his equites to supplement the garrison until Mungo had returned. One of them was Adair who had fought so valiantly for me before. Prince Pasgen said, "It is kind of Captain Tuanthal but I think we have enough horsemen. Besides we have little enough forage for the winter anyway. Why not keep them with you as your bodyguard until you return to the stronghold again."

It was a sensible suggestion and it allowed me to explore more of the land which was further afield. We managed to cross to the southern end of the peninsula. It was beautiful and rugged country but there were places where I could see we could settle more of our people. There were bays for fishing ports and sheltered valleys which were perfect for sheep and cattle. Once we began to grow then we had room to spread.

When we returned there was a message from King Iago. I read it and turned to Pol and Pasgen. "It seems we are invited to Deva. The king wishes to invest his son with the title Prince of Deva and, as the man who saved his son, he wishes me to be there."

Prince Pasgen furrowed his brow. "I can only spare a few men Warlord. Perhaps we could send to the island for more?"

I shook my head, "I think Pol and these four warriors will be more than enough. There are no Saxons now to worry us and the king will have his whole army at Deva. I think we will be safe enough."

The prince was not convinced but he bowed, "As you wish Warlord. When do you leave?"

"The ceremony is the day after tomorrow. We had better leave now. We can stay overnight at the monastery."

"Very well I will send word to Myrddyn, Garth and your wife where you will be."

We took two spare horses for our armour and we left in the early afternoon. We would reach the monastery by evening and I knew that we would have a warm welcome from the new bishop, whoever he was.

The monk who greeted us was the one who had brought the news of the bishop's death and the monk whom Bishop Asaph had leaned on in his latter days. "Welcome Lord Lann, I am Bishop Stephen. Will you stay the night?"

I grinned. "We were rather counting on it."

The meal was well cooked but simpler than in Asaph's time. "I am sorry that the food is plainer than it was but we now believe that we must adhere to Christ's principles and live a life which is more austere."

"Do not worry bishop, we are plain folk ourselves. We enjoy rich food but so long as our bellies are full… Are you pleased that the king has secured the borders?"

He frowned a little. "I am not sure of what to make of King Iago. He wanted to enlarge the monastery."

"That is a good thing surely?"

"Perhaps but the price we would have to pay would be to call it St. Beli after his father."

"Was his father a saint? I did not know that."

He grimaced, "I am not even sure he was a Christian but he was no saint. If we were to name it after anyone it would be St. Kentigern its founder or Asaph. Anyway, I told him we would have to deliberate. He did not seem pleased." He took a sip of wine. "It seems to me that he does like opinions which differ from his own."

"No, he appears to want his own way. Still so long as we have stability."

"Yes Lord Lann. That is a good thing. We shall have accommodation for you on your return."

"Thank you, bishop, this is always a beacon for us; a place of sanctuary."

We rode easily down the vale. This time we were not hiding and we could use the main roads. Two of the equites rode ahead of us and two behind affording Pol and I the chance to talk. "Are you still happy about being my standard bearer?"

His face fell, "You would get rid of me?"

"No, you misunderstand me. I thought you might want to join the equites, there you could have the greater opportunity for glory rather than just watching my back."

He laughed, "The greatest glory I can have is holding your banner and watching your back. Do you know how many others would give their teeth for such a chance? No, Warlord, I am happy with the arrangement.

Of course should Hogan wish the honour then I would not stand in his way."

"I do not think Hogan would be content to hold the standard. I think he dreams of glory; as I did. Besides he must be trained to lead men. Soon the duties of being a squire will pale."

"But no longer eh Warlord?"

"When you have seen many brave comrades die in battle then the glory does not seem so great." I looked at the sky. It was coming in to rain. My wolf skin would keep me dry, and Pol had one too, but the four equites would suffer in the storm which was about to break. "Let us kick on a little."

We dropped over the vale and down into the flat lands which lay before Deva. There was a little shelter here from the bushes and trees which not only lined but also overhung the road. "That's better!"

Suddenly the two equites ahead of us were attacked and felled by men dropping from the trees above the road. "Ambush!" I drew my sword and prepared to defend myself. Four men ran at me and I chopped awkwardly down on one and he crumpled to the ground with his brains showing through his skull. My horse reared and that saved me for its hoof caught the warrior attempting to spear me. I turned and saw Adair and the other equite behind me being chopped and hacked by five warriors. The ambush had been so swift that they had no time to defend themselves. Pol had despatched his men and I shouted, "Ride to the left!" I noticed that the ground dropped to a small valley and I hoped to hide there. As we raced I saw that the four equites were dead and the ten or twelve men who remained from the twenty or so who had ambushed us were chasing. Fortunately, they were on foot while we were still mounted. There was a slight chance that we could still escape. Then there was a flurry of four or five arrows. I saw Pol's mount stumble and gamely try to carry on but it was no use, it was dying. "Jump clear and climb up behind me."

Pol was a skilful horseman and he managed to avoid injury as he dismounted on the run and then I reached down to haul him up on my horse. We lumbered on, a little slower now, but continuing to out pace the men on foot. I saw the stream ahead and behind it a hedgerow and a field. I was contemplating what to do when I noticed my horse labouring. Pol said, "There are two arrows in its hindquarters. She will not last long."

That decided me. I headed into the stream. "Get off and jump into the bank on the left." As he did so I dismounted and slapped the horse's rump. Without a rider she galloped off along the stream. I joined Pol and we lay down behind the bank of the river hidden by the grass which was still long from a hot dry summer. Our cloaks covered us and I looked down the stream. My horse still ran on splashing through the water and then something must had scared the beast for it jinked to the right.

Just then the men reached the water's edge. This was the moment of truth. Would they find us? I heard their voices and they were Welsh, not Saxon. "Which way did they go?"

"There I can see the tail of the horse. They are going downstream come on quick."

"If we don't bring back the bastard's head the king will have ours!"

I kept my head down as they splashed into the water and waited until the sounds had faded. I lifted my head and saw that no-one was in sight. "Quick Pol on your feet." I contemplated going back to the ambush site and gamble on the fact that they would all be searching for me. That was not the sensible option and we needed to get away. "Over there!"

I led Pol through the blackthorn bushes away from the river. It was thick and tangled but we had mail and wolf skins. It would not harm us. We pushed on through increasingly thick bushes until suddenly we found a path. Left would take us back in the direction of the monastery some fifteen miles away. Right would take us towards Deva some ten miles hence. "We have a choice Pol,. Deva or the monastery."

He managed a wry smile as he adjusted his shield across his back to make it more comfortable. "You have already decided have you not?"

"Aye, we head for the monastery. They were Welsh warriors and not bandits. King Iago wants me dead; he sent them for us. This was a trap."

We headed down the path and made much quicker time than before. "I thought they were not Saxon and wondered why I could understand them. But why does he want you dead?"

"I believe he sees me as a threat. I am not a threat but men who are devious themselves see cunning in others. He does not trust me."

We made good time until we suddenly found a place where the steam had flooded. The way ahead was impassable. "We will have to find a way around. You stay here Pol while I seek the way. You will need to direct me for I will not be able to see far ahead and I may become lost." I took out my long dagger and began to hack at the brambles and briars which seemed to form a fence. The ground was wet and sucked at my boots. Even the wolf skin did not seem immune to the thorns.

"My lord you are going too far to the right. Cut left!"

I turned to the left and saw a large patch of water. I had no idea how deep it was. I hacked down four or five huge weeds and laid them like a mat and then placed them over the water. When I stepped on to it I was pleased that it took my weight. I leapt from it and found solid ground and I saw the path reappear before me. "Pol, follow my tracks, I am almost there."

When I reached the path I looked at the state of my boots and my cloak I was now a shade of brown mud. When Pol appeared he looked the same except he also had cuts on his face. He only had a conical helmet. "I think that, when we get out of this we will have the smith make you a better helmet." I noticed that he still clutched the standard. "You could have ditched that you know. Your life is more valuable."

He shook his head. "No, my lord. This is worth ten Pols in battle. We have never lost when it has been waved. Let us not tempt fortune."

We pushed on hard and the ground began to climb. We took a rest. When we were not moving I heard the sound of the chase. They were behind us. I could not see them because of the bushes but they would be able to track us that I knew. We had had to cut through bushes and grasses; even the poorest tracker would see our route. I looked up at the sky. Night was rapidly approaching but we needed an escape quickly or we would not see the night. The path continued to twist up the slope and the brush gave way to woodland.

Suddenly I saw a patch of rocks to the left of some trees and I made for them. "Follow me." The rocks went ten paces into the woods. I spied an oak with branches low enough to climb. "Quick up the tree!" We both made the branch and then I looked around for the next path. The branch crossed the branch of a smaller tree quite close by and I edged, gingerly along the limb until I could step, carefully on to the next branch. It held but only just. "Wait there Pol until I find the next one." I doubted that this branch would take the weight of two of us. I walked to the bole of the tree and saw another large round rock beneath. I jumped and managed to avoid slithering off. "Right Pol follow me and I will catch you when you jump."

We had both just dropped safely behind the rock when I heard the sounds of men crashing through the bushes some fifty or so paces away. There were more than ten. They moved on and then there was silence I breathed a sigh of relief. Pol opened his mouth to speak and I put my mailed glove across it. A few moments later I heard voices again as some of the hunters returned. "The footprints stopped here!"

"Well they can't have just disappeared, can they? They have to be close. What do you think they did? Fly?"

"I dunno. He has that wizard Myrddyn you know? He has powers. Don't you remember that story we heard how the wizard made him disappear so that he could get into Dina Guardi and kill Morcant Bulc."

"Just keep looking. I don't want to have to tell King Iago we lost them."

"Can't we just say they died in the river."

"Nah! He will want the head and if he is alive and reappears then it will be our heads stuck on a spear."

"You never know he might get to Deva himself and save us the trouble. He might think it was Saxons who ambushed him."

"I hope he does. There are a hundred men on the roads just waiting for him. But I think the crafty bastard is here in this forest."

They began to beat around on both sides of the path. I think that they were hoping to make us bolt but we were like two statues not moving and hardly daring to breathe. At one point one of them reached the rock behind which we were hiding. I had my dagger in my hand ready to rip his throat if he stumbled upon us then I heard. "Let's try back tracking. They might have tried the horse trick."

"Let's go and get the dogs. They'll find them."

"Aye well that is what we might as well do. They can't get out of here. We have men on both ends of the path. We just need to be patient."

The night darkened and human noises ceased. Soon the only sounds were the animal and bird noises of the forests. "We cannot use the path but we are off it anyway." I tried to visualise the land as it had been in daylight. "The path was going uphill. We are now parallel to that path. If we continue going uphill then we will end up on the ridge again."

Pol was just happy to still be alive. "We can get by without the food Warlord but I am powerful thirsty."

"As am I; we will just have to hope for a stream."

There was no moon which made it difficult to keep moving in a straight line. I always went up the slope and tried to avoid deviation. The higher we went then the fewer the trees and it became easier. I was no longer worried about leaving tracks. If they were close enough to track, then we were dead anyway. I just hoped that we could emerge away from a party of Welshmen hungry to feast on Warlord.

When I aw the hillside growing lighter I knew that we must be close to the top. I held my arm out for Pol to halt. I was panting. I was not as fit as I had once been. I listened. At first I heard nothing and then, in the distance, I heard the faint neigh of a horse. We had avoided stumbling upon them. We edged forwards until the tree line ended. We crept out on all fours and peered down the ridge line. The Welsh guards had made a cardinal error. They had lit a fire and we could see it about a mile away. I knew, from countless nights on guard duty, that their night vision would have gone and I hurried Pol over the top of the ridge to the welcoming trees on the other side. We had to get as far down the ridge as possible. They would bring dogs as soon as dawn broke and search the forest. They would pick up our trail and so we had to disguise it as best we could.

I waved the weary Pol down the slope which led to the monastery. We were still at least ten miles away and by daylight we would still be well short. I was searching for two things, a stream, we needed water and it would throw off the scent, and some animal dung. It would only confuse the dogs but confusion would slow them down and we needed every tiny particle of time we could grab.

The stream was only small but it was all that we needed. We drank first and it tasted like nectar. Then we walked down the middle of it oblivious to the cold and the dampness seeping through the seams of our boots. I spied a deer in the woods. It ran off but I searched around and found its dung. "Step in this. Get it over your boots." Pol looked at me sceptically. "This may save your life. Just do it."

He did as he was ordered as did I and then we followed the trail left by the deer. It didn't matter where it was going it would confuse the dogs. Luckily it was going downhill and that suited us. After a mile I deemed that we could head for the monastery. I wanted to be well down the valley before sunrise. I could see that Pol was tiring. It was not that I was any fitter but I think I had more stamina. It was mid-morning when we heard the dogs over the ridge. Pol shot me a look of terror. "Do not worry Pol. They still have some miles to travel. Look yonder, the smoke of the monastery." I stopped, partly to let us both get our breath and partly to make quite clear what I intended. "We will head across the vale as though we are going over the ridge. We will find another steam and then back track. I want them to follow us to Mona." Enlightenment filled his face. "It is what they expect we will do and the dogs will persuade them that this is so."

When we reached the other side of the valley I could hear the dogs much clearer but we could see nothing. When we found the shelter of the trees and a stream I stopped. "Take off your boots!" Pol obeyed me and we both became barefooted. “Walk in the water and head downstream.” The icy water of the stream woke us up but I was counting on the change of smell throwing the dogs. By the time we reached the bottom my feet were blue and I had little feeling left in them. Once again we used stones to disguise our exit; by stepping on them we left no prints in the mud. I could see the monastery some eight hundred paces away. It would not do to be seen and we sprinted from bush to bush and tree to tree until we reached the shelter of the monastery walls. We both slumped to the floor and a surprised monk found us. “Warlord!”

“Find Bishop Stephen! We are in trouble!”

Chapter 10

Bishop Stephen took one look at us and had his monks escort us, not into the main hall, but to the animal byre. He asked us to climb up into the higher level, the hay loft. I said not a word. Shelter, rest and food were our priorities and the bishop looked like he knew what he was doing and had a plan. As soon as we were inside he dismissed his monks after asking them to bring food and drink for us. I quickly explained what had happened. He did not look surprised. "I suspected that you were in danger and that you were being hunted when I heard the dogs. The smell of the byre will confuse them. Here give me your boots and I will wash them. Take off your armour and clothes and I will send a monk's habit. It anyone comes in here then begin to tend the animals. Hide your armour and weapons beneath the hay. If they search there then it means the ruse has not worked."

"Do not put yourself at risk bishop."

He smiled, "Jesus told us to help those who needed help and you two need help. I am doing the Lord's work!"

As he left I turned to Pol. "Let us do as he asks but I hate to put these good people at risk. We will try to escape on our own as soon as possible." We stood there naked until the monks reappeared with habits and food.

While we dressed Bishop Stephen made sure our clothes, weapons and armour were well hidden. He leaned towards us. "They are on the far side of the valley. Whatever you did it confused the dogs but they will visit here. Keep your cowls up and do not speak if they come. Some of the monks have sworn an oath of silence. It will not seem unusual if you do not talk." He beckoned us. "Come and join the other monks in the chapel." My face must have shown my surprise for he smiled. "I do not think that God will send a bolt of lightning to destroy my church because I protect a good man." He shrugged, "But if it helps to make you a Christian…"

We climbed down from the loft and followed the bishop towards the church. I resisted the temptation to look in the direction of the howling and baying dogs but it was hard to keep my eyes fixed on the ground and the hem of the bishop's habit. The church, I was pleased to see, was dimly lit by smoky candles. I also noted that the monks all knelt and had their cowls up. The bishop gestured for us to kneel next to two monks who had left a space for us. They smiled and nodded at their hands which were folded together. We copied them.

Although I know some Latin, I did not understand much of what was said, sung and chanted but I stood when the others did and knelt at other times. The whole process seemed to go on for hours and was as exhausting as the practice for the shield wall! Eventually the bishop walked out and everyone filed behind in pairs. I tried to make a pair with Pol but the monk next me smiled and pulled Pol next to him and I followed. As soon as we emerged into the bright, almost blinding light, I saw why. We stood out as a pair because we were so much bigger than the others. This way we were less obvious. To aid the illusion I stooped. Everyone halted when the Welsh voice spoke. I recognised it as one of the men who were hunting us.

"Bishop Stephen, we are seeking two bandits who have murdered some men and fled into this valley. They are both armed and dangerous. Our dogs lost them on the far side of the valley. Did they visit here?"

"Last night?"

"Probably."

"No-one came to the monastery last night. We have the gates locked to keep us safe from bandits." I smiled at the half truth. He had not lied and he had answered the question as truthfully as he could manage.

I heard the disappointment in the man's voice. "We will keep watching then. They cannot have gone far. They are on foot."

"If they come here I will tell you. What are their names?"

I heard the panic in the man's voice. "Do not approach them or speak with them. If you see them then lock the gates. They are dangerous and should not be spoken with. Thank you for your time bishop. Right lads. Back into the hills. We'll get the dogs going again."

After they had left the bishop led us into his rooms. "They will watch."

"I cannot put you and the monastery at risk bishop. We will leave."

"We will be in greater danger if they see you leaving here."

"Then we leave after dark. We can spend the day resting."

"Very well but there is no time limit. You may stay as long as you wish, or need to."

When we were, once again, in the loft I explained to Pol what we would need to do. "I am worried that the attempt on my life was a precursor to an attack on our land. I could not tell the good bishop that but we must return as soon as we can."

"It is over forty miles to the island lord."

"True but it is only thirty to the fort of Pasgen and I hope he has men patrolling. It will be a long walk Pol. If you think you are not up to it then remain here and I will bring help."

He shook his head angrily, "Warlord what kind of oathsworn would I be if I allowed you to go alone amongst our enemies while I remained here in safety?"

"Very well Pol, but we keep going no matter what we feel like. It is our island which is under threat and all of our people. Much rests on our shoulders."

We slept well and awoke before dusk. Bishop Stephen fed us well and then gave us food for the journey. "These are honey and oat cakes and they will sustain you better than bread alone. This liquor is a spirit. It will purify any water you drink and give warmth in the night for it is becoming colder."

"Thank you bishop and I will not forget this kindness."

He spread his hands and looked like one of the statues I had seen in Civitas Carvetiorum, the White Christ, "A true Christian is charitable."

We headed, not up the valley sides, but towards the sea. I reasoned that they would be seeking us along the most direct route. The coastal way was slightly longer but it had fewer rises and falls. I had made the decision and we followed it for good or ill. As we were travelling at night it also made it easier for us to navigate as we had fewer trees to worry us. We just had to follow the stream towards the sea. By the same token the lack of trees meant a lack of cover. For the first six miles or so the land was flat and featureless but I could see a ridge of hills looming up and, in the near distance the foothills of Wyddfa came alarmingly close to the sea.

When we reach the col at the neck of land which jutted out into the sea I stopped for some food and to see how Pol was doing. His breathing had been more laboured than mine. I had asked him to leave the banner at the monastery but he stubbornly carried it. He took his duties seriously. The honey cakes were delicious and they seemed to make us both feel better just by eating them. There was no water nearby and so we both took a sip of the aqua vitae neat. It warmed, tingled and burned a little as it slipped down but we both felt warmer.

As we were at the top of the col we were able to view the darkened road ahead. There was the hint of a moon and it showed that the next few miles would be perilous indeed. The trail we would take was narrow. It looked, from where we stood, to be less than two hundred paces from the sea to the rocks and foothills. If the Welsh had their wits about them then this would be the perfect place to keep warriors to watch for us. We would have to tread very carefully.

The track was little more than a well-worn sheep track but it meant that there were few loose rocks to disturb and we made good progress. We both moved silently; there was no need for words. I strode ahead and Pol trudged behind. It was because of the silence that we heard the waiting warriors. Instead of waiting and watching, they were talking. I could also smell the wood smoke and knew that they were not far ahead. I waved my hand for Pol to lie down and then, drawing Saxon Slayer I edged up the rocks to my left to peer ahead and spy out the land. I was totally dark with my helmet and wolf skin covering my head and not even the whites of my eyes showed as I peeped over the rock. There were four guards and they were seated around the fire. Two were sleeping and the other two looked like they were playing a game of dice. More importantly there were two horses tethered to a large rock. That decided me. I had been contemplating sneaking around them but that was a risk. When I saw the horses I knew that they would catch us but they were a gift from the gods if we could slay their masters.

I retraced my steps to Pol. I took the standard and laid it down. I mimed taking out a sword and then pointed in the direction of the fire and held up four fingers. I pointed to the left and then at Pol. We had fought together long enough for us to understand without words. He nodded and then dragged his finger across his throat. I nodded and smiled. He hefted his shield and slipped up the rocks. It would take him longer to reach his position but he would be able to see the four men clearly. I would have to remember where they were as I went along the easier route. The danger was the horses which might give the alarm when they smelled a stranger. I had no choice. I had thrown the dice and I would have to see which way it fell.

The going was much easier for me and I found myself below the level of the track. I could see that the men had their backs to me and the fire was before them. When they turned at any noise I would be, briefly invisible and I would have to take my chances. Luckily for me they were not wearing armour and I still had on my mail. I boldly stepped forwards and, miraculously the horses did not neigh nor did they appear to hear my approach until I was three paces from them. The man who was to my left must have sensed a movement from the corner of his eye for he stood and stared at me. I did not hesitate. I swung Saxon Slayer and it struck him between his head and his shoulders. I withdrew the blade and swung backhand at the second surprised warrior who half turned to see me just a pace away. His head flew across the trail. Pol had leapt towards the sleeping men. He hesitated to kill them and they sprang up at the noise. He reacted then and killed one but the second had been sleeping with a dagger close by and he stabbed at Pol, the blade sliding across the mail. I stabbed him in the back and he fell to the ground.

"Secure the horses!" While Pol did so I checked to see if there were any other warriors hiding or sleeping nearby and there were none. Pol returned and I saw a tendril of blood. "Come you are wounded." He looked down at the blood in surprise. I ripped a piece of linen from one of the dead men and balled it and then poured some of the aqua vitae on to it. "Jam this under your mail and tighten your belt around it. We have no time to look at it now." He took the damp linen and grimaced as the fiery liquid burned the wound. "You were lucky Pol! You could have died. Never hesitate. If you can kill then do so! Mercy is for the Christian and not the warrior."

"I am sorry Warlord but he was asleep."

"Unless you want to sleep forever just kill them. It matters not if they are awake or not. Now get the precious standard and we will get out of here."

By the time he had returned, chastened, I had checked to see if they had anything of value about them and they did not. "Here, help me throw their bodies into the sea." He cocked his head and looked confused. "It will take them some time to discover what has happened to them. When they come here and find no horses and no guards they will think they either deserted or pursued us. Both suits us." After the bodies were thrown into the sea we went to the horses. I laughed, "Now I see why they did not give us away. They are our horses captured in the ambush!" *Wyrd*!

We now had less than twenty miles to go, we were horsed and we were still armed. "We now take a chance and ride. If we see any Welsh warriors before us then we will just ride through them. They will think we are their own men until it is too late."

It was dawn by the time we saw the island of Mona in the distance. It loomed like a dark shape from the sea but to me it looked beautiful for it meant home. We were still not safe but we were close enough to be able to touch the familiar rocks of our land and that was enough for me. I saw a glow ahead and wondered if it was the fire of Prince Pasgen's sentries.

When the Welsh voice shouted, "Slow down you mad buggers! Where's the fire!"

"Ride like the wind!" I drew Saxon Slayer and ploughed through the small camp. The Welsh warrior who had spoken died with my blade in his throat. I heard a scream from my right as Pol killed another. A third loomed up on my left and hacked at me but the blow was taken by my shield and I punched him away, his weapon still embedded in the wood and metal. And then we were through and it was an open road.

"Warlord! They have horses and they are pursuing us."

Our horses were tired and this looked to be a short escape. I leaned over the saddle, "Come on girl! Not far to go now." I stroked the mane of the huge chestnut and she kicked on. Her companion copied her and we began to pull away a little. I knew that it could not last for we were mailed. If these were like the other sentries then they were not armoured. Suddenly I detected a faint glow and it looked to be less than two hundred paces away. It was Pasgen's fort. I began yelling for all I was worth. "Wolf Warrior! Wolf Warrior ho!"

Then Pol shouted, "It is the Warlord of Rheged!"

I had no idea if they had heard us until there was a whoosh of arrows over our heads and then a light as the gates were opened showing us the way ahead. We had survived and we had returned safely to my land.

It was one of Aelle's men who greeted me. "We thought you were in Deva! Who was chasing you?"

"The Welsh. What happened to them?"

"Four of them are dead and the rest have fled."

"Good. Take me to the commander of the fort I have much news."

The first thing that I did was to put the fort on war readiness and then I sent two riders, one to Mungo's Burgh and one to my stronghold requesting a meeting with my leaders. It was lucky that I had returned safely to my fort or the whole of my land could be in danger. For all that I knew King Iago was marching towards Mona right at that moment. As I drank the watered wine I made sure that we had Pol's wound dressed. It would not do for him to die of a poisoned wound.

The garrison had all been alarmed by my sudden arrival and they were all alert to danger. I was pleased to see that two bolt throwers had been manufactured already and the road leading to the gate would be a death trap to any attacker. "How many men do you have in the garrison Captain Calum?"

"Twenty archers and forty warriors. We have five scouts too."

It was not as many as I had hoped but it would be enough to deter a quick attack. My worry was that King Iago was close by with his whole army. The fort was solid but lightly armed men could still cut it off by scaling the slopes of the hillside. We had not yet completed those defences. Perhaps this was a good thing and we could see how we might need to improve the defences. The problem was that we had planned on fighting the Saxons and not our allies. We were now in the same position that Raibeart, Pasgen and Aelle had been in Rheged. We were surrounded by enemies and without friends.

"We will need them and more. I suspect that King Iago may be coming to try to take Mona and your men are all that stand between him and the bridge!"

It was close to sunset when we saw the Red Dragon banner of King Iago Ap Beli approach from the north. The coast road twisted and turned making it difficult to estimate numbers. It looked like it was just his bodyguard but I was under no illusions. The rest of the treacherous snake's army would be close at hand. "Make sure the bolt throwers are loaded."

This was where I missed Miach's archers. Had they been present then we could have picked off any of the Welsh we wished. It was not worth showing them our secret weapon for such a few men. I waited with Pol next to me on the newly finished gate. He had my banner but it remained furled. I peered down into the ditches; as yet they had no traps or lillia in them. We would need to remedy that soon. Perhaps it was no bad thing for I saw King Iago giving both my fort and the ditches a close inspection. I was glad that we had built three ditches. It looked like we would need them.

We had made the fort like the Roman ones with a gate at each end allowing for swift passage of troops. I heard the clip clop of hooves and turned to see Prince Pasgen and his equites. He waved a greeting and I felt much better. We could now deal with this king, whatever he threw at us. We had the best soldiers on the mainland and they were all gathered in this fort.

The king and his banner rode forwards. "Who is the commander of this fort? I bring news of the Warlord of Rheged, Lord Lann."

I nodded to Calum who spoke, "I am Captain Calum, your majesty, what is the news?"

"Surely you will not keep the king of this land outside you fort to bandy words like a seller of fish?"

The words sounded reasonable but I was more than a little suspicious. There was a ridge running along the coast which could hide thousands of men and the king must have known that he only needed a few to overwhelm the half staffed fort. I shook my head at Calum.

He spread his arms, "I am sorry your majesty but the lord of this land is Prince Pasgen of Rheged and I cannot admit anyone without his permission. Were it just myself I would admit you in an instant but the prince is a stickler for protocol."

I saw the prince laughing as he heard his name taken in vain. King Iago began to become angry. He was unused to be refused anything. "Prince Pasgen rules this land with my permission. I am your king."

"I am sorry your majesty but none of the men in this fort, or indeed the island has, so far as I know, sworn allegiance and fealty to you." He paused and glanced mischievously at me, "Not even the Warlord. What is this news? The last we heard he was visiting you at Deva."

I suspect that the king was now unsure of my whereabouts. He had expected either me to speak or, at the very least, be granted admittance. Now that neither had happened he was puzzled. "That is my news. He did not arrive and when we searched for him we found some Rheged warriors slain. They must have been ambushed by bandits or Saxons."

"That is grave news. I will send a messenger to Prince Pasgen immediately. Thank you for the news. Our dead comrades, were they buried?"

Again the question had not been expected. The king looked desperately for help and then said, "I believe my men did see to them."

Calum should have been an actor. He smiled and said, "We are grateful to you for that and we thank you for your news."

Suddenly the king erupted with rage. "Enough of this. I demand that you open the gate. Do so or you will all be slaughtered!"

Calum's tone became more serious. "With one hundred bodyguards? I fear that many of your oathsworn would die in the attempt."

The king laughed and wheeled his horse around to retreat behind his shield wall. "Perhaps this may change your mind!" The dragon standard lowered and raised twice and suddenly there were three thousand warriors lining the ridge and the road. "Now, see sense and let me in. If he were still alive then the Warlord would order you to do so."

I now understood the king's attitude and stance. He had been told that we made the fort but I was slain. I remembered the attack and the blows we had taken. Pol's blood would have made them think that one of us, at least was wounded and whoever led the men had gambled that I was, at least, wounded.

I nodded to Pol and stepped forwards. As my banner was unfurled I said, "I would not presume to take my name in vain, Iago Ap Beli. My captain has done all that I asked of him and, as I recall, the hacked and chopped bodies of my bodyguard were left for the crows," I paused and pointed a finger at him, "by your men acting under your orders!"

While that was not news to his own men, to the garrison it was shocking and startling. I heard a murmur run around my fort. I held up my hand for silence. "What say you to that? Is it honourable to invite a man who was your ally to your home and then to have him ambushed and murdered? I know that your father would not have done so and I cannot see your son doing that either."

"My father was a great king but he was not strong enough. He should have shackled you years ago and I will now do it. I know that you have less than fifty men in the fort and you will all die unless you surrender."

Pasgen joined me at the gateway and said, quietly. "We have a hundred men from the island on their way here now."

"I am not worried. They cannot take it now. Have your men come to the walls but remain hidden. He will have a shock soon enough."

"I am waiting and I am not a patient man."

"Oh I am sorry. Were you expecting me to wet my breeks and surrender in the face of your army? Remember Iago Ap Beli. I have been fighting better warriors than yours, the Saxons, for my whole life and I see nothing before me that makes me worry. Do your worst but I warn the men of Gwynedd. If you start a war against my people then you had better win for we do not forget treachery." I paused to let my words echo around the cliffs. "And you may have a dragon on a banner but I have Myrddyn the Dragon Wizard and I know which one I would fear!"

I could see that my last barb had struck home. The men of Gwynedd were fearful of magic and Myrddyn was renowned as a magician. I could see them look at each other in apprehension. King Iago roared, "Enough of this! Attack!"

I nodded at Calum whose archers were ready with their bows. They stood and the twenty bows loosed their arrows. The Gwynedd standard bearer saved the life of the king as he thrust his shield to protect him but four arrows pierced his neck and he fell dead, the standard dropping to the ground.

"See how the Dragon Standard is fallen. It is an omen. Myrddyn is not here but his magic protects us all." I saw Pasgen look at me and I gave a slight shrug. I said to him, quietly, "Had I the men then I would not need deception but I use every weapon available to me."

The archers continued to loose their arrows as the bodyguards dragged the king away from his dying horse. The first of the shield walls came bravely on. The narrowness of the land meant that their wedge was only ten men wide but fifty deep. I hated to be so ruthless but I had to teach them a lesson. "Bolt throwers ready! Aim at the wedge."

When they were just ten paces from the first ditch, their shields covered in arrows I roared. "Now!"

At that sort of range the bolt went through men as though they were parchment. They tore through mail, bodies, armour as though they were not there. There were two lines clearly visible in the demoralised shield wall and my archers took advantage, raining their lethal flights on the stunned men. The bolt throwers reloaded and I dropped my arm again. The effect was just as good and there were now fifty dead and dying men. They were brave but they turned and ran. They had never fought against such lethal machines before and they had no answer to them. I saw Iago's shoulders slump and he ordered a withdrawal. He had planned a sneak attack and it had failed. His men, holding their shields up for protection, trudged back along the coastal path. Thanks to the foresight of Myrddyn and Brother Oswald we had a weapon hundreds of years old which terrified our enemies.

Chapter 11

By the time that Mungo's one hundred men had joined us I felt much happier. Mungo's Burgh was still adequately defended and I knew that Tuanthal, Myrddyn and Garth would soon be joining me. Mungo's men were solid and dependable fighters. I gave Calum and Prince Pasgen a brief explanation of what had occurred and then made sure that Pol got some rest. His wound was not life threatening but I needed my brave standard bearer well again. I thanked Bishop Stephen for his liquor had, no doubt, helped to save Pol's life.

I went to the stables to see the brave mount which had carried me to safety. Pasgen was just as keen a horseman as I was and he joined me as I went to rub down the chestnut and feed her some grain. "This will be my new horse." I looked at the saddle which was hung nearby. Sometime the equite would mark the saddle with his name or that of his horse. I did not want to rename the horse unless I had to. The equite had been able to write and he had carved his name in the leather. He had been called Seargh and I now remembered him. Tuanthal had had high hopes for him. I would thank him for his horse in the afterlife. He had also carved the name of his horse under his own, Scout. "Well Scout, you are my horse now." She nuzzled my hand when she heard her name. "A strange choice for the name of a female but it seems to suit."

Prince Pasgen nodded. "Perhaps there is a story behind her naming. It does her rider great honour that the Warlord chooses to ride her. Seargh will be happy beyond this life now."

It was half way through the next day when the others began to arrive. My captains, wizard and son arrived first and I had to spend some time telling them of our adventures. Myrddyn did not seem surprised by the treachery. "The dream Warlord, it did warn." He smiled. "It appears that my former countrymen can be cowed by the threat of a wizard. Perhaps we should bear that in mind for the future."

"I am just glad that the bluff worked! Come let us use the Praetorium to discuss what must be done."

When we were seated around the table we were crowded as the room was small but I enjoyed the intimacy. I felt that it made us closer both physically and strategically. There was much outrage, especially from Prince Pasgen about the treachery from an ally. My brothers said little. Hogan, for the first time at such a meeting was quite outspoken.

"We teach this King of Gwynedd a lesson. We know our men are superior to his. We know that are our arms are the best. Let us defeat him and conquer the kingdom!"

Prince Pasgen clapped him about his broad shoulders. "Here we have a true warrior of Rheged! If my son had lived I would he had been as you are."

"Any other comments?"

Hogan and Pasgen desperately looked around for support. Miach said, "We have still to replace the archers we lost. I know that they were a small number but they take time to train."

"The bolt throwers worked well."

"I know Prince Pasgen, but they need the enemy to attack us. I am quite happy to stay on the defensive and let the enemy bleed upon our walls. I am just uncertain about our ability to go to war and bring them to battle on the open field." I pointed to the west. "Even now we have depleted our forces on the island. We have to build up our army. We knew we would have to do it anyway for the Saxons would return but this means we have to do this thing urgently. So long as they outnumber us then we will defend."

"Perhaps we need do nothing about King Iago."

We all stared at Myrddyn. He rarely said anything which had not been soundly thought out and I waited for him to continue.

"Young Hogan is right; the men of Gwynedd cannot compare with our men. They have just fought two battles with the Saxons and they are in no position to fight us. It is coming on to winter and this is no land to fight when there is snow on Wyddfa. We need do nothing but watch and be vigilant. The Saxons will return and they will come set on revenge. They will want Iago and they will want you. Iago was not interested in Mona before because the Hibernians kept attacking and his men or his father's men got wet each time they were summoned to repulse them. He had no trade. Look at him now; he has no ports and lives far from the sea. It was Lord Lann who made the island attractive by building our bridge and defeating the Hibernians. He built up trade and made the island a safe place. It is why the ones who were here already do not resent us." He paused to allow his words to sink in. "We build up our forces and let the two armies destroy each other."

"That is not particularly noble."

"Was it noble Prince Pasgen when your father was murdered and your family slaughtered? It is war and war is not a game. The Warlord knows that and I am certain that is the reason your father named him Warlord. You need a warlord who understands war and how to win. Lord Lann does."

"Any other comments?" While listening I had made my decision. "We will build up the army. Calum will be responsible for the warriors here. Miach I want your best archer to take charge of the archers, slingers and bolt throwers based here. We will increase numbers when you have trained them. Until I say otherwise every freshly trained man comes here. We also need to stay ahead of the enemy with our weapons. I want every man in the shield wall to have a helmet with cheek guards. They will all have a leather padded coat beneath their armour. Pol nearly died because of a dagger. I want half of Prince Pasgen's equites and half of Tuanthal's men arming with a spear which is three paces long. Like the lance they used to scar the White Christ."

"Are you becoming a Christian brother?"

"No Raibeart but I had time, at the monastery, to look at the paintings and that was on one of them. I saw how it could be used to reach beyond the enemies' own spears. They will also have the biggest horses for I want the horses mailed too. We need the equites to be as heavily armoured as the shield wall."

"Is that all?" Tuanthal shook his head. "Where will we get the horses? The armour? Neither are cheap."

"No captain, it is just the start and you are right, they are not cheap. Raibeart and Aelle, you need to get your people to produce as much of whatever it is they produce so that we can sell it at the markets and then buy leather for the coats and iron for the armour. I know that we can go back and dig up the treasure from the field of death but not yet. I want us to become the people the whole world trades with."

I paused for breath, if nothing else. Captain Calum asked, more for clarification than anything, "So we stay behind the walls and do nothing?"

"Not quite. Captain Tuanthal I want you to take your equites on a long patrol to find King Iago and see what he is up to."

Prince Pasgen went bright red and leapt to his feet. "That is the job of my equites!"

I was not a man to shout and I said, "Sit down!" It was said firmly and without shouting but he must have seen my face for he did as he was told. "You will do as I say or you will be replaced. Your job is to keep the mainland and the bridge safe. Tuanthal can be spared from the island you cannot. Do you think I can afford to have a handful of men defending this fort when King Iago could be around the corner? This is not your personal battle. You will have to man the southern wall as well as the fort. Mungo and his men will have to keep the bridge on their side of the narrows and you could be cut off at any time. I need you here. I need you in charge not being a hero and getting your men killed!"

He paled and Aelle said, "That is cruel brother!"

"Having a death wish when men follow you is cruel." I softened. "This is no game Pasgen. You are a good leader. You are like your father and not your brother but you have to begin to think of the bigger picture and not just what you are doing moment to moment."

He nodded, "You are right and you were right to say it. My father chose well Lord Lann. I am sorry."

"There is nothing to apologise for. In this room we can all say what we want." I pointed at the door. "Out there we do not argue; in here it is a different matter. One last thing; I intend to get Gwynfor to try to get us two ships. I want to be able to reinforce here even without the bridge and Brother Oswald told me that we can put bolt throwers on the ships as the Romans did. I would use the ships as a floating fort." I paused again. "I have spoken much. Does anyone want to speak?" I had come up with these ideas whilst lying in the monastery hay loft and I had had to get them all out in case I forgot any.

There was silence but I was gratified to see smiles from all of them. They had approved of my words. Myrddyn said, "I think that King Urien and Brother Osric would be more than happy with their choice of leader. You have grown Warlord."

Later when I was travelling back with Hogan, Pol and Myrddyn my son kept looking at me strangely. "Have I grown two heads son?"

"No father but I saw a different Warlord tonight. You frightened me at times and yet excited me beyond words at others. How did you think of all those things?"

"Every waking moment I am thinking of my people. We may not live in Rheged any longer and we may have acquired others but they are all my people and my responsibility. I have no time to think of me. I have others to think of and so my mind works all the time." I nodded at Myrddyn, "And I have had two good teachers. You can learn even when you are a man my son. Remember that."

I could hear Hogan telling Pol everything which had transpired during the meeting. Despite the tempers and raised voices I felt happier. Today all my men knew where we were going and that we were together.

Raibeart and Aelle were heading back to their people to be leaders in a different way from before and they were both happy about that. Aelle had long since been a leader of people rather than a war leader and Raibeart's wound had made him realise his own mortality. Neither man wanted war and that suited me. I was the brother who was the warrior and nothing would change that. My men had also thrown themselves into the new conflict. Tuanthal was already riding the foothills of Wyddfa while Miach and Pasgen were moulding a mighty army to withstand the hordes of King Iago and the men of Gwynedd.

When I reached my stronghold, I was tired but I knew I had one more journey to make before I could rest. Myfanwy took one look at my face and was about to berate me when Hogan, surprisingly put his arm around her and, after winking at me, led her away. "I think that the Warlord would like a decent meal tonight after he has visited Caergybi. Now I thought…."

Myrddyn laughed, "Your son is growing up and handles women far better than his father ever did!"

"You are right. Come Pol, one more ride to the port and then you may rest for a few days and Myrddyn can heal your wound."

The word had reached Gwynfor and Gareth of the ambush and the concern on their faces was touching. "He was always a bad 'un that Iago. I remember when he was a young man he would tear up the countryside whoring and carrying on as though he was a brigand instead of the son of the king. He was not like his father. There was a real king who kept his people safe."

"What I need, from both of you are your thoughts on ways to increase trade and how to buy two ships."

They looked at each other and Gareth said, "If you get the ships then trade will increase because there are places who don't trade with us yet and we could make profits from them."

"And I think we could build a ship. It depends on how big you want it."

"It should be able to sail to Gaul at least."

"It will cost timber and there is precious little here."

"How about," suggested Myrddyn, "we build a saw mill on the mainland and we build the ship in the Narrows."

"Aye we could do that. Old Tam, he is a shipwright. His sons both died. It would give him something to occupy his mind and stop him drinking."

"Good. I leave that with you. Just tell Brother Oswald to get you whatever you need. Gareth, I have told my brothers to increase the production of everything. We need as much trade as you can create. The work you do is as valuable as that of any soldier."

He swelled with pride. "I'll not let you down Warlord."

Once Hogan and I returned to the stronghold I set about, with Brother Oswald, to work out how to improve the defences. We were many miles from King Iago and the Saxons but I remembered that the Hibernians had raided us before and with so few men to defend our land we needed the strongest walls that we could.

There were just the three of us who ate together that night. Myrddyn and Brother Oswald were busily planning walls and ditches. They were both in their element. Myfanwy watched with satisfaction as my son and I devoured all the food she had ordered for us. Although we had cooks she supervised the cooking and watched the whole process. The meal was as much hers as those who had toiled in our kitchens. "It is good to see my two men eating so well and it makes a change for us to be a family."

I sensed criticism but I had learned, with Aideen, to keep my mouth shut. As I was eating this was not a problem. Hogan was much better with women than I was and he grinned at Myfanwy. "We get much bigger portions this way. I agree with Myfanwy, father. Let us keep it private all the time."

"No, Hogan, I did not mean that. I know that the Warlord has many duties but I think every now and then we should be alone when we eat."

I had finished my food and I sat back. "I think that is an excellent idea. We entertain too much anyway." I was grateful to Hogan for his intervention. Once again he had steered me in the right direction. I looked over at him. He was now a man. He was as tall as I was and nearly as broad. I struggled to remember his age but the number was irrelevant it was more important that he was ready for more responsibility. "Hogan, you are now almost full grown. You deserve more than to be just my squire. What would you wish to be?"

"I am happy to be your squire."

"You and I know that you wish more. Be honest with me son. I always try to be honest when I speak. It is the only way."

"I think I would be an equite. I envy Tuanthal when he goes off on his adventures."

"It is more than an adventure Hogan. It is not a game."

"I know and I do not mean to make light of it. I mean that I do not wish to compete with you. You are the Warlord and the master of the shield wall. I want to be my own man." He paused. "Does that disappoint you?"

"No son. It makes me even more proud of you. When Tuanthal returns I will speak with him and you can begin your training as an equite." I remembered my decision about heavier equites. "And I would look for a larger horse and then you can be one of the first to wield the long spear." His face lit up and I noticed the nod of approval from Myfanwy. I was becoming better at this.

The next day the three of us, Pol, Hogan and me, rode through the island seeking bigger horses. It was only then that I realised that the only horses we had we had brought from Rheged. Hogan was as disappointed as I was when we reached Mungo's Burgh and we had not seen a suitable mount. "I think that we will need to breed our own."

Hogan's face fell, "That will mean we will be without the horses we need!"

Pol pointed to the mainland, "Perhaps not. Remember Warlord, when we passed through the flat lands to the east of Deva there were larger horses pulling ploughs."

"Plough horses!" snorted Hogan.

"I did not say our men would ride plough horses but if we bred them with our horses then the animals produced would have the best qualities of both." Pol had trained Hogan and knew when to be patient and explain things; this was one such occasion.

Hogan brightened at that. "That sounds like a plan."

"Except that the horse lands of which Pol speaks are now under the control of King Iago. Let us wait until Tuanthal reports and then we will know what we must do."

Once we returned to my stronghold I spent the rest of the day talking with Myrddyn and Oswald. I was so engrossed in their plans that I lost all track of time until Pol, uncharacteristically, burst in shouting, "There is a messenger from Gareth. Mungo's ship has been sighted!" He was suddenly aware of the stares of those in the room and he murmured, "Sorry for the interruption but I thought…."

We all laughed. "Do not worry Pol. I would have been as excited. I will carry on this discussion this evening for I too, like keen young Pol, would like to find out if he was successful in his hunt for new warriors."

We galloped hard to Caergybi and reached it quickly. It was a bare two miles hence. When we reined in Gareth was pointing at two ships which were edging into the port. "It seems he has brought friends."

I was intrigued. The first ship I knew; it was the one he had set sail in but the other was new to me and had a different rig to the first. We made our way down to the quayside. As soon as the first ship touched, before they had even tied up, Mungo leapt from the side and almost picked me up. "It is good to see you Warlord and we have been more successful than you can possibly imagine!" He turned and roared, "Come on boys and meet the Warlord!"

The sides of the ship seemed filled with huge men, some armoured and others with just leather but they were all armed. They leapt beyond the poor seamen who were busy trying to tie up the ship. "Come let us take them away from here." I pointed to the market square which was now empty. "We can meet them there."

I was aware of many voices speaking in Mungo's dialect. I felt like a stranger in my own land. I reached the square and stood at the steps. The second ship was disgorging its passengers and there appeared to be almost two hundred men who were coming to the square. I also noticed some and a few women with babes in arms. Mungo cleared a space around me and then raised his hands and there was silence. "This is Lord Lann, the Warlord of Rheged. I know you have all heard of him for that is the reason you sailed with me. Now that you see him in the flesh, do you still wish to serve him?"

There was a chorus of "Wolf Warrior!" and I wondered if this had been rehearsed.

"Good. Now the more difficult part. Warlord, do you wish this rabble to serve you as warriors?"

I do not think that Mungo thought I would answer in the negative but the men looked at me in a mixture of apprehension and awe. "Welcome brothers. I am honoured that you choose to fight with me." I turned to Pol. "Take them to the warrior hall. Unfurl the banner." He looked worried. "Do not worry, they are on our side." I waved my arms to get the attention of the excitable warriors. "Follow Pol and the Wolf Banner and he will take you to my hall and your home until we get you settled."

When they had left there seemed an unreal silence in the square and the bemused men and women of the port looked at the departing army.

Mungo walked with me and I led Scout. "You have a tale my friend. Out with it."

I could tell that he was eager for the telling; he began speaking as though it was a torrent of water from a waterfall. "We arrived unseen and the captain said he would find a port and meet us at the bay he had left us in four days time. We split up and all agreed to meet back at the anchorage in four days. I returned to my old village in the hills and found that it was burned and empty. I wondered if our trip had been in vain but suddenly, out of the forests, came many men. It seems that the Saxons had captured the villages and enslaved the women and children while the men were away fighting. Many of the men died as they tried to rescue their families but the families had been taken far away. As soon as I mentioned your name and Myrddyn's then they wanted to join you. They begged me! Runners went to find other groups hiding in the hills and we made our way back to the meeting place. There were many others who wished to fight. They were the remnants of the army but most had lost their weapons and could no longer fight. When we reached the meeting place the ship was not there and we became worried in case something had happened to our ship. I did not fancy another walk through the country, especially without you and Myrddyn to guide us. The captain returned after three days and was full of apologies but it seems he had met a captain who was bemoaning the lack of trade. When he told him of the opportunities in Mona he and his crew volunteered to join us. That is why there are two ships but we were chased by some Saxon ships and had to sail to the west, out of sight of land to avoid them."

"You lost sight of land?" It was almost unheard of for a ship to sail beyond land. Every sailor was afraid of falling off the edge of the world.

"It was either that or be captured and we thought that the unknown was preferable to slavery. We waited a day until we were sure that they were no longer waiting and then headed back."

I clapped him on the back. "That was bravely done by both you and the captains. You are a sight for sore eyes and I cannot thank you enough." I then told him of our new problems.

His happy face darkened, "The treacherous bastard! What a snake! I got back just in time then."

"Aye, Pasgen is busy organising the defence but, as you can see, we now need more foot soldiers to defend the bridge and Oswald's southern wall will become even more important than it was." As we entered my stronghold I could see that he was working out which men to keep and which men to send to others.

My resourceful triumvirate of Myfanwy, Myrddyn and Oswald had organised food and beds for the warriors so that by the time we arrived my stronghold was a place of serenity and peace. While Mungo went to check on his countrymen I sought Oswald and Myrddyn. "These men can fight but they need arming."

"We have many weapons and armour from the Saxons but they are not up to our usual standard. We were going to melt them down and forge them as better weapons."

"We have no time for that. Issue them; we will worry about the quality when we have the time. And we have a new ship here. Get to the port tomorrow. We will pay the captain to go to the land of Gwyr. They have much iron and we can trade wheat with them. At this time of year it will be more valuable than gold and we should make a healthy profit."

Myrddyn laughed, "It is not just your brothers who have an eye for business."

"If it pays for warriors then so be it." I pointed towards the port. "We also need a couple of bolt throwers for the boat and four men to man them for this trip. They can train the seamen. See to it!"

I was so engrossed in my tasks that Myfanwy had to force me to bed. "It will do no one any good if the Warlord is too tired to think and I have a feeling you will want to go with them to the other end of the island tomorrow." She knew me well and I went reluctantly to bed.

The men of Strathclyde were all as taken with Mona as the rest of us had been. It was totally unlike the glens and forests they were used to. I saw the wives and the children looking enviously at the neat huts and villages through which we passed. I was riding with Mungo, Hogan and Pol. "I think that the men with families should be based on the island."

Mungo looked at me, "Why, Warlord?"

"It will be much safer for them and it is only fair. The mainland will be a place of war. Let the single men settle there. In time we may well be able to make the peninsula safe but for now let us be cautious."

The numbers worked out well. There were forty men with families and they began to build dwellings close to the fort as soon as we arrived. The other one hundred and thirty men were ferried across to the mainland. We went before them and both Calum and Prince Pasgen were delighted to see so many reinforcements. My only worry was that Tuanthal had still not returned. I had come to rely on Tuanthal as one of the most dependable warriors I had ever met. I decided to stay the night for I was anxious to see how they had improved the defences.

We rose early the next day and Calum proudly took me on a tour while Prince Pasgen patrolled beyond the walls to see Tuanthal and to train his six new equites. As I crossed to the southern wall I saw Miach with twenty trainee archers. He was bellowing and complaining, as usual, but when he gave me a half smile as I passed him I knew that things were going well. Hogan had hinted that he would like to ride with Pasgen but I was determined that he would be trained by Tuanthal. Prince Pasgen was a brave horseman but I knew who I would prefer to guard my flanks in a battle.

"See, Warlord, we have built three ditches. The slopes on the far sides are steeper than those close to our walls. If any one is trapped there it will be a killing ground for they will not be able to climb out and regain their own lines. We have incorporated a stream into one of them so that it hides the lillia on the bottom." He smiled, "For a priest Brother Oswald can think up some devilish ways to kill." We climbed the gate house which looked identical to the one at Civitas Carvetiorum. "We have built two bolt throwers but we are short of bolts." He shrugged. "We can send sharpened stakes if we have to they will still kill." He showed me the two towers at the ends of the wall. "Luckily we have much stone and so the two structures are solid but I think we will add more in the winter when I wish to keep the men warm and active."

As we approached the front gate I heard a cry from the sentry. "Equites approaching!"

Tuanthal! I saw Hogan begin to become excited. In truth I was too for I desperately needed to know the information he had. As they rode through the gates I could see that they had had a hard time. There were two empty saddles and at least one horse missing. Tuanthal gave a brave smile as he entered the gates. He turned to his second in command. "See to the men and horses they need a good rest."

"As do you Tuanthal. But if you could indulge me and make a short report…"

"Of course Warlord." He grinned. "Even after you and Pol had walked for two days you still found time to speak with us and I have just been in the saddle!"

The four of us went to Calum's office and I poured a beaker of wine for him. He quaffed it swiftly. "You cannot know how good that tastes, my lord. On with my report. When we left here we headed for the monastery. I spoke with the bishop. The king thought that you had been aided by the monks and he was not happy but as he wished to keep on the good side of the church he left them alone. They were a day ahead and we followed their trail. It was easy. They are not a tidy people Warlord! They tried to ambush us once, which is where we lost the three men but the eighty men they used all died. We buried their arms as we could not carry them with us." It seems there was much armour and many arms waiting for us when the time allowed. "Eventually they reached Deva and King Iago set about adding to the defences. I think the Saxons had tried to damage it when they left. He will be there for some time." He took another drink.

"Your opinion, Tuanthal, will he attack before spring?"

"If he does then we shall easily win. The roads are becoming impassable." He pointed to Wyddfa. "We could see the snow atop the mountain all the way back. He has a month at most and then he will be stuck in Deva until the warmer weather."

"Excellent and you have done well but before you take a well-earned rest I have a boon to ask."

"Warlord, you can just command and it will be done."

"I know, which is why I shall ask and you can refuse." I saw Hogan's nervous face from the corner of my eye. "My son would be an equite and I can think of no better teacher than you."

"I am honoured by both the request and the sentiments. I would be delighted."

Hogan was still enough of a child to show clear unbridled joy on his face. "When you have rested perhaps you could take some wagons and recover the two piles of arms. We shall need them and perhaps see if you can buy some plough horses from the low lands before King Iago returns. We shall need to breed some larger horses for our heavily armed equites. I think that Hogan would like to be one of the first. Pol can accompany you to show you where we buried the arms." Pol showed the same delight as Hogan and I felt much better with the report. We had breathing space and it was thanks to the Saxons. ***Wyrd***!

Chapter 12

Before I left I spoke with Prince Pasgen. He too had been worried about the larger animals we would need. "I am trying to get breeding animals. The island will be perfect for them but it will take time. Let us just try to use the lances first."

"I agree. The men will find them unwieldy at first but we will persevere. How long do we have?"

"I cannot see them being ready for war before the spring and that gives you time to work with Calum and Mungo. The three of you must be of one mind. You need to have signals ready to send for help should you need it. I will not be close at hand and I will rely on the three of you to make the right decisions. Remember you will be the rock on which Iago's armies break."

"We will not let you down."

"I know it which is why I will be at peace while I am at home."

"Or as much peace as Myfanwy will allow."

"And that too."

I rode alone across the island feeling more at peace than I had a right to. There was still a threat from King Iago but it was distant. We were now aware of the problem. The other problems, the Saxons and the Hibernians, were also still there but Mungo's story had shown me that we had done the right thing. The land was now settling down for winter. The summer had been a good one; it was not always so and the crops had done well. The wheat we could sell would make us stronger. The people were happy and waved at me as I rode across the island. The old Roman Road had been a little overgrown before we had arrived but now the trade and the warriors kept it weed free and well-used. I wondered what my parents would have made of it all. I suspect my mother would have expected it for she was still in my dreams and those of Myrddyn. But my father… I never got a chance to know him and to talk with him. I determined that I would take more opportunities to speak with Hogan. Myfanwy had opened the door and I would not close it.

I had a good Yule for it was full of surprises! Firstly Hogan returned with Tuanthal and Pol. I could see from their expressions that they had enjoyed being away from me and with a young leader like Tuanthal. I was not jealous. I would have been surprised had it not been so. They had brought back great quantities of arms and armour. The better pieces were already with Mungo's men while the others would be smelted and used to make the horse armour, helmets, arrow tips, bolt heads and all the other pieces of weaponry we needed to be ahead of our enemies. Hogan was even happier about his training as an equite. Tuanthal confided in me, privately, that he was the most proficient of his equites with the new longer lance. I suspected it was because it was new to him and he had not used a spear for as long as the others had. He learned to use it as it was meant to be used. We decided that he would lead the lance armed equites leaving Tuanthal to command the rest. The horses they had brought were also welcome. He brought two breeding mares. They looked enormous to me but my horsemen assured me that the stallion we had would cope. He had told me with a twinkle in his eye which showed me that he was happy. They had captured a couple of stray horses on their travels and were already training new warriors.

The good news from Brother Oswald was that he had set up trading links with the people of the Gwyr. They were more than happy to let us have the iron and they needed the wheat but the real reason was that King Iago had begun to make incursions into the lands to the north of them and they saw him as a predator. The people of the Gwyr were our first allies.

The captain who had joined us from the north was also happy. The bolt throwers meant that he did not fear pirates and the sea voyage along the coast was much less perilous than the one he was used to. As the shipwrights had laid the keel of our first ship we were on target for the spring. The only delay had been acquiring the wood but once the mill had been built, within Pasgen's walls, then it soon began arriving and the work began.

However the biggest surprise came from Myfanwy who told me that she was with child. I was shocked. I had thought I was beyond that stage. I knew that my wife was young enough to have children but I now had grey in my beard and in my hair. She had laughed when I told her. "No husband. You will father many more children."

Amazingly Myrddyn had not only foreseen the event he agreed with my wife. "You will sire many children Lord Lann. It is written and they will be powerful allies to you in the future."

Myrddyn could be so damned enigmatic. He gave you a taste of the future and then let you stew. But I was happy. I knew that Myfanwy would be a good mother, I had seen that evidence already. I had been worried about Hogan but he was even happier. "I am old enough now not to worry about who will have the affection and I can be the older wiser brother. Besides it will not be long before I sire your grandchildren and so it will be good practice for all of us!"

That stunned me more than anything else. My son was almost a man in every sense and yet, to me, he was still a child. I also felt just a hint of sadness for I knew his mother, Aideen, would have been proud of him and as excited about him taking a wife as he was. It made me wonder if he had anyone in mind. I decided that the next time we hunted I would ask him.

Once again we had a winter without snow on the magical island of Mona. To those who had only recently travelled from Rheged and Strathclyde it was nothing short of a miracle and the priests we had made much of it telling the people that it was the work of the White Christ. Of course Myrddyn and those of the old religion dismissed that for the Mother was known to love Mona and to treat it with special care. To me it mattered not so long as people did not starve or freeze to death. As Myfanwy was not far into her pregnancy I took the opportunity of visiting Pasgen's Palace as Garth and Ridwyn named it. There was a little rivalry and some jealousy between the three of them. I would have expected it of Tuanthal but he seemed above it. Miach was a law unto himself and never worried about anyone else's position so long as he was in charge of his precious archers.

Myrddyn and Pol accompanied my son and me. We rode with Tuanthal's equites. It was not because I was afraid of ambush but because we needed the two leaders of equites to share their experiences of the new weapons and armour. Hogan had become better and better with the lance and I think Tuanthal was anxious to see if the nobles of Pasgen's command could match him. Our first ship was a month away from sailing and we needed a quay or dock building close to Mungo's Burgh; I had had enough surprises at Yule, I wanted none from King Iago.

The settlement close to the island fort was well established and the women bowed as we rode by. After the uncertainty of life amongst the Saxons their new life must have seemed a world away. The walls of the new fort bristled with bolt throwers and sentries. Prince Pasgen had used the new timber mill to build huge stables and warrior halls for his men. The recently acquired armour and weapons were worn with pride by the men from Strathclyde. Prince Pasgen's personal quarters were also well apportioned. Although he did not have the hypocaust we had had in Rheged he had fireplaces in every room and it was very comfortable even when the wind was blowing from snowy Wyddfa.

I was, therefore, somewhat surprised when Myrddyn suggested that we spend a two day trip ascending Wyddfa. Pasgen and Tuanthal were also less than happy.

"You want to take the Warlord up a mountain which may be teeming with Iago's men?"

"I do not think Iago's men will be teeming anywhere at the moment. Besides it will be safe."

"I can ill afford to have horses breaking their legs for no reason."

Myrddyn gave an exasperated sigh, "Prince Pasgen who said anything about taking your horses?"

"What about an escort?"

"We need no escort. We will take Pol."

I smiled at the reaction. All of them, thought that I would be mad to do as my wizard asked but I trusted him. He had never lied to me and never told me anything which did not come true. If he said we would be safe then we would be. "I am going. Would you like to come too, Pol?"

He grinned, "Of course, Warlord!"

We left the next morning. I knew that Pasgen would send Aedh and his scouts out to watch us but I knew that Myrddyn would have a good reason for the journey.

We headed south and meandered our way up sheep tracks. Scout was a surefooted horse and I did not worry that he would lose his footing. Soon we left the spindly trees behind and there was snow underfoot. Myrddyn obviously knew where he was going and we rode around the side of the mountain towards the eastern side. I saw only the tracks of birds and wild cats. There was no sign that either man or horse had ever been up here.

"There is a good reason why you have brought me here Myrddyn. It is not just to annoy my captains and make me cold so pray, tell me the reason."

"I have told you of the power of the mountain and at this time of the year the power is at its greatest as the mountain awakes from its winter sleep. There is a cave and it delves deep into the heart of the dragon. We will sleep there and we will dream."

I heard the sharp intake of breath from Pol. "And what of Pol. You and I know of the dreams but not Pol."

Myrddyn was silent and then he reined in his horse and turned to face me. "The spirit who will visit us Warlord, who is she?"

"The spirit of my mother."

"That is the form and the voice she takes and do you think that she will harm Pol."

His words were those of a mother chastising a child for being afraid of the dark and I did feel foolish. "You will be safe Pol but if you wish to sleep outside of the cave then I will understand."

"No Warlord, I am your standard bearer and I face the same dangers as you." His words sounded brave even if they lacked conviction.

We reached the cave towards mid afternoon. We had to dismount to enter. I wondered if our horses would enter but Myrddyn spoke kind words to his and led him in. I stroked Scout. "Come girl, I know that you will not be afraid." She walked calmly in as though it was not a deep black hole filled with shadows and shapes.

It took Pol some time to persuade his horse to enter but I did not embarrass him by waiting. There was just a dim light in the cave but Myrddyn had brought kindling and soon he had a fire going. I saw that there were dead branches around the sides as though others had done as we had. The light helped Pol's horse to settle and we took off their saddles and fed them grain and water. We tied their halters to rocks and then Pol and I explored the cave. It went back some three hundred paces and lowered quite sharply. Even at the end we could feel air and so we knew that the cave went on further. The dim light did not let us see how far and we returned to the fire where Myrddyn was fiddling on with a small cauldron.

Pol stood, his mouth open, "Are you conjuring or making a spell?"

"No, I am getting us some hot food. Now it you want to help rather than asking foolish questions go outside and bring me in some snow to melt for water."

I laughed at Pol as he scurried out, bright red. "It was natural you know given that you are a wizard."

"And in all the years you have known me have you ever seen me with a cauldron, making spells?"

"Well no but…"

"Potions to heal? Yes I made those but I need no spells. I have magic within me. You do too Lord Lann although you do not know it. I hope that tonight you will see some of that magic and that power."

As Myrddyn prepared our food I took a branch and set it alight. The walls had strange shapes painted on them. "Did you do these Myrddyn?"

"No they are from the time before man knew about time. They are from the first peoples who worshipped here at this mountain. This has been a holy place forever."

"You have been here before then?"

"Many times. The first time was with my grandfather after my parents were killed. Each time I come here my power grows."

Pol asked the question which was on my lips. "Then why not come here more often?"

"Even a wizard can only take so much power. If he has too much then it can destroy him. It is like that with kings. King Urien was content with the power he had and was comfortable with the king that he was. King Morcant Bulc wanted more power and he did not like who he was. It will be the same with King Iago. His father was happy with his power but Iago craves more. He defeated the Saxons and thinks he is invincible." He suddenly looked at me, his green eyes piercing, it seems into my head and heart. "When you fight a battle do you always know that you will win?"

"Of course not. We have fought against great odds where I expected to lose but we always win. I know what you are trying to get me to say but I do not take for granted that we will win. You tell me you have not foreseen my death and that is comforting but I still fight and lead as though I could die at any moment."

"And that is why you do not get beaten but King Iago believes that he cannot be beaten which is why he ran from your fort. He did not want to lose. You would not have run in the same position." I remained silent and Pol looked at me. Myrddyn nodded towards me, "The Warlord would have worked out a way to defeat those in the fort and not rested until he had a plan. That is the difference. And now I shall sleep. Whatever you hear tonight Pol it will not harm you and if you do dream then remember those dreams."

Pol looked at his empty bowl. "Did you give me a potion?"

Myrddyn laughed, "No I gave you rabbit stew. Now sleep."

I must confess that I was both excited and afraid when I laid down on my sheepskin. The cave was, despite the cold outside, remarkably warm and the fire flickered and danced on the roof of the cave. It was mesmerizing and then….

A huge dragon rose from the fire and leapt to the roof of the cave. It seemed to fill the cave and its breath was monstrous and choking. Fire leapt out at me and I held my shield before me to ward off the flames. I heard Pol crying out and then Pol became Hogan and he was trying to escape but the

dragon had him in his claws. I struggled to draw Saxon Slayer; my arms seemed incapable of holding it and suddenly I held it in my hand and I felt power surge through my body. I hacked at its claws but the sword, inexplicably bounced off and Hogan was screaming and then in his other claw I saw Myfanwy with our baby in her arms and she too was screaming. I hacked and slashed impotently at the dragon but its skin was too tough. I found that I could barely lift the sword.

Suddenly I felt a woman's hand upon my shoulder. I turned and it was my mother. She whispered in my ear. "You must climb closer to the beast. You must take its head. Do not be afraid. Your armour will protect you and your sword is more powerful than you know. Believe in the blade and believe in yourself." And then she was gone.

I climbed up the beast's legs. His reptilian eyes sought me out and fixed me. His foul breath surged towards me and I held my shield up. The wood and the metal became so hot that it hurt but it did not break asunder. As I struggled to climb his chest I saw that his mouth could not burn me any longer and I lowered my shield and there I saw that his neck did not have the same scales as his legs. I drew back Saxon Slayer, even as Myfanwy and Hogan screamed in pain and I thrust it deep into the neck of the dragon. It twisted and turned and still I held on. Foul green blood gushed from the wound but I held on and its death throes began and it tossed its huge head from side to side. My sword was torn free but I held on to it and then I was falling, falling, and there was no bottom; I was falling into the pits of hell.

I was cold and I opened my eyes. Through the entrance of the cave I saw the first rays of the new dawn. I sat up and stared around. Where was the dead dragon? And then I saw Pol and Myrddyn watching me. My wizard had an amused look on his face but Pol looked at me in awe and wonder.

"You dreamt too Pol?"

"No my lord I watched as you fought the dragon and the beautiful lady handed you your sword and you slew the dragon that was as big as the mountain."

"No Pol, that was a dream. I had one similar to that."

"No, Warlord, you are wrong. It was real and I felt the heat and I heard the cries."

"Myrddyn?"

"Who is to say that Pol does not have the second sight too and can see the future? What we saw or dreamt or heard is personal to each of us. Pol, you can never speak of this night. We are all joined by this bond."

Pol nodded, his eyes still wide with wonder.

"But what did it mean Myrddyn?"

"It can mean many things Warlord," he saw the look of annoyance which crossed my face. I did not like these games. "However I think that the dragon is King Iago and it means that he is the enemy and not the rest of his people."

"You mean I should challenge him and kill him?"

He laughed, "Do you think, for one moment, that he would face the warrior who has killed more Saxon kings and champions than any other man? He would be a fool to do that and he is no fool. No it means that you must ruthlessly pursue your war against King Iago."

Pol could not stop talking about his vivid dream in the cave and Myrddyn had to patiently explain that it had been a dream but the dead spirit he had witnessed was my dead mother. It changed his life that day as it did mine. The dream had been my most vivid and, like, Pol I had thought it had been real. I had smelled the brimstone!

There was great relief from all within the fort when we returned. I think all of them had thought that we were mad to venture out to such a dangerous place and to risk invoking the otherworld. Perhaps they were right but with Myrddyn as a guide you always felt safe. Even now he still looked like the young men who had sought employment all those years before and he did not appear to age. The other young man who had sought my employment, Brother Oswald, now appeared to be even older than I. It is strange how life treats us.

The next few days were spent watching the new equites training and the archers performing for me under their new captain, Walch. They set up a two bolt throwers to show me how fast they could use them and they were impressive. Walch was an interesting man. Like Aelle his mother had been taken by a Saxon and used as a thrall. When we had rescued his mother he had been but a child and had grown up at Glanibanta. He had joined us on our southern journey and Miach had spotted his potential. It showed me that Saxon Blood was not necessarily a bad thing but perhaps the Saxon way of life was.

On my way home we called to see how my brothers were doing. Raibeart looked well after his wounding and had begun to put on the weight of a man who is not training with sword and mail each day. Aelle looked disturbed and I asked him what was amiss. "It is Lann Aelle." Lann Aelle was his eldest son and named after me. He was now almost fourteen summers old and was beginning to show his Saxon heritage with blond hair and beard. His mother had roots beyond the seas and more than a hint of Saxon blood so it was no surprise that Lann Aelle should look more like Aelle's father than his mother. "He is restless on the land. It is not for him and he would become a warrior."

"Is that such a bad thing brother? We all became warriors and we did well when we did so."

"But look at him. He shows the Saxon blood in him. I fear that there are warriors who might pick on him or bully him. He is a proud youth and would say nothing." He looked around to see if anyone was listening. "He is a lonely child and does not play with others. Perhaps it is my fault. I was so busy building Glanibanta up that I neglected him a little. He would follow me around when I was working and did not play with the other boys. I just didn't notice."

I felt for my little brother. He rarely showed his emotions but I could plainly see his distress. "If he was a little older and could ride I could put him with Hogan's equites."

He shook his head. "He would stick out like a sore thumb. He is a fair swordsman but not in the class of Hogan."

One of the effects of my time in the cave apart from my new-found calmness was the fact that I sometimes heard voices in my head. They were not the voice I had but normally that of my mother or sometimes, bizarrely, Myrddyn. This was one such occasion and my mother's voice seemed to whisper in my ear. "He could become my squire. I have none at the moment and it would mean that I could train him. Pol did a good job with Hogan and I am sure he would look after Lann Aelle." Aelle's face lit up. "And then, when he is trained, he can do as Hogan did and choose his own destiny."

"Thank you, brother; you still watch over us after all these years."

"That is an oath only broken by death. Freja knows that he will be leaving and living away from her?"

"She knows that and I am sure that she would be happy knowing he is with you."

"I am always in danger. There is a risk he could be wounded or die."

He spread his hands, "*Wyrd.* What will be, will be but you are the luckiest warrior I know. Raibeart and I can no longer fight but no wound slows you up and your skills are never diminished. No I am happy knowing he is your hands. They are the safest hands I know."

Lann Aelle was delighted to be with his famous uncle and showed his gratitude by tears and an embrace for his father. The look on Aelle's face was worth a dozen victories. Pol was also happy to be training a new squire. He had been my first squire and knew how important it would be to the boy. He put a brotherly arm around his shoulder. "The first thing I must show you is how to keep Saxon Slayer sharp. We will see if you can make it sharp enough to shave with!"

"You appear to be more settled now that you are back home husband. Why is that? Did the wizard do something to you and Pol? You are both different in some way."

"We visited a cave and spent some time alone." I looked at Myfanwy, now heavily pregnant, "Are my changes such a bad thing?"

"No, in fact quite the reverse but I wondered how they were achieved. You know I do not care for magic."

"This was not magic. This was just a night in a cave with my thoughts."

I spent more time with Myfanwy and our unborn child than I had ever spent with Aideen. It was not because I loved Myfanwy more, Aideen was still the love of my life but I wanted to enjoy every moment of this special time and the world, remarkably was at peace. I knew it would be a brief moment in time; Iago or the Hibernians or the Saxons would become belligerent again but I took the chance to savour it. My parents had been taken from me too quickly; I had not had long enough with Aideen and my daughter. I would have to be apart from Myfanwy and so I indulged her and I watched her as she grew. I hoped that I would be granted the opportunity to see my new child and that Belatu-Cadros would not call me to arms quickly. My prayers were answered for in the spring when the first hardy flowers peeked above ground my daughter was born.

I was summoned to Myfanwy's chambers when the labour began. The midwives and women tried to shoo me out but my wife half rose and said, "He is the Warlord and it is his child. He has every right to see it born!" I leaned over to kiss her. "You are safe then?"

"Forget me, how are you?"

She gave me a wry smile. "Men! If you had had to have the babies then you would know. I am fine or at least I will be when our child joins us. Now stand over there and keep out of the way."

Thus dismissed I watched as the birthing began. I thought I would be distressed but I found it quite moving to watch. There seemed to be little fuss and the women were supportive. I would never experience that sense of unity in peace but I did in war. My oathsworn were like the women around my wife; they were there to protect and to help. The birth was uncomplicated and I had a daughter.

We named her Nanna after the goddess of flowers and it seemed to suit her. All fathers think their daughters are beautiful and so it was with me but even Myrddyn seemed taken with her and played the nursemaid on more than one occasion. She became someone other than me who commanded his attention and that was a rare thing. I also sensed within her the spirit of my mother. That may, of course, be wishful thinking but, as events showed; there may have been more than a hint of truth in that.

We had barely two weeks together before a messenger arrived from Mungo; our scouts reported movements from the men of Gwynedd. Pol, Myrddyn and I left. Garth and Ridwyn resented being left behind and I had to take them to one side to explain my thoughts. "We cannot keep attacking larger armies until we have built up our own strength. My shield wall had many more men in it when we were in Rheged. Now there are barely forty warriors left from that time. We need to break Iago's heart before we break his will. I intended to let him attack our stone walls. We have new weapons which we can use but they are not ready yet. Let us breed our horses and build our ships. When every warrior has a shield such as yours Garth, a helmet such as yours Ridwyn and a sword such as mine then we will be ready and we will go to war." I saw them nod their understanding. "And I would have you protect my family from the Hibernians. They have been too quiet for too long."

I think the other reason why the two warriors were unhappy was that I was escorted by Tuanthal and his equites. They saw Hogan's appointment as some sort of favouritism, not realising that it had been my son's wish. There were now fifty equites and ten of them, led by Hogan were armed with the long lance. Hogan had also somehow managed to procure a slightly larger horse and his wore a mail head piece protecting his nose and neck. His armour also reflected that he had spent some of his own money on the best mail and helmet he could get. His helmet looked like mine and had bronze cheek pieces and strengthening. I was proud of my son as we rode east.

Lann Aelle looked as though he had died and gone to heaven as he rode behind me, next to Pol in his new mail armour and helmet. Hogan had given him his short sword which had served him so well and his old horse. It showed how much Hogan had grown over the winter. Like Pol he looked with affection at Aelle's son, his cousin.

Hogan had pennants fitted to the lances and they fluttered in the breeze as we rode. I could see even Tuanthal looking enviously at them. They would add nothing to the effect of the lance but they did to the appearance of the warriors. Hogan had also asked if he could make a copy of the wailing dragon pennant used by Prince Pasgen. Although I could not see an objection I thought it wise to ask the last member of the Rheged royal family for permission.

While we waited for the bridge to be readied I spoke with Mungo. "Are your people happy?"

"They want me to return home and bring more of their families." He shrugged, when time allows then I will do so but not while King Iago is still at large."

"You have seen evidence of him?"

"My men patrol the coastline to the north and they have seen his men in increasing numbers coming towards Wyddfa. He is coming but he is showing caution."

"How many men do you have now?"

"There are two hundred warriors. We have fifteen archers, ten slingers and we have managed to train twenty hammer throwers."

That was good news. Angus, who had been my friend, had led the men of Strathclyde to decimate the Saxons at Dunelm; I missed him for he had died fighting Aella on the Dunum. It was a weapon almost as fearsome as the bolt thrower and the men of Gwynedd knew nothing of it. "And on the mainland?"

"Many of the warriors I brought are over there. Calum has two hundred warriors including another ten hammer throwers. There are forty archers and twenty slingers. Prince Pasgen now has seventy equites." I did not say anything and he added by way of explanation, "We thought it best to keep the bulk of our men there where the danger is."

"As I said to Prince Pasgen I put the three of you here because I trust you and I see nothing wrong in your dispositions and I like the idea of bringing more of your people. We need children to become farmers and warriors if our people are to survive. The last of the Britons live here on this island."

Prince Pasgen was delighted to see us. He had installed a stone water chamber in case of siege and in the months since I had last been there more of the land around the walls had been cleared. "We now control four hundred paces in every direction. The bolt throwers are on every wall and they can clear any enemy who approaches."

"And where were the enemy seen?"

He pointed to the north. "Aedh and his scouts said that they were camped between the monastery and here. He said that there were four camps and they numbered four thousand warriors."

"Then we had better gather our leaders and decide what we will do."

Chapter 13

Prince Pasgen was all for showing off his new weapons and warriors. I, of course, wanted nothing of the sort but I had to let my other leaders speak. Myrddyn was, unusually for him, itching to speak but a slight nod of my head silenced him.

"Well I could bring over some warriors from my fort to help you defend this one."

Prince Pasgen smiled, appreciating the support of his friend, "Thank you, Mungo, but you will need to defend the bridge."

"My archers will be needed on the walls."

"As will my warriors. The plain fact is, Prince Pasgen that we do not have enough warriors yet."

"But it means that when there is a battle my equites and those of Tuanthal will be twiddling their thumbs while others fight and die."

"I hope that it is us who fight and the men of Gwynedd who die."

Myrddyn nodded his agreement and also the fact that I had spoken which gave him the opportunity to give his opinion. He unrolled the map he had been drawing over the winter with the help of Brother Oswald. "Look at this map. We have a toehold here at the very edge of their land. The mountains and the sea make it very narrow. The only opportunity for an attack by the equites will be when we drive him back to the monastery and there the open land will suit us and allow you to charge, to encircle and to use your superior weapons and armour. But until he has bled a little that will not happen."

Pasgen looked at the map and then at me. "I am sorry Warlord. You are all right and I am wrong."

"No Prince Pasgen, it is not wrong to want to fight with your comrades." I stood. "We have brought more arrows and bolts. The first of our ships will be ready to sail within the week and Gwynfor himself will bring her over. We will use some of Mungo's men to help man the bolt throwers and, when this is over, give some thought on the best way to use and to man our two boats. We will keep them on the far side of the narrows so that they will not be seen until the time is right." I looked at Calum. "The signals work well?" We had used the Roman system of flags to signal between our two forts and I had yet to see it in operation.

"Aye my lord. It is a great boon and saves much time. This way the bridge stays on Mungo's side until we need it and by the time we reach the Narrows it is ready. It saves time and, I believe, it will save lives."

Just then we heard a call from the gate and a short while later, while we were still poring over the map, Aedh came in. "King Iago is now two miles down the coast. He has brought his entire army and they have cut down two mighty oaks which I believe they intend to use as a battering ram."

"Well now it begins. The equites can remain close to the southern wall and provide guards there. Every archer, slinger and warrior will be on the northern wall."

Calum looked first at me and then at Myrddyn. "How do we deal with the rams?"

"Have your men bring as much sea water as they can and flood the approach to the gates. They would struggle to span the ditches anyway." Two of the ditches had bridges which we removed until needed while the other was drawn up before the gate. The ram would have to breach three ditches and pierce two gates. If we did nothing then they might succeed but we would be picking off their men while they toiled to drag the trees.

"Right my captains. To the walls!"

Lann Aelle was ready with my armour and my sword. I saw Pol nearby and knew that he had supervised every action. When I was dressed I said, "That was well done squire. Now has Pol told you of what you must now do?"

"Aye Warlord. I stand behind the two of you and stop anyone getting behind you and I run messages when you send for me."

"Good." I glanced down at his armour and weapons. "I see you have Hogan's old buckler?"

Pol patted his arm. "It was mine before his. It is the heir loom of the squire. It will protect you and the warlord, believe me."

When I reached the wall I saw the last of the warriors hurling buckets of sea water to make the ground slick and muddy. It would drain away and dry but not for a few days and by then it might be slick with blood too. It was an anticlimax when they did not arrive that day. I think that King Iago was trying to avoid another embarrassing about face and wanted to arrive when everything would be in place. Captain Calum took the opportunity of wetting the ground even more and laying a few more lillia in the ditches.

I stood with him, watching the sunset over Mona. "It is a pity we do not have a stream here on the northern edge and then we could be surrounded on three sides by water." Already he was thinking of how we could improve our defences.

"Ask Brother Oswald. He may have some ideas about how to divert the flow to both sides." I pointed to the mountainside. It was steep and covered in scree below the tree line. "And what of an attack from that direction?"

He laughed. "We sent up some of the boy slingers to see how solid it was and even they could not keep their footing. Once you are beyond the trees then you cannot move and the trees are three hundred paces from the walls."

"They could use archers. They would be above us and even their bows might have the range."

"They would have to emerge from the trees and our archers could pick them off."

"Still I think that we might cut the trees back another fifty paces or so. The wood will come in handy for more ships."

"As you wish Warlord, but that is one part of the fort I feel happiest about."

The sentries alerted us early the next morning before it was light. The garrison was up but the start of their attack caught us unawares. King Iago was showing that he had thought the attack through thoroughly.

A line of warriors bearing shields led the way and we could see the two rams being pulled one behind the other. A second line of warriors protected the men hauling the huge sharpened tree trunks. Darting archers and slingers jinked their way between the rams and the warriors ready to let loose when the order was given. King Iago was at the rear and I saw that he, his bodyguards and his son, were all mounted. They were the only horsemen he appeared to possess. Aedh had told us that but it was good to have the intelligence confirmed. There was little point wasting bolts on the warriors pulling the ram. Our archers were good enough to pick them off. Despite being protected by shields there was always a piece of bare flesh which could be struck and an injured arm or leg prevented the warrior from doing his job.

I could see the nervousness of the warriors as they moved slowly forwards. They would have spoken of the terrible weapons we had unleashed upon them around their winter fires and they would be waiting for the crash of the deadly war machines as the bolts were launched. And we waited. The first of the ditches was fifty paces from the one closest to the walls. That had been a deliberate ploy by Myrddyn and Oswald when they had designed it. The side facing the enemy was steep and would be difficult to climb. The forward slope was shallow allowing not only their men to escape but to afford no shelter from our arrows. We wanted them in the ditch; we wanted them in the killing zone. It was like the game we had played as children where one child was facing away from the others and the other children had to creep closer and closer. The game would be won by the one who could touch the first child's back but if they were caught then they had lost. The men of Gwynedd were coming closer and closer and waiting for the trap to snap. Every step closer to their goal brought them closer to the trap they could not see. I had been in the wedge which attacked a defensive site and it was a terrible place to be when fighting an unknown enemy.

The shield wall approached the first ditch. The slope was slight but the slippery and muddy surface made it as treacherous as ice. In addition the sticky mud clung to the bottoms of their shoes and boots making the next steps even worse. They held their shields anticipating the arrows but none came and I could see their confusion as they looked to their chiefs for leadership. Still we did not release our arrows. The machines remained silent and the shield wall approached the edge of the ditch. There was no easy way down save jumping and that was when the eerie silence was broken as they jumped into a trap filled, watery ditch. I swear that I heard at least one ankle break before the screams began. They tried to return the way they had come but more men were piling in and the only way they could go was forwards. The second rank had less of a problem as they stepped over their wounded comrades, lying injured in the bottom of the ditch. Most of them would never fight again; a broken leg or ankle rarely heals perfectly. The chiefs and leaders who had survived began to organise their men, no doubt grateful that the deep was not as steep on our side. As they reached the top of the slippery bank, the only way out, they began to lose their footing and hands, which should have held shields, grasped the ground for support.

Walch grinned as he ordered his archers and slingers, "Loose!" Every arrow and stone was deliberately aimed. Although there were only sixty of them there were able to reload and release five times in a few moments. The ones who had reached the top of the ditch fell backwards to knock others into the deadly trap now filled with the dead as well as the wounded. Men were suffocating beneath the bodies and more of them tried to escape but, for most, it was a struggle in vain. Eventually some of them managed to clamber over the bodies of the dead to reach their own archers who were busy trying to hit our men on the walls. They were having little success as our men were protected by the walls and had a height advantage but I could see that Walch did not want to take chances. "Change targets. I want those archers dead!" They were a smaller number and were encumbered by warriors trying to flee through them. There were not many archers but within a couple of heartbeats there were none and the men pulling the ram were exposed as they, too approached the ditch.

Suddenly I saw a messenger race from King Iago; it looked to me like his son Cadfan. The rams halted and the warriors gathered around it with their shields. He had seen the futility of trying to get the ram across that ditch of death.

I turned to Calum, "You might as well feed the men. He has to rethink his strategy."

Myrddyn nodded. "He will now build a bridge."

Calum looked at the wizard, "Are you looking at the future now?"

I smiled, "No Calum. It is what we would do. It is the only way to get the ram over. He will cut down some trees and then try again. They will probably attack later this afternoon."

It was closer to noon when the warriors brought the logs to the ditch. Walch knew what was coming and his mouth formed an almost wolf like snarl as he said, "Pick you targets and kill them!"

The men carrying the logs only had their helmets and armour for protection and at that range it did them no good. The ones at the back fared better as they were protected by the bodies of the warriors who fell before them. More men took their places and the logs began to move across the gap but incredibly slowly. King Iago was buying the crossing with the lives of his warriors. The only good thing to come out of it was that his warriors could cross the ditch over the bodies of the dead. Once the bridge was complete fresh warriors came to pull and to protect their precious charge. At the same time a line of warriors locked shields and stepped across the human ditch. Walch and his men ignored the ram and picked off warriors as they crossed. The men pulling the ram could not believe their luck until they struck the slippery land before the next ditch. As soon as they struck the mud their feet slipped and they could gain no purchase. The mud then now mixed with Saxon blood, began to suck their feet into it. It was then, as they struggled to stand, that Walch started to kill them. The ram reached halfway across the ground between the ditches before there were not enough men left alive to pull it. The men of the shield wall, who had reached the second ditch, huddled under their shields around the precious ram.

More men struggled up and this time they brought rushes with them which they laid on the muddy ground before they began to pull, this time protected by the shields of the survivors of the first attack. Walch and his men were still striking the men of Gwynedd but this time they were not killing. They were wounding and maiming but Iago's men stuck to their task and the ram was finally across the bridge allowing even more men to come forwards. It was now mid-afternoon and they still had two ditches to go.

Myrddyn came to see me. "I think I can prepare a little surprise if you will excuse me." He disappeared leaving Calum looking bemused.

"It will not be magic, Calum, but the enemy will believe it is. Whatever he is planning will be outside the scope of the minds of Iago and his generals."

I heard Lann Aelle ask Pol, "They have lost so many men why they do not go away?"

I turned. "Because he has paid a high price already it will be even higher if he has to leave and start again. If you were Iago you would see that you were very close to our gates."

"But the ground is muddy and there are even more traps."

"The king thinks he has the solution, look."

Even as we discussed Iago he was sending up more logs to bridge the second ditch. I assumed there would be more trees for the third but I was not going to let it get that far.

The second ditch was a repeat of the first. When I saw the calibre of warriors Iago was using now I could see that they were neither the best armed nor the best armoured. He was saving those for his final assault. As soon as he had his ram half way across the second body filled ditch I nodded to Calum who ordered his men to pick up the specially made spears. Brother Osric had written about a Roman spear called a pilum which had a soft piece of metal holding two halves of the spear together. When it struck anything the soft metal broke. The spear hinged in two and could not be thrown back. It only had a range of twenty or so paces but thrown from a wall it could easily reach the men at the ditch. As the shield wall came up, two hundred pila were thrown. Those that did not strike flesh struck shields and the weight of the broken spear pulled them down and they were slaughtered by the archers and slingers.

This time they retreated well outside the range of the archers and we were almost back where we started. My squire became quite animated, "We have won! We have won!"

"Not quite nephew. They will come under cover of darkness and they will think that they will suffer fewer deaths."

His face fell, "Then they will win!"

"Luckily it is not all black and white. Just because we haven't won yet does not mean we will not win. Myrddyn has plans of his own. We will wait until he returns."

Myrddyn was back well before dark. He had with him three rough clay pots and he had with him three men from Strathclyde. "I took the liberty of finding these three. They are some of the hammer throwers Mungo was telling us about."

We all peered at the containers and wondered what was within. "Come wizard and tell us or do you want an amazed audience when you pull your magic trick?"

He sniffed, "A little appreciation is all I ask."

"Myrddyn!"

He grinned and relented. "Within here are some oils and powders. I discovered the mixture when reading Brother Osric's papers. The liquid is thick and burns well. It sticks to whatever it strikes. I have three prepared for the ram will be difficult to hit in the dark."

One of the warriors laughed. "What hit yon wee log from here? Man I could do it without my hammer."

"Warriors!" Myrddyn shook his head. "In that case you wait until your friends have thrown and if they hit then you can try for the far ram."

"Right let me..."

I held up my hand. "Let us wait until they attack. We will demoralise them even more." I looked at my wizard. "Do they take long to light?"

"No but what we will do just before is throw three containers with some of the fiery liquor brewed by the monks and the men of Strathclyde. When the burning mixture strikes it will burn quicker."

I held my hand up. "From now on no talking from anyone. We need to know when they approach. Just wave your arm when you hear anything." To help me I took off my helmet. I smiled as my squire and Pol did the same. We could hear the crash of the waves along the nearby shore and I knew that would disguise some of the noises but metal on metal makes a distinctive noise as did the noise of someone slipping and sliding in mud.

Pol held his hand up and pointed into the dark. I listened and I too could hear the laboured breath of men as they crept forwards. Once we heard them we could look for the changing shadows which would show they were men. I saw shapes crossing the first ditch and touched Myrddyn's arm. He tapped the arm of the first warrior who hurled his pot. It crashed and broke on the log. Myrddyn slapped him on the back. The noise made the enemy stop for a moment but as nothing happened they moved forwards and we saw them approach the second ditch. Myrddyn did not need my help and he judged the moment well. He lit the pot and, as it flamed the warrior hurled it through the air where it looked like a comet. It lit up the space before the fort and we saw the upturned faces of the men of Gwynedd as they massed for an attack. The pot struck the soaked log and it erupted in flames. Splashes flew to the sides where men were waiting to begin to pull the ram. They too began to burn.

The next pots were thrown at the second log. It was further away but at least one of the pots of liquor struck and both fire pots did. Soon both rams were ablaze and the men around them were dying as Walch's arrows struck home. I watched for a while and then went to my chamber. There would be no attack this night and I had seen enough useless slaughter.

Myrddyn and I went to see Calum and Pasgen at the southern wall. They were disappointed that no one had attacked them but when I told them that only the archers had been involved then they were a little happier about the situation. "So far we have their measure but tomorrow is another day!"

I awoke the next morning to the smell of burning. Lann Aelle was awaiting me and helped me to arm. "Will they be gone Warlord?"

"I do not know. It depends on how badly he wants this fort. We shall see. There is little point in worrying about things over which we have no control."

As we viewed the scene we could see the bodies still lying where they had fallen. The two rams were still burning and smoking away. Even if they wanted to use a third tree trunk they would have to wait until they had cooled down. The question I needed the answer to was, were they still camped close by? Did I dare risk some scouts? We had not lost a man and, looking at the bodies there had to be more than two hundred dead warriors before us and there would be many more wounded who had been taken back to their camp. I made a decision. “Captain Calum I want a hundred warriors. We shall go and see if they have left.”

“Isn’t that dangerous Warlord? Perhaps we should send out some scouts.”

“I am taking a hundred men because I am certain that if this is a trap then we can fight our way back. You may come with us if you have a mind but I will be taking my wizard too.”

I think it was the fact that I was taking Myrddyn which persuaded Calum that I was not losing my mind. At the gate I made sure that Pol, Myrddyn and Lann were protected by a solid phalanx of Calum’s oathsworn and they were safely protected by the bodies of men from Strathclyde and Rheged. “Open the gate and lower the drawbridge.” I was pleased to see the bolt throwers manned and the ramparts lined with archers. I did not think this was a trap but Brother Osric had once told me a story of ancient Greeks who pretended to leave and then sneaked back inside. We would take no chances.

There was still heat being given off from the rams and we had to step across the bodies in the ditch to avoid them. The gases in the stomachs had not built up yet but it was still an unpleasant sensation stepping on men who had been alive the previous day. I hoped my squire could cope with the experience. Myrddyn’s mind was a calculating one and he could not help but look at the bodies as we crossed them. “There have to be over two hundred dead bodies here. These ditches were quite deep. And it looks like we may be able to recover some of the arrows.”

“Myrddyn, these were warriors. They may have been our enemies but they deserve some respect.”

“Sorry, Warlord, you are quite right.”

Once we passed the last of the ditches I ordered a wedge formation. Their camp should be just around the headland half a mile away and we would not be able to see it until we were almost upon it. It was one of the peculiarities of this particular coast that it twisted and turned without any apparent pattern. I led the wedge towards the sea in order to ensure that we had the best view of their camp. As we stepped around I was expecting to see it deserted but, as we cleared the cliff I could see that they were still there! King Iago had not left.

This was where the training of my warriors showed itself to be superior to other armies. “About turn and double back to the fort.”

I was now the rear man and I slipped my shield over my shoulder to protect my back. I heard Pol say to Lann. "Just don't fall, whatever you do!"

I hoped that my wizard would heed those words too. Although he had trained for the shield wall it was many years since he had been subject to its discipline. I heard a roar behind me as the whole Gwynedd army launched itself after us. Although we had a lead of over eight hundred paces I knew that some of them would catch us. I just hoped that my archers would make the difference. We crossed the first ditch successfully and I began to think we would make it and then Myrddyn tripped. I knew others would help him and I turned to see where the enemy were. To my horror there were ten of them less than twenty paces from me. I swung my shield around and unsheathed Saxon Slayer. The first warrior impaled himself on my sword in his eagerness to kill the Wolf Warrior. I punched away the second with my shield and blocked the sword thrust from a third. When the fourth warrior rushed at me with a spear I thought I was dead until Pol grabbed the spear head in his left hand and pulled the man onto his sword. Lann stabbed the stunned warrior in the throat and then four arrows took out the rest.

"Warlord, the wizard is safe. Run!"

There were hundreds of warriors who were now less than forty paces away and we ran for the gate. I heard the whoosh and crack of the bolt throwers and then the screams of the dying as they were mowed down by bolts and arrows. When I heard the drawbridge slam into place I smiled.

Calum wagged an admonishing finger at me. "Next time, Warlord, we send scouts, wizard or no wizard." He threw an angry look at a shamefaced Myrddyn and then stormed up to the ramparts.

"Sorry Warlord. I am a little out of practice."

"These things happen Myrddyn," I turned to the two who had saved me, "but I am grateful for you two. Without you at my side I would have been a dead man. I thank you both." Pol had been praised before but I think that day marked a change for Lann Aelle and he realised he could be a warrior and he could protect his Warlord.

When they pulled back we saw that they had left another pile of bodies to the original charnel house. We estimated there to be over two hundred and fifty dead warriors. The men of Gwynedd had paid a high price already. "They will begin to smell soon."

"I know. Captain Calum, get the metal and weapons from those in the first ditch. The archers can cover you. Then put kindling on the bodies. We will burn them tonight and that may stop any night attacks. In the morning we will do the second ditch and then we will send out the scouts as you so wisely suggested."

The weaponry and metal was collected without incident although the men of Gwynedd posted guards to ensure we did not launch a sneak attack. That night as we watched the bodies burning, we held cloths around our noses to keep out the smell and I said to Myrddyn, "I am surprised. I thought Iago had some sense about him. Surely he can see that he cannot breach our defences?"

"I do not think he is finished yet my lord. He has lost many men but most of them were lightly armed. His best warriors were kept in reserve." The wizard pointed down to the dark sea. "He could avoid a frontal attack and come by the shore. Our defences are weakest there."

"True but we could then use our equites. A charge along the beach would be perfect for them. But you are right that may be his plan and he does not know that we have all of the equites here. We shall see."

The next day we managed to strip some of the bodies but that was all for they began their second attack. The rams had now cooled and largely crumbled. The bodies in the first ditch were now just ash and I think their king thought he had to show us that he was still a general. Calum's men made it successfully into the fort and we stood on the ramparts ready to fight. He looked to have brought his best warriors for they stood in a shield wall three lines deep behind the third ditch. They had left their dead in the ditch and I suspected they would be walking on them until I saw them bringing out small bridges made of logs. The warriors used them as giant shields until they were close to the ditch and when they had laid it a handful raced across to make a shield wall. This happened in ten places along the ditch and they were soon over the barrier of the dead.

I could see no log ram and wondered if he would try a frontal assault. Suddenly there was a cry from behind me. "The mountain side! An avalanche!"

I turned and looked up at Wyddfa. His men had climbed up into the trees and had loosened rocks and chopped down trees. They then began to roll them down the mountain side. Even as I watched a wall of rock and stones hurtled down the steep stone littered slope gathering pace and material as it did so. At the same time the warriors to our fore rushed at the walls. They were brave men and my archers and bolt throwers took a terrible toll but then the rocks struck our fort and our men. One huge rock demolished a bolt thrower and crew as though they had never been. We were fighting two armies; one of men and one of rocks and trees!

"Repel them!" They were empty words for men were watching over their shoulders for the rock which would kill them instantly. King Iago had shown cunning. "Myrddyn, see to the wounded and send for the equites. We need them this day. Pol, Lann, be ready!"

They had no ladders but their plan was obvious. They had a wall of warriors protecting ten axe men who were busily hacking the drawbridge to pieces. The two remaining bolt throwers were slowing down their reinforcements but the archers and the slingers had been damaged in the attack. They were not as effective as they had been. The bolt throwers could not hit the men at the wall. I could see that some men would break through. I grabbed fifteen warriors from the walls. "Come with me! Calum, use the pila!" As I said it I did not know if the captain still lived but I hoped someone would hear the order. "I want a shield wall behind the gate. Pol and Lann stand behind me and unfurl the banner. Let them know who they fight. When they break through we become the gate." I turned to look at these warriors whose death I had probably just ordered. They were grinning and eager for battle. "Are you with me?"

"Yes Warlord!" It was a small roar but it heartened me nonetheless. We had to hold them until the pila had taken their toll and the enemy were so weakened that the equites could terrify them into fleeing.

I suddenly saw the gate before me shake and knew that the drawbridge had gone. I knew that Walch and his men would keep loosing even when exhausted. They would whittle them down and we had to buy the time. "These are men with axes coming through that means no shields. One man takes the axe on the shield and the other kills. Lann you see any flesh just stab it. The gate lintel will stop them swinging their blades so stab and slash. Our armour and weapons are better than theirs and besides…" I paused to turn around, "Myrddyn hasn't seen my death yet so it must not be my turn to die eh?" Their laughter gave me the confidence I needed and I slipped my dagger into my left hand as the first sliver of light could be seen through the gate. I knew that, when the gate went, it would go quickly and it did.

The first warrior who broke through hit the gate so hard that he fell at the feet of the man next to me who stabbed him in the neck. The others tried to enlarge the hole and five of us stabbed with our blades into unprotected stomachs and legs. The other gate breakers swung at the shattered wood enabling us to kill more of them until there were no axe men left but the gate was shattered and could protect us no longer. Through the opening I saw the warriors massing to attack us. Unless Tuanthal and Pasgen arrived quickly then it would be too late.

Chapter 14

They say that things look the blackest before the dawn and in this case they were right. A wedge of warriors came towards us and I led my handful of men into the gate. We were six abreast and so far none had died. The enemy were eager to get to grips with us and came at us individually. They were not difficult to kill; we parried and blocked and then stabbed and they died but someone organised them. Soon a solid wall of shields and blades came at us. They meant to push us through the gate and with their weight of numbers they would succeed. I was wondering how long we could hold them and then I heard the unmistakable crack of bolt throwers but they were coming from the sea and soon I heard cries as the men behind their shield wall began to die. The pressure slackened as more bolts crashed through their lines and then I heard the wail of the dragon standard and knew that the equites had arrived.

I heard Tuanthal yell, "Warlord, clear the gate!"

I did not need to look to know what they intended and I roared, "Wheel right and back." The surprised attackers suddenly thought they had won for the gate was empty and then Hogan and four equites with lances smashed into them and the front ranks were hurled back. When Hogan had cleared the gate another five smashed through the next line and then another five. It was relentless. Attacked from the walls, the sea and now by horses the men of Gwynedd fled the field. Their best warriors lay butchered and now the rest were almost surrounded. They ran and they kept running. No amount of exhortation from their king would bring them back to face the wall of death from land and sea.

I did not wait to see the outcome; I raced up the stairs to the gatehouse. I saw the ship we had been building fitted with four bolt throwers and the weapons were scything through the enemy ranks. Over a hundred equites had spread out in a line with the lances of Hogan and his men at the head of the wedge. The ditches which had been a barrier to the shield wall were no obstacle to the horses and the men of Gwynedd could not defend themselves. It was to be expected that they would flee. We had won. I looked to see the damage the rock fall had done. There were dead and dying men lying everywhere. I could not see wounds from blades, only from rocks and flying trees. Calum and Walch came over to me. They had not escaped and there were cuts and bruises which showed where the rocks had struck.

Calum shook his head, "You were right Warlord. I should have done something about the rock side."

"Well nature has done it for you now. On the side away from the sea there was now a wall of rock and wood which was higher than the rest of the fort. With a little work and steps, it would mean it would be more secure than any other of the fort's walls.

Walch looked at it, "*Wyrd.* It is as though Wyddfa herself helped us."

As I went to help my healer with the wounded I too wondered about that. We had lost men but the cost had been less than had we lost the battle and we were now secure. King Iago would not return for some time.

By the time the equites had returned the wounded had been looked after and the dying put out of their pain. Even though they were tired Calum's men began to pile up the bodies which had accumulated. The ones from the earlier attack had begun to swell and we did not want disease and pestilence. I took the opportunity of riding to the shore to speak with the captain of the ship which had saved us. Gwynfor's smiling face greeted me with Mungo next to him.

"I see you are getting a taste for sailing Mungo. But it was well done. We may have lost but for your timely arrival."

"We would have been here a day earlier but it took longer than we thought to fit the bolt throwers."

"I think the timing was perfect. Thank you, Gwynfor. We now need a captain for this vessel I would not like to take you away from your fishing."

The old man pointed to the tall sailor next to him. "With your permission, Warlord, my grandson Daffydd would be honoured to captain this ship."

"If you recommend him then the role is his. You get a share of all profits Daffydd. How does that sound?"

"I get to captain my own ship and make money? What is not to like about that?" He laughed and it was a deep rolling laugh. He was a sound and dependable captain who served us well. "I will get some of the boys I know to crew these bolt thrower things as soon as your general here shows me how to use them."

Mungo nodded, "That should only take a few days." He pointed to the mountain side. "Did we lose many in the rock slide?"

"Not as many as we might but too many. King Iago timed it well but so did you and our new equites acquitted themselves well."

"Was that young Hogan I saw leading the charge?"

"It was. They are impressive with those lances. He has learned much since he began to serve with Tuanthal."

"You should be proud." He pointed down the coast, "And here he comes."

Tuanthal and Prince Pasgen led my son and the rest of the equites along the beach from the north. I could not see any empty saddles but few of them still had their lances. I rode down to meet them. All three of them grinned at me, their helmets on their pommels and their sweating faces showing the exertions. "Well done my equites. That was a brave charge."

Tuanthal pointed to Hogan, "The lances worked well and your son is truly a great warrior."

Hogan looked embarrassed as Prince Pasgen said, "He reminded me of my father when he led the charge."

I rode next to my son and embraced him. "Well done my son."

The equites banged on their shields and roared, "Wolf Warriors!"

I wheeled Scout around and we continued towards the fort. "How did the lance and the extra armour feel?"

"We will need bigger horses if we are to have more armour but this mail saved my mount's life for a warrior tried to strike at his head with his sword but it failed to penetrate. I think an axe or a club would be useful. When you strike with the sword it can become tangled in the mail. One of my men lost his sword that way. A metal headed club would be as effective and with the added speed of the horse would cause more deaths amongst our enemies."

"Good. See Tuanthal and try it out. Speaking of enemies what happened to King Iago?"

Tuanthal turned around in his saddle to tell me. "They ran into the forest at the foot of Wyddfa. It would have been suicide to follow them there and the horses were tired but there are many dead twixt here and there."

"I think it will take the King of Gwynedd some time to become a danger again. We have bought the breathing space we needed but the cost was amongst our most precious archers. Miach will have to train more."

Prince Pasgen laughed. "Something else for him to complain about but if he cannot complain he is not happy!"

It was late in the day when the fort was made secure again. Calum and his men would have many days repairing the gates and the wall. After we had eaten I told the officers what our plans would be. "I will take the iron back to the stronghold to be made into more weapons. We will take the ship so that Gwynfor can return home and Daffydd can recruit his men. We will then use it to patrol as far as the vale of Asaph. Tuanthal can remain here for a while to ensure that King Iago has truly left the region. Then we will patrol for thirty miles in each direction. I know that it will be hard but the riders do not need to be armoured. We need advanced warning of Iago's moves."

Myrddyn pointed to the east. "We could build a watchtower on the slopes of Wyddfa. Eight men could man it and they could signal the fort. If we gave them horses then they could evacuate it if danger threatened."

I looked at Calum who shrugged. "We are short of men."

"These would not need to be warriors. They could be slingers or scouts who are in training. It would be their eyes we would need and not their battle prowess. They could even keep a flock of sheep up there and earn their keep." I was thinking back to my days as a shepherd and thought that the plan could work. "We were lucky today and learned some lessons. The fort will hold Iago but we need to make it even stronger. I will send Brother Oswald back with our ship to improve the defences as we discussed." I paused, "Make no mistake, King Iago will be back. We are now an itch he cannot scratch. He could ignore us before and pretend we did not exist but now his men will tell tales of our weapons and our men and horses. It will be a constant reminder of his defeat and humiliation."

Hogan asked, "What is the name of the ship?"

I had not thought about it but I looked at Myrddyn and smiled. "Why, The Wolf of course!"

Everyone thought that was appropriate and Myrddyn added, "There is a good carver of wood in Caergybi; I will commission a wolf head for the prow. If we paint it black it should terrify other ships."

"It is not a large ship, wizard." It was smaller than the ocean going Saxon ships.

"Yes Warlord, but just as with men and wolves, it is not the size that matters but the heart, and that ship has a good heart."

Scout was a little wary of boarding the ship but once aboard and tethered to the rail she appeared unconcerned with the motion. I found it a speedier way of travelling and I got to see the island from a different perspective. I could see how perilous the settlements by the coast were. If raiders came, either Saxons or the men of Gwynedd, then there was little to stop them. I pointed this out to Myrddyn. "Yes Warlord and that is our fault. We have bred success into their minds and they feel safe without walls but it is pure luck that has kept these people alive."

"When I return to my stronghold I will send for Aelle and Raibeart." I had divided the land between my two brothers at the Roman Road. I did not obligate the people to fealty but my brothers would both be responsible for part of the land. I would ask them to oversee the building of defences to deter any attacker. Once Tuanthal and his men returned we would have warriors who could reach any part of the island in less than half a day. I would resurrect the beacons we had used in Rheged. There would need to be more of them here but it would save lives.

Myrddyn smiled and I knew he was thinking. "Come on wizard, out with it. What is going through that fertile mind of yours?"

"I was just thinking that if the castle in Rheged was Castle Perilous then your new one is Castle Peace or Castle Calm."

"I would not tempt the gods and *wyrd* by naming it Peace but Castle Calm seems appropriate. I certainly feel at peace there." And so we named our castle although the way they pronounced it on the isle was Castle Cam. It did not displease me. The name was not the issue so long as it had a name.

I left Gwynfor and Myrddyn to see to the unloading of the ship and I rode with Pol and Lann to Castle Calm. I went to my chambers where Pol and Lann helped me out of my armour. "You two see to the horses. I will not need you again today and ask Brother Oswald if he will travel on The Wolf and oversee the new defences at Pasgen's fort. It is important that we begin to improve them before King Iago gets more ideas."

I went to see my wife and my daughter. It had only been a short time but I had missed them both and I was determined to spend as much time with them as I could.

"Well wife and little Nanna, your father is home and he is unwounded!"

Myfanwy laughed, "At last you understand my priorities."

Part 3
The Hibernians

Chapter 14

By the time summer had arrived we had two ships. The second was named The Dragon by Myrddyn. I think he intended it as an insult to Iago. He must have been thinking of the name for some time for he had had a figure head similar to the one for The Wolf carved in preparation. Another of Gwynfor's many grandchildren became her captain and Daffydd crew trained them to use the bolt throwers. Raibeart and Aelle were pleased to be tasked with building defences. Both of them felt that they were skilled in the creation of good forts and I think they were right. They both still wanted to fight but their injuries meant that they could not. This gave the two men, both of whose children had now left for their own homes, something creative and useful to do. They did good jobs. They had both chosen one settlement each which was in the middle of their coastline. They told me that the size of the burgh was irrelevant for the neighbouring villages could seek refuge there. They had come up with this clever plan of building one and then the next ones would be between their first and Castle Calm and then the next between there and Mungo's Burgh. We now had two forts on the two coasts. With Castle Cam and Caergybi at one end of the isle and Mungo's Burgh and Pasgen's Palace at the other we had enough places for the islanders to seek sanctuary. It was a number we could keep increasing as we grew.

The towers that we built made a cross across the island and Brother Oswald took that as a sign that we would all soon be Christian. He may have had a point. The islanders who were here first and the newcomers from Strathclyde were all Christian and there was a church in every settlement but I left it to each person to choose for themselves. Each of the towers was manned by locals who farmed or worked close by. The key ones were in the settlements and every town and village had men who took it in turns to either guard the gates or watch for enemies. We still only had one ally and all the rest of the people close by were enemies.

We were also surprisingly graced with a visitor from Constantinople. It was an envoy from the Emperor himself. Andronikos was a warrior like me but he had been wounded in the arm and the Emperor had tasked him with visiting their trading partners with a view to making them allies. I liked him. He could converse in Greek and Latin. I had a smattering of Latin and so we had to employ Brother Oswald as an intermediary when the language barriers became too great during our discussions.

He firstly gave me a present. "This is what we call a mace. It is an idea we took from the Persians and Parthians. It is the weapon of a Cataphractoi." Neither of us had heard the term before and he graciously explained. "It is a horseman and horse completely encased in armour. They have a long lance, a bow and a mace. They do not need shields."

Oswald looked at me and said, "*Wyrd*!" as he made the sign of the cross.

I saw the question on the Greek's face and I explained. "I have just begun to put armour on some horses and to use a long lance. My son leads twenty such men."

He smiled, "I had heard that you were a strategos and now I understand."

"Strategos?"

"Yes, it is another word for Warlord. I was a strategos before I was wounded. Here feel the weight of the weapon."

It was a wooden weapon covered with metal at the end from which protruded some wicked looking spikes. I swung it and found it remarkably light to use.

"With your permission, strategos I will give this gift to my son. He was looking for just such a weapon and I believe this can be made by my smiths."

He spread his arms, "Emperor Phocas just wished to give the Warlord a gift. I am a soldier and, like you, I would like to see a fine weapon used and not kept as a ceremonial piece. Speaking of weapons, Lord Lann, I have heard much about this sword of yours. There are many documents in the library in the city and some of them mention your weapon."

"Saxon Slayer?" I gestured for Lann Aelle to fetch it.

He covered his smile with his hand, "I am sorry, Warlord I mean no offence but it is only in the legends of the past that men name weapons."

I smiled to show I was not offended, "Then perhaps we are a throwback to the time of legends for men believe that the sword has magical qualities which help us to win battles."

"Ah that I understand for we carry religious relics into battle and there are other stories of ancient swords which could help men to win battles and wars."

"I am sorry but my men would prefer to follow a weapon carried by a leader who knows how to use it." Lann entered with the sword still in its scabbard. "This is the weapon, please give it to this gentleman Lann and then find my son."

Andronikos swung the sword and watched Lann as he left. "I thought that was your son as he was called Lann."

"No he is the son of my half-brother Aelle."

"The half Saxon." Someone knew a great deal about me. "Intriguing but then everything about you is intriguing, Warlord; the shepherd boy who becomes a strategos without any training; the callow youth who defeats champions and kings. It is the stuff of legend and with a half-brother from his enemy's tribe as well. You are truly a remarkable man with an equally remarkable family." He returned the sword to the scabbard. "A fine and well-balanced weapon and the steel of the blade is the finest I have seen outside of the Empire."

"It has served me well and it has never let me down."

"And I hear that on this island you sometimes challenge a champion to avoid unnecessary deaths?" I nodded. "That is like the legends of Hector and Achilles."

"It does not always work out that way but I have fought kings and champions."

He shook his head. "It is like travelling back to ancient Greece. Do not get me wrong. I like it but it is many miles from the intrigue and politics of the imperial court."

Hogan walked in and I introduced them. "The Emperor has sent us a gift and I would wish you to have it." I gave him the mace and he swung it. His face lit up.

Andronikos laughed. "Here is a warrior if ever I saw one. No words just a smile as he swings his weapon and I suspect, Hogan Lann that you cannot wait to use it?"

Hogan blushed and began to apologise. I waved my arm, "Go and use it. We can speak at the feast in honour of the strategos."

After he had gone Andronikos said, "A fine boy. And I can see you are proud of him."

"He is the finest horsemen we have and was instrumental in defeating our enemies in his first battle. I have been lucky."

"I believe that people make their own luck."

He seemed to appraise me for some time and we sat in silence. I broke it first. "It seems to me that you want something from me Andronikos. I am a soldier, you are a soldier. Tell me, soldier to soldier, what it is you wish."

"I think I was chosen because I too am plain spoken. The Emperor would like an alliance with you."

"I am flattered but I am not even a king. I control one little island and everyone is my enemy."

"There you are wrong. Our sailors have been returning to us and telling us that Rheged and Roman Britannia are alive and well which as we both know is ironical given that the legions slaughtered those who lived here." He waved his hand, "But I digress. Given the support of the Empire you could become a king and your lands could be increased in size." He leaned forwards, "Between you and me it would help the Emperor in many ways if you became his ally."

"What would it cost?"

"Nothing! The Emperor is rich beyond words but this would be the first step to reclaiming those provinces which have been lost and the fact that you are not a king helps him."

"How?"

"He would make you Dux Britannica, the Roman ruler of the entire island."

"That is ridiculous I only control a tiny part of it."

"When we had governors, they controlled small areas not much larger than this island besides you underestimate yourself. You managed to march to the furthest extreme of the old Roman Empire and destroy your enemies. With the Emperor's help you will become even more powerful. We will increase the trade links. We will pay whatever price you wish for your wheat and add a quarter. We would share with you our technologies. Not just the mace but Greek Fire too."

"I cannot see any reason why I should refuse but I would meet with my closest counsellors and discuss what we ought to do. Does that displease you?"

"No, for I expected it of you, Warlord."

"We have guest quarters for you. We also have a bath house, not as good as the ones you are used to but a place to become clean after the long sea voyage."

"Thank you I may take you up on that but I believe you have some writings from a priest of Rheged, Brother Osric. Would it be possible to read them?" Both Oswald and I had the same quizzical look on our face. How did he know of the writings? Andronikos had lived in the political world of the Byzantine Empire for some time and he spread his arms in apology. "Brother Osric wrote to a friend of his in Constantinople and told him of Rheged and his writings."

"Aah, I do not think we have any objections. Brother Oswald can show them to you and then join me in the Praetorium."

I sent one of my men at arms to fetch the others and I seated myself at the table with Lann behind me. "Remember Lann, whatever you hear in this room stays in this room. You are privilege to hear more than most men. Do not abuse the trust."

"Of course Warlord and I am honoured."

My men quickly joined me, Garth, Ridwyn, Tuanthal, Hogan, Miach, Myrddyn and, finally, Brother Oswald. When they were seated I gave them the gist of the conversation. "But before we discuss it I would like Brother Oswald to give me his opinion and when you have all spoken I will give you mine."

"I was as taken aback by the offer as you were Lord Lann but I understand it. This is a new Emperor who overthrew and killed the previous Emperor. He is a soldier himself which is why I think he chose a soldier and not a diplomat for this task. The Emperor has many enemies in the east and the west. If he can bring back Britannia into the Imperial fold it will be a mark of his power. If Brother Osric was, as it looks at the moment, a Byzantine spy then the Emperor is basing his plan on his knowledge of you. He sent you, deliberately in my view, the man you would trust the most; an honest and wounded soldier. Someone who suffered almost the same wound as your brother Aelle. They are devious and convoluted in the east and this is how they go about things. And before we speak, in my opinion, we have nothing to lose by entering into an alliance."

"Thank you Oswald. I now understand more than when we were in the room with the strategos. I thought we were an insignificant speck, a throwback to the days of Rome but I can see now that others have a different view." I leaned back in my chair. "What should we do?"

"If we accept that Brother Osric was passing information to the Greeks then some things which appeared strange now make sense. When King Urien came up with the title of Warlord it seemed a peculiar decision given that he had sons who could have removed the title but if it came from Osric then it is logical. He was thinking of the Greek strategoi. And what of the ships which suddenly began trading with us? I thought it was the magic of the isle but now I see that it was politics and he was spying on us whilst still conducting trade."

"You sound disappointed. Are you Myrddyn?"

"A little, but that is disappointment with the gods. I am flattered that the Emperor thinks that we can be of use to him." He grinned, "And I would like to get my hands on this Greek Fire and the other exciting inventions from the East."

"Garth?"

"I would like an ally but I think they are a little far away to help us."

Hogan reached down and brought out the mace, "If they can give us weapons like this then I am in favour of it."

I shook my head at the distraction. They all spent some time admiring the weapon. "Enough! Weapons apart what else do we think?"

"I am with Oswald. I can see no argument against it."

"Thank you, son. And you Ridwyn?"

"I am with them. I like the idea that you would be Dux Britannica. There must be others like the men of Strathclyde who wish to join us with that title then they might flock here."

"You forget, Ridwyn, that the news will be in the court of Constantinople, not in Britannia."

Brother Oswald coughed and said, "Not true, Myrddyn. This will be like when you drop a stone into a pond. The circles move from the middle. There will be others who hear of this. When they do we may receive embassies from them as well. What the Warlord decides today may well be the most important decision he has ever made."

"It will be our decision Oswald."

"No Warlord, the priest is right. This is your decision. You have to become Dux Britannica. It is not up to us, it is up to you."

Myrddyn was right. "Before I make that decision, does anyone here object to an alliance?" I looked at Tuanthal, who had remained silent throughout. "And you Tuanthal, what do you think?"

He laughed and looked suddenly young again, "No Warlord, I am like Hogan. I just want to get my hand on maces!"

"Horsemen! No objections then?" They all smiled and shook their heads. "Then, thank you for your advice and I will tell the envoy of my decision at the feast. Oh by the way Oswald, do we have any copies of Osric's writings?"

"Part of it but it is not as good as the original."

"It matters not. We need a gift for the Emperor and I can think of nothing else. Bring them tonight and I will give them to him and we can get some monks to make copies."

"Where will we get monks from?"

"We can ask Bishop Stephen. When he hears that I am to be Dux Britannica it may make him our third ally."

Myrddyn laughed, "I can see you becoming more devious by the moment, Warlord."

As we were dressing for the feast I told Myfanwy of the offer. She did not seem surprised. "Here, hold Nanna while I prepare myself." I had never nursed my own children before but my wife thought that I could and, I found that I quite enjoyed it. The gurgling child seemed to enjoy entwining her tiny fingers in my beard and she giggled at the silly noises I made. "I think it is a good alliance. Heaven knows we need all the friends we can get and I prefer the title to that of king. I do not think others will try to take the title from you." And so the decision was made. I became Dux Britannica because no one could think of a good reason why I should not.

We had invited all the senior officers as well as Gwynfor and Gareth. It was too far to send for Aelle and Raibeart as the envoy had to return the next morning but it was a grand occasion and Myfanwy, despite the new baby had excelled herself. Brother Oswald had used the last of the decent wine we had although I was sure that it would not compare to the wines Andronikos was used to.

After the meal I stood and nodded to Lann who scurried away. "Today is a most important day for us here, at our home and our castle. We have been invited by the Emperor Phocas himself to join him as an ally. We have decided to accept this offer of friendship." They all banged their beakers on the table, much to Myfanwy's annoyance. I glanced at Andronikos who smiled and nodded. "And we have a little gift for the Emperor. It is a poor copy but it is some of Brother Osric's writing. Next time a ship arrives from Constantinople there will be better copies ready."

I could see from his face that the Greek was touched by the gift. "I thank you Warlord and can I ask, have you accepted the title."

"Yes strategos, I will be Dux Britannica."

"Then you will need this as well." He took out a wooden chest. I did not know how he had brought it in unseen. He took out a chain with a pendant. There was a golden image of the Emperor and around the side writing which said, Dux Britannica. He placed it around my neck and bowed and then he took out a magnificent silvered helmet. It had mail hanging from it and enclosed the face apart from the eyes and the mouth. Unlike my Saxon helmet it was made in one piece. The top had a white plume sticking from it. It was the most beautiful piece of armour I had ever seen.

I saw the envy from my warriors and admiration from my wife who said, "Well go on, put it on, you know you want to." She knew me so well. I put it on and heard the cheers and roars from the room. It felt light and I found that I had good vision. It was cleverly made.

When I took it off Andronikos said, "It is the type worn by our Cataphractoi. This one was mine."

"I cannot accept your helmet!"

"Please I will never need it again and," he gave a wry smile, "I have seen yours and this guarantees that you will live a little longer."

The celebrations went on long into the night but Andronikos like Myrddyn and me, drank sparingly and the three of us were the only ones up early the next morning. We took a stroll along the cliffs to the south of the castle.

"This is a perfect spot for a castle and this looks well built. I noticed, as we sailed north, that the only solid looking castles were Roman and the rest were built in wood."

"They call us the last of the Romans and we like the stone forts."

Myrddyn had been desperate to ask questions and now he began, "Strategos, the Greek Fire recipe?"

He smiled, "I have a copy in my room I shall give it to you."

"The Warlord has not asked but how will we communicate?"

"A good question, Myrddyn. I will send letters with the ships which call here. There will be a ship a week from now on. I hope that you will have plenty to trade."

Myrddyn gave a confident nod. "We will. Now that we have the alliance we can plan accordingly." Myrddyn should have been a Greek and I wondered what was running through his mind.

"I would like to have some of your younger officers visit with me so that they can learn of how we make war."

"I can already think of a couple who would like to do that."

"Good. Let me get back to Constantinople and make the arrangements. I am glad that I was chosen to meet you."

"And I am pleased too. It was beginning to feel lonely here at the edge of the world."

"Well now you are closer to the very centre of the known world, the Emperor."

Chapter 15

The signal towers proved their worth as the days began to shorten after midsummer. The sentries could see far out sea and the odd ship which had come close to the isle had been seen and reported. The wheat was growing well and both Gareth and Brother Oswald were calculating our profits. The first of our new horses had been born and, although we would not yet see how good they would be they were at least healthy. That month also saw the birth of many children on the island the result of unions between young girls and widows and the soldiers who now wanted families. It did seem particularly precocious of the gods to smite us with the Hibernians. The signals came from the north reporting that Irish ships were in our waters. Tuanthal led his equites, now eighty strong, to assess the threat. Garth and Ridwyn made sure that the warriors were ready to march and Miach prepared his flying column of archers. Our plans had long been in place.

As Lann polished my sword, which he had already sharpened he said, cheerfully, "You will get to wear your new helmet Warlord. Are you excited?"

How could I tell him that it was not exciting it was a deadly business? He had been spared the true horror of war in his first fight but I knew that when we stood in a shield wall and fought another then he would know that war was not exciting. "I have worn it before."

"Yes my lord but the enemy have not seen it! They will flee when they do."

"I hope so," I said wryly, "it will save many lives."

We now had to wait until Tuanthal returned although I hoped that our two ships would see the signal and investigate. An attack from sea would disturb an enemy's plans. Then signals began to come from the south too. Had we two attacks? I summoned Aedh and Miach. "Investigate the southern course. I hope that we do not have two attacks. Take your mounted archers; you may be able to deter them a little." No matter how many men invaded or attacked us I was confident that I could defeat it if it was one force but I had not enough men for two attacks. We had three hundred warriors for we had had many recent volunteers but I would need to leave at least one hundred to defend Castle Calm and Caergybi. I intended to fight with two hundred warriors, eighty equites and sixty archers. I knew that every settlement would have up to one hundred men who could fight and some had more. I hoped that the signals had ensured that everyone had made a fort safely.

One of Tuanthal's men galloped in just before noon. His horse showed how hard he had ridden. "Warlord, there are six Hibernian ships. They have landed four hundred men." My mind took in that they must have been big ships or very overcrowded. Then it struck me that some may have landed and returned to Ireland. "The captain is watching them."

"Have they destroyed anything?"

"They have burned a small village but it was empty. They have reached your brother's Burgh." Aelle's calm demeanour would make everyone feel safer and with my horse watching them they weren't going anywhere. Had I not had the second signal I would have taken Garth and a hundred men and sent the Hibernians packing but I had to delay. I would not risk a trap.

I sent for Garth and Ridwyn. "Ridwyn take eighty men and march to Aelle's Burgh. There are forty foot archers who can accompany you. Your presence may send them home."

"Do you want us to attack them?"

"Only if you think you can win. We will have to wait until we see what is going on in the south."

They were ready to march and they set off. They were fit men and could travel almost as fast as the equites. "Garth, make sure the men have been fed. We will have to march fast."

Aedh's scout galloped in with the bad news from the south and Raibeart's Burgh. "Ten ships have landed close to your brother's fort. There are five hundred Hibernians and they have surrounded Lord Raibeart's Burgh. Captain Miach is harassing them with arrows."

"Myrddyn, you take charge of the defence here. Let Tuanthal know the situation and send a messenger to Mungo. If they have not already sailed I want The Wolf to the south and The Dragon to the north. Garth, get the men and let us march. Lann, lead our horses." It was not fair to ride while my men marched and it would save Scout in case I needed some hard riding later on.

We took the coast road along the cliff. It would afford us a good view of their ships and was the shortest way. I smiled as Lann struggled to keep up. He had the horses to lead and it was a little unfair but he had to learn about war the hard way by doing it. We were five miles from Castle Calm when we saw the first burning farm. I sent one of the scouts to investigate and his bleak face told the story before he opened his mouth. "They are all dead!"

Garth shook his head, "Perhaps they were the first ones and had no warning."

"Perhaps."

We saw the ships and they were lying less than half a mile off shore. Their captains must have been confident for there were many rocks in that part of the sea and if the wind came up they could be wrecked. Garth came next to me. "How do we do this, Warlord?"

"Not the way I intended. We will have to do it the expensive way; a wedge to break them up and destroy them. We have to get across the island. Tuanthal and Ridwyn cannot defeat four hundred men, they can only watch."

Raibeart's Burgh was built on a low ridge above the sea. He had wooden walls and a single ditch but he had no bolt throwers. They had been planned for the future. If Miach was harassing the enemy with his archers then we might be able to reach them before they had breached the gates and walls. As we reached a rise about a mile away I saw that the Hibernians were already at the walls and were trying to fire them. I could see tendrils of smoke rising. "I want us to double time to reach them. We will go in a column until we are a hundred paces from them and then we go into wedge formation. Garth you will be on my left; Lann and Pol behind me. Tie Scout and the other horses to that tree." As Lann obeyed me I put on my new helmet and the men cheered. We began to run.

The Hibernians were using the tactic used by Iago's men. They were hacking at the walls with axes. I could see the defenders loosing arrows, hurling spears and throwing rocks. Miach and his archers were trying to thin out the Hibernians but the shield wall was holding. I would not give them the chance to form ranks and face us; we would make a wedge at the run. I trusted my men and their training. "Wedge!" I would be the point of attack and I focussed on the warrior I would strike. I led us towards the extreme left of their wall. He was, by his armbands, weapons and stature a chief and we needed to take those warriors and leaders out first.

Between the roar of their attack and the crash of their weapons they had no idea we were coming. I knew that Miach and his archers had seen me and that they would aid us with their missiles. We were less than twenty paces from them when we were seen and by then it was too late. "Unfurl the banner!" Raising my sword I roared, "Rheged!" and smashed my blade through the helmet of the surprised, shocked and soon, very dead chief. The weight of warriors behind me took us into the flank of their attack. The men on either side of me slashed and hacked too and soon we were deep in the heart of their shield wall. Only their shields faced us and they struggled to turn to present their swords, axes and spears. Many were simply knocked to the ground. Some of those were trampled to death while others were stabbed by the men in the middle of the wedge. The warriors who were attacking the wall were suddenly aware of the slackening of support and Miach and his archers took advantage to thin them out too. Already we had achieved our first objective; the settlement was no longer under attack and I hoped that Miach and his archers would join the defenders. Their arrows would do more damage from their ramparts and they would join Raibeart's men in a joint arrow attack.

I heard the sound of drums ahead and knew that we would soon be surrounded as our wedge drove deeper into their lines. As I took off the head of the man before me I said to Garth, "We need to get in front of the wall. We need to wheel right!"

"Aye my lord!" It was a difficult manoeuvre. The left side had to hold while those from me to my right had to turn right and clear the men who were attacking our flank. We would then have to retreat backwards and I hoped that Raibeart and his men would be ready to support us. Garth shouted. "Right wheel!" As he held his position I gave a half turn right to stab Saxon Slayer through the unguarded side of the Irish warrior next to me. Pol was stabbing with the banner; it now had a spear head and was a lethal weapon while hacking with his sword. Lann's seax flashed out like a serpent's tongue to strike flesh whenever it could and then we had a shield wall.

"Rheged! Walk backwards." We began to retreat the thirty paces to the damaged wall. We had some space for the Hibernians were still disorganised but that would only be a brief respite. Once they saw that we were moving backwards they would hurl their warriors at us in that wild way the Irish had. The wedge had become three lines with a small gap between them. The first of the Hibernians came at us one by one and they died to a man. I had drilled into my warriors that the enemy had to be killed, even if it took two or three men to do it. Then a huge bare-chested warrior wielding an enormous war hammer threw himself at us. An arrow flew from behind us and struck him in the shoulder but it did not slow him up. The hammer connected with Con, the warrior next to me and his whole skull disintegrated. I dropped to one knee and drove my sword up through his stomach, through his chest and out of his back. As I stood I punched with my shield and his body slipped noisily from my blade and crashed into two warriors behind him.

Pol shouted, "We are at the wall!"

"Here we hold them. Lock shields!"

With our shields together and our blades before us we were like a huge piece of armour and the half-armoured Irish rushed at us. There were so many of them that, had we not had the wall behind us, then they would have driven over us but all that they did was kill their own warriors in the front rank when they drove them on to our weapons. All the time they were pushing hard to get at us arrows and stones were flying over our heads from those on the walls to kill those behind who were giving their weight to the attack. As the pressure slackened then the bodies would fall and another warrior would be pushed forwards onto a blade. Our shields were too good and our weapons were superior. The end was inevitable and they fell back leaving a wall of dead before them.

I heard a cheer from within as the Irish stepped backwards over the dead and the dying. We had stopped them but what I did not know was, had we won? They retreated back to the shore. I heard Garth yell, "Get any wounded inside the burgh. The warriors at the front, despatch the wounded."

"I want a prisoner!"

"You heard the Warlord, the least wounded can be captured alive."

I did not take my eyes from the Irish in front of me. We had hurt them and, had I had Tuanthal with me, then they would be defeated. However there still enough of them to attack again. Then I saw them move slightly south to a sandy ridge. It soon became clear that they would be making camp and I sighed with relief. I hated fighting when I did not know all. I needed to know how many men were left in this burgh before I could plan on defeating the Hibernians.

Behind us the gates opened and the men at the rear began to enter. Raibeart came out and embraced me. "You came just in time. We had killed many but this was a huge warband." He patted the wooden walls, the walls which were now charred in places. "Thank the Allfather you ordered these to be erected." As I took off my helmet he added, "Miach told me of the attack on Aelle's Burgh. How did they fare?"

"I know not. I sent Tuanthal and a handful of warriors and archers for it was a smaller band." I looked out to sea and saw the ships slowly moving down to the camp site. "How many ships landed these warriors?"

"There were twenty."

As we went in I rubbed my beard. "There is something amiss here brother. I cannot see twenty ships here."

"Nor can I but my men told me that some of them disappeared over the horizon after they had landed the warriors."

"Which makes me wonder why and where did they go?"

"Let us feed you and your men and clear away the damage. We can talk better on a full stomach." He looked at the helmet in my hands. "The new helmet stands out on the battlefield. It appears to shine like a beacon. It is a fine piece of work."

I handed it to him for him to feel the weight and examine the skill in the manufacture. "It is and I barely noticed that I was wearing it. It is cunningly made. Ralph, my smith, has been trying to copy it, without success I have to say. If we all had these then we would have an advantage over any foe."

Garth and the last of our warriors entered and deposited the arms and helmets they had gathered. "There is still more to be gathered, my lord."

"I will get my people to do that brother."

While Raibeart organised the collecting Garth took off his helmet. "We lost fifteen dead. It could have been worse."

"We had surprise on our side. They did not expect us to attack as soon as we arrived. They will now be planning how to end this."

"They lost many men, Warlord. I do not think they can defeat us now."

"If this was the only band then I would agree but what of the band on the other coast? What if they joined here? They have cleverly divided our forces. It is not like the eastern end of the island where the two forts can see each other; here we are vulnerable to an attack from anywhere. We will have to prepare for the morning and see what comes. Organise the men. Pol and Lann go and fetch the horses. Scout will be fretting to be so close to a battle and not be involved. I will find Miach."

Miach strode over to me, a large cut running down his grizzled cheek. "Did you get too close to one of them?"

"Aye, the little bastards hid in the dunes and tried to pull us from our horses. They failed. We lost five good men though."

"It was worth the cost for it held them until we arrived. Gather any spent arrows and after food we will plan the morrow. Send one of your men to Tuanthal to discover how it goes there."

Raibeart told us, over food, about the attack. "The men on the tower saw the ships as they approached and lit the beacons. The people began to come in but there were few from the north and the beacon there was not lit."

"I believe that is why we received the message late. They must have landed men up there and they killed those close to the beacon. Someone has been spying."

"When they landed they formed into a shield wall on the beach and then advanced. The ditches and the arrows slowed them down a little and we killed many but there were too many of them. When Miach arrived and began harassing them at least it stopped them trying to burn the walls."

"I think we need to add some stones and extra ditches to prevent that in the future and we need bolt throwers here too."

"When this is over I think that the people will gladly work to prevent this happening again."

"Did you lose many?"

"A handful of warriors only; the ramparts protected us and they still have piss poor archers. My men were laughing at them."

Miach snorted, "If we had had all of our archers then they would already be on their boats and fleeing. And they still do not wear as much armour as they should if they are going to fight the Warlord and his armoured giants!"

I nodded to Miach. That was rare praise indeed. "I am grateful that they do. This is why we always strip the bodies. I know that our enemies think that we desecrate their dead but it keeps us ahead of them. And now Garth, let us go and speak with this prisoner."

The wounded man had had an arm removed but the application of a burning brand staunched the bleeding and meant he would not die, yet. "You are a brave warrior. What is your name?"

"I am Boru and you are the Warlord; the warrior with the magic sword. Where is your evil wizard? Has he disappeared and vanished into thin air again?"

I smiled; Myrddyn's legend grew even if he did nothing. "We did not need him for your band of brigands. Who is the leader of this little raid?"

"Little raid?" He spat at the floor and Garth began to move forward but I restrained him. "This is no little raid, Roman. Soon you and all those who fled from Rheged will lie dead or enslaved and King Felan will rule here."

I now knew their leader. I had fought him before. "So he has named himself king has he? King of what? A little shit hole in the middle of a bog?"

That stung him. "He has more men that you can imagine." A sly grin came over his face. "You are not the only one with allies and cunning plans."

That was all that we could get out of him. Garth wanted him tortured but I restrained him. "He is a chief and he will not talk under torture but do not give him water and we will see what the morning brings." As we went to our quarters I felt uneasy. "The last time Felan allied with someone it was Aethelfrith. I had thought that he would be licking his wounds after his drubbing by Iago."

"Perhaps he meant Irish allies."

"It could be but it could also be King Iago and that worries me for where are our ships? Why has Mungo not sent riders following the lighting of the beacons? We do not have the whole picture yet and I am loath to make a decision on such scant information. Let us see what the morrow brings."

Chapter 16

We discovered the bad news that the new dawn brought when the early morning fog disappeared. We saw a horizon devoid of Irish ships and, even worse, the camp was deserted. They had gone in the night. Despite brutal questioning from Garth our prisoner refused to give us any more information but the sly grin on his face told me that he knew that this had been planned. I allowed Garth to give him a warrior's death for he had been true to his lord. We were now in a worse position than we had been the previous day; we had no idea where they had gone.

Raibeart was as puzzled as I was. "I did not think that they would go so tamely. It is not like them."

"No, there is more to it but we are in the dark."

Just then a rider galloped in from the south. "Warlord, King Iago is attacking the bridge. He has an army to the south of the Narrows and began his attack yesterday." Garth threw him an accusatory look and he continued. "Four riders before me tried to get through but there were Hibernians who ambushed us."

"That is where they are brother!"

"Not necessarily, Raibeart. Those Hibernians must have been there yesterday and it explains where those other ships went. They dropped another warband to aid Iago and now we know who his allies are."

"Shall I begin the men marching south, Warlord?"

Something troubled me in the back of my mind. If the attack on Aelle and Raibeart had been intended to draw us off then why had the Irish not stayed to hold us here? It made no sense for we were as close to Mungo's Burgh as we were to Castle Cam. And then it hit me. The Irish were attacking my barely defended home.

"Pol. Ride to Tuanthal and tell him Castle Cam is under attack. He has to get there as quickly as he can."

Garth and Raibeart looked at me dumbfounded as Pol leapt on his horse and galloped off. "Have you become Myrddyn? How can you know this brother?"

"Lann get our horses." As my squire ran I explained my thinking. I saw the wily Miach nodding. "Miach get your archers mounted. Garth, bring the warriors north as soon as you can."

Raibeart said, "I will bring as many of my warriors as I can spare. It will not be many but it may help."

We mounted our horses and galloped north. Miach rode next to me while Lann proudly held the Wolf Banner. "This is a risk Warlord. Suppose they have gone to attack Mungo? They would be hard pressed to fight off two armies, especially if one has landed on the island."

"It is a risk but if I gamble on that outcome then I am gambling my family and our people. I can recapture a fort I cannot make people."

We galloped in silence. "And that is why you are Warlord and I am a mere captain of archers."

"It does not make it any easier making the hard decisions." The only positive thought which sustained me as we rode north was that it was Myrddyn who controlled the defences but I knew that he did not have enough men to man the fort at the bridge and the castle. I assumed that he would abandon the bridge to the main island and that alone kept me going.

I could see smoke over the ridge to the north of us and my heart began to sink. I urged Scout on and was aware that I was leaving my escort behind. I cared not. It was imperative that I get there first to assess the damage. My men would be coming but they would be arriving in dribs and drabs and I had to have my mind set on a plan. When I reached the ridge my spirits rose. The smoke was coming from three of the Irish ships which were burning. I could see that there were twenty ships now. They had obviously used two diversionary attacks before launching their main one. The other ships were pulling away from the deadly fire. The catapults were hurling Myrddyn's new weapon, Greek Fire and there was no answer to it. Even as I watched another ship was hit and seemed to explode into flame, the crews leaping into the sea. I had to admire my two enemies and their cunning plan. It was well thought out and, had I taken the bait then my family and my home would soon be gone. We had little chance even now but we did have a chance and I would seize it with both hands.

I saw that Myrddyn had, indeed abandoned the bridge forts and retreated behind the main walls. There was fierce fighting at the walls of Castle Cam but the Irish had not secured the bridge forts, they had just passed through and that was a mistake. When Garth arrived he could plug the hole and the enemy would be trapped between two sets of defences. Miach joined me. "We will secure the forts and use that as a base. When I raise the Wolf Banner then they will know I have come but they will not know I bring only a handful of archers."

"Do not worry Warlord, if my lads are firing from those gatehouses we will slaughter any who get close. We have full quivers."

It was eerie to approach so close to a battle and to be almost invisible. The land close to the bridge fort was lower than the land around my castle and no-one could see us approaching. Once we reached the small fort we tethered the horses and closed the gates which led to Holy Island. Miach stationed his men on the walls and then I ordered Lann to unfurl the banner. Although we were a mile from the castle the defenders would be able to see the banner and they did. Even at that distance I heard the cheer. Soon the Hibernians would have to decide what they should do. Would Felan continue his attack on the castle or would he divide his forces? If he continued his attack then I would have to go on the offensive but I counted on Irish arrogance and recklessness and they did not disappoint. "Lann go and find me a bow and a quiver. There is an armoury down below. Get one for yourself. This will not be sword work for a while." As he disappeared I glanced south and saw the column almost running to reach us. It would be a close-run thing.

The first of the Hibernians came in a loose line with no order and I knew that Miach's men would choose their own targets. The leading warriors seemed to run into an invisible rope as they were thrown back by arrows. There were only twenty-one bows but while the enemy were few they would be lethal. Once they formed a shield wall then we would face a different enemy.

Lann almost fell up the last steps in his eagerness to join me. "Steady squire. Do not let the fort wound you."

It was not my own bow but it was a good bow and I notched and loosed an arrow to fly beyond the first warriors and strike one who was encouraging the others from behind. He might not have been a chief but he was a leader and any dead leader would demoralise them. I saw that Myrddyn had moved the bolt throwers and the bolts began to slice through the warriors attacking us. It was a risk but the bolts which passed through the Hibernians just embedded themselves in the lower walls. Miach grunted, "If that wizard hits any of my men I'll have his balls for breakfast."

"Do not worry Miach, he built them and he knows how to aim them. It is working. None have shields on their backs."

I heard the tramp of feet coming up the stairs and Garth, puffing and panting led his men to the walls. "I need to work out more my lord."

I pointed at the field. "Myrddyn is thinning them out. When Tuanthal arrives…"

"If he arrives."

"When Garth, when, then he can charge them. As soon as you see him then put your men behind the gate. We will open it and clear a space for the horsemen."

Garth nodded and took one of the pila which were stacked on the ramparts. The Irish had been too eager to attack the castle and had missed some valuable weapons. Soon the Irish attack was faltering and whoever was leading this attack drew them off away from the bolts and protected from our arrows by a wall of shields. An archer shouted, "Horsemen Warlord."

Knowing it had to be Tuanthal I said, "Get your men down there now while there is a lull. They will attack you but you are better armed. When I give the order then split and allow Tuanthal and Hogan to do their worst."

When the Hibernians saw the gates open they surged forwards to be met by a hail of arrows which punched them backwards. Some brave souls reached Garth and his unformed shield wall but they easily despatched their would-be attackers. Confident that Garth could handle the warriors close to him I turned to speak with the horsemen who were arriving. "Tuanthal, Hogan, Garth has cleared a space for you there is one warband attacking the castle and the other are attacking us. Dispose of this war band first." I looked at Hogan, "Destroy them, completely!" My son nodded and I knew that it would be done.

Pol reined in and raised his hand. "Lann go and give Pol the standard and then fetch our horses." I saw the clear disappointment on his face. "One day you shall carry it but for now give it to Pol eh?" He grinned and ran off. I handed our quivers to the nearest archer. "Miach keep after them. When these are destroyed then mount and relieve the castle." Although I was worried sick about my wife and daughter I knew that I had to rid the area of these warriors first. As I descended the steps I saw another two ships blazing, the Greek Fire had done its work and the new alliance had paid dividends already.

I tagged along behind the column of equites who emerged through the line of warriors and began forming a line. I joined the second rank for I had neither lance nor spear. Hogan and Tuanthal had both and they suddenly roared their charge and galloped towards the Irish who saw the wall of metal and horseflesh and ran. The wooden wall close to the rocks barred their way and they clambered and hacked their way through and over it but to no avail. The line of horsemen swept imperiously through the warriors brave enough to attempt to stand. I saw the lances thrusting and then withdrawing, the blood from their victims dripping from the heads of the lethal weapons. When the lance was broken some used a spear and I saw Hogan laying about him with the mace. Neither shield nor sword could stand against its force and he cut a swathe through the unfortunate warriors. Soon we were spread out across a wide front and I was able to hack and slash at the backs of the running men. If they turned to face us they fared no better for our weapons were superior and our horses were a weapon they could not face. Soon there were no warriors left on our side of the wooden wall and they were streaming towards the beach. I raised my helmet. "Garth! Take your men and finish them off. Tuanthal, reform."

Miach and his archers rode up. "Where would you like me Warlord?"

"Join Garth and finish the Irish off. I want no survivors. We were kind last time and we have been repaid by treachery. Kill them all!"

Tuanthal and his horses were blown but I knew that we had one more charge left in us. As they rode up I heard my son shout. "Collect any spears and lances we may need them."

I pointed to the warriors some half a mile ahead who were oblivious to the disaster which had befallen their comrades. They were still attacking the walls and were so close that the bolt throwers could not strike them. "One line and charge into the back of them. We will then withdraw, dismount and fight on foot until Garth can join us." Their looks told me that they doubted my judgement but I knew that neither of them would gainsay me.

"Yes Warlord."

We were soon in one line beneath the Wolf and the Dragon Banners. It was time to announce our arrival. "Charge!" As we gathered pace I roared, "Wolf Warriors of Rheged!" The wailing of the Dragon Banner added to the effect.

The whole line took it up and soon the cry was echoing across the field making the Irish there turn around. There may have been hundreds of them yet alive but all they saw was a line of horsemen who seemed to fill the field and of their comrades there was no sign. King Felan tried to organise his rear ranks into a shield wall but many had no shields and others had no body armour but they tried to do as they were ordered. The equites with lances and spears struck first and the line burst open like a ripe plum. We were like an arrowhead and we could choose who would die. I saw an older warrior turn with his shield held close to his body and his spear pointing over. He had seen many battles but I could see, in his face, resignation. It was a battle of wills, who would strike first? Scout was taking me at a fast pace and he made the decision for the veteran. He stabbed at Scout and my sword snaked out and removed the spear head and then back slashed when I was beyond him to lay open his unarmoured back. He crumpled to his death.

The ditch and the wall were looming up and I reined in Scout. I saw Pol and Lann were still with me. "Back to where we began the charge and dismount."

As we rode back through the scene of the charge it was like trying to cross a sea of bodies. As we halted our exhausted horses I saw Garth and Miach leading their men from the beach. "They are all dead, Warlord, and their ships are coming in to take off the rest."

I turned and saw that our last charge had broken them and they streamed towards the beach and safety. Like their dead comrades they had to negotiate a wooden wall and that gave us time to reform and march in three lines towards the beach. I was in the front rank with the warriors, Tuanthal and Hogan led the equites and Miach brought up the rear with the handful of archers. We kept our lines as they ran heedless of obstacles towards the beach, the sea and the safety of their ships. Perhaps Myrddyn had run out of Greek Fire for he had to resort to stones and the bolt throwers. Both were effective and another ship began to sink.

There were just three hundred or so warriors who were still streaming towards the beach. As we passed the wounded or the exhausted, they were slain. I could see King Felan, he was wounded, and his oathsworn were protecting him with a ring of shields. His bodyguards were stripping him and themselves of armour to enable them to swim out to the waiting ships.

"Charge!" Although on foot we had the slope with us and the Hibernians had destroyed the wooden wall. We piled into the demoralised and disorganised Irish. They all fought bravely knowing that they would die. They would die to protect their king. Had they had our armour and our weapons then it would have been too close to call but we had the advantage and we used it. Hogan caused much devastation with his mace which nothing seemed able to withstand. One huge warrior tried to take him on with his axe and shield but Hogan took the axe blow on his shield and smashed the mace onto the Irish warrior's shield. It shattered and must have broken his arm. Hogan raised his mace and brought it down with such force that the warrior's head looked like an egg had been smashed open and not a skull.

The Hibernians did not surrender. Most of the oathsworn were slain where they stood but a few managed to swim out to the ships. When another ship was sunk the last three hoisted sail and headed out to sea and out of range of the deadly war machines. The beach then became an abattoir with the last remnants of the warband being slain along with the wounded. Finally we had won but what of my castle and what of my family?

As soon as the last warrior was slain I turned and ran towards the castle entrance. I could see that they had tried as hard as they could to break the defences and the ditch was half filled with their dead. I saw too some of my warriors, some with whom I had stood in the shield wall, greybeards, and they, too, were now dead. I would mourn them when I knew that all inside were safe. My heart almost stopped when I saw the bare feet of a woman covered in a blood-soaked shroud and then dismissed the idea. The lady of the castle would not be left to lie dead outside. Myrddyn rushed over to see me. He had wounds to his face and he held his arm. He saw my concerned expression and smiled. "She and Nanna live. They were safe throughout the whole battle." I glanced down at the dead woman. "Her husband was wounded and she rushed out to aid him, a spear aimed at someone else took her. *Wyrd*!"

I took his good arm. "Thank you old friend. We will talk later."

"Go, Warlord, your family waits."

I ran through the doorway still guarded by two warriors who grinned and nodded as I raced by. I ran up the stairs to our chambers and there, with Nanna and eight of the slaves and servant women was my wife. "There," she said as I entered, "it is the Warlord and so it will be safe for you to leave my room."

They giggled as they ran by and two of them surreptitiously touched the hem of my mail shirt. "I reached out to hug her and Nanna gurgled happily. "You are both safe, thank the Allfather!"

She snorted, "I think I would have been happier on the ramparts with a sword in my hand than stuck in here with those simpering fools wailing on about being raped by Irishmen." She pushed me away and glanced up and down my body. "You are still whole then? Despite fighting the whole Hibernian tribe on your own."

"I did very little fighting, well less than many."

"Aye and more than most! I can see the damage to your armour." She half glanced out of the window, "Hogan, Pol, Lann? They are safe too?"

"They are all safe and the only warrior I have not seen is Ridwyn but he is too awkward to die."

"Well you have seen us now you can go and see the others. She is due for a feed and a change anyway. Now go!"

Myfanwy was the most practical and organised of women. As much as I had loved Aideen, I loved Myfanwy just as much. Myrddyn and Brother Oswald were busy bringing the interior of the castle back to some sort of order. I could see great armfuls of iron being brought in and I knew that Garth would be organising the funeral pyre for the dead, both Hibernian and Roman. Despite what our enemies thought, we always honoured the dead of both sides. It would not do to meet a warrior in the Otherworld whom you had dishonoured. Pol and Lann led in our mounts. Tuanthal and Hogan would have taken theirs to the stables which were between the castle and the bridge fort. Had the Hibernians been cleverer they could have caused much damage and hurt us for the future but, thankfully they had not. The damage they had done was superficial. We would rebuild the wooden walls but in stone this time.

I wandered around the castle, asking warriors who had been wounded how they were; I was already planning for the future. We had to have a bigger army. With the Imperial alliance we could afford it. I knew, from conversations with Brother Oswald, that in paying us more than the wheat was worth they were, in fact, subsidising us. If that meant we had a bigger army and we survived then so be it. I was also determined to increase the equites. They had almost won this battle on their own. I would give Hogan his own company. First I would send Hogan, Pol and an archer to Constantinople to study with the strategos. It was even more vital now. My son and Pol would learn to become Cataphractoi.

Myrddyn found me, his arm in a sling. "Come Warlord. You must tell me of what went on outside of the walls and I will give you a brief account of our travails."

When I had told him he frowned. "I like not this alliance Warlord. We can ill afford two enemies at either end of our island."

"And that is why I ordered the raiders slaughtered. If fifty escaped in their handful of ships I shall be surprised."

"All dead? You have changed Warlord."

"I suppose I have. Since speaking with Andronikos I have seen our place in the world. We are the last of the Romans. I had thought we were the last warriors of Rheged but he has shown me a different perspective. I want future generations to remember this as a golden time and not a time of blackness and evil." He nodded and looked strangely happy. "And you Myrddyn, how did you fare?"

"Gwynfor came during the night and told us that he had seen the Irish ships sneaking up the coast and so I deduced what would happen. I abandoned the bridge fort; seeded the ditches with lillia and brewed up some Greek Fire, not enough as it happens, but it saved us nonetheless. When they attacked we were ready. Brother Oswald armed every man we could. The whole of Caergybi was within our walls and we had more men than we ought to have had. The Greek Fire and the bolts took the heart from them but without your timely intervention they would have won. We need to build towers to allow us to clear the walls from the sides. We will work on it."

"We must speak with my son and Tuanthal. I know nothing of the fight in the north."

The weary leaders of equites trudged through the gates. I knew both of them would have seen to their horses and to their men before they came to see me. It was not disrespect it was how I had trained them. "I saw the lance and the mace. They were both impressive weapons."

Hogan looked as he had when he was a child and I had complimented him. He looked proud enough to burst. "Thank you. That means much. And I cannot wait to wear the new helmets; if Ralph ever manages to make one."

"Do not be unfair to Ralph. He is doing his best and besides I have a better plan."

He was intrigued, "Tell me more."

"No son, that can wait until Captain Tuanthal has made his report."

"When we reached Aelle's Burgh they were massing outside and trying to burn the walls. We used the archers to break them up and then we charged before they had time to form a shield wall. Once they were broken they withdrew and we entered the burgh. The next day they were gone."

"Aye it seems the Hibernians are beginning to learn about following orders. It seems that this is a plan of Iago's and he launched an attack on Pasgen while we were preoccupied. I think his plan was to draw us to

Mungo's Burgh while his allies destroyed this castle and then he expected us to tramp back north to deal with the dead."

Tuanthal; smiled. "Then he underestimated the Dux Britannica." He became serious. "So we know not what happened there."

"No and I intend to ride there this evening to discover what happened."

They looked at each other. "Then we will bring the equites to protect you. "

"No, I will take Hogan and ten only, the rest will need to join Aedh and scour the island for any Hibernians who escaped the slaughter. There is a band in the east who slew the scouts."

Myrddyn and Myfanwy agreed that I should go but I could see that they were both happy that my son was my escort. As a horseman he had no peer. We left in late afternoon and we took it steadily for our horses were tired. We wore no armour to save weight. If we saw an enemy then we would run. As I said to Pol and Hogan as we rode east, I was not expecting a disaster. "I left three good leaders there and if they have failed then we will all eventually fail for I trained them."

The sun was setting behind us as we rode the Roman Road and it cast long shadows before us. It reminded me of the warriors in the past whose long shadows were before us; Julius Agricola and Emperor Hadrian. Both were great leaders and protectors of Britannia. I was now their heir and I took that responsibility to heart. "I have in mind for you two to go to Constantinople and spend the winter learning about that great city and how we can become better warriors. How do you feel about it?"

The two friends roared with delight. Hogan reached over to put his huge arm around me. "That is the best present you could ever give me."

"You will have to work and to learn but I believe the strategos will be good for you both. You need someone other than me to be your teacher and I need some of the ideas from the east. I will ask Miach to select a young archer to go with you and perhaps one of Brother Oswald's acolytes. But you Hogan, as the son of Dux Britannica, would have to be responsible for all of you."

"I will not let you down father."

The two of them began talking animatedly about what they would do when they were there and what the voyage would be like. I rode next to Lann and saw his downcast face. "Do not be unhappy nephew. This will be the first of many such visits. Be patient. You are now where Hogan was last year and Pol the year before. Watch and learn and be ready when the opportunity comes your way."

We became alert and focussed as we approached Mungo's Burgh. We could see, across the water the glow of burning. Had the wily Iago managed to defeat my men and was he waiting now inside my forts to fall upon us? Hogan sent one of his men forwards to the gatehouse. He was challenged and he answered. If this was a trap then we would know when the hordes of warriors fell upon us. He came back smiling. "It is not taken my lord. I know the guard. They are lowering the drawbridge."

"Nonetheless be ready for a trap. Until I see Mungo I will be sceptical." We rode forwards with swords drawn. The bridge dropped and then, as the gate opened I saw framed in the light, the unmistakeable figure of Mungo."It is good to see you old friend."

I dismounted and walked towards him. He clasped my arm and looked at me in surprise. "You came alone? Where is the rest of the army?"

We continued walking onto the inner yard. "With respect Mungo I need to know what happened here and I need to know now."

"We lit the beacons as soon as the attack began. I sent Wolf and Dragon to assist Prince Pasgen. When we received the request for help we could not do so for I did not know if we would be able to hold them. The king attacked with new allies and along the length of the southern wall which, as you know is weaker than the north. Calum sent a signal asking for reinforcements and I sent all but fifty men to aid the defence. That was this morning and I have received no signals since."

That worried me. I had seen fires burning. "Are the two ships still safe? And the bridge?"

"Aye my lord, it was not touched. The ships were still sailing when night fell and I have ten men guarding the bridge at this end."

"Then while your men get us some food, for we have not eaten all day, we will tell you how close Iago came to defeating us."

When Mungo heard all, he hung his head. "I am ashamed to say, Warlord, that, when you did not come, I thought you had abandoned us. Please forgive me I should have trusted my heart and not my head."

"There is nothing to forgive. I should have sent a clearer message and we need to improve our own communications. If they survive still on the mainland then we need not worry."

Hogan belched and said, "Sorry. Fine meal Captain Mungo but you need fear not. Prince Pasgen and Calum are both good commanders.

When Tuanthal and I were based there, I saw that they would not be easily shifted. They will be there on the morrow."

I did not sleep well, despite my exhaustion and I dreamed...

I was in a den with a she wolf and two cubs. Some hunters were outside and they had lit a fire. The fire was throwing off copious amounts of smoke and I was torn between saving my cubs and fighting off the hunters. I leapt out and there was a ring of Saxons with spears levelled at me. As the she wolf and the cubs came out I leapt at the warrior with the longest spear and I began to tear his throat. Spears plunged into me and I was suddenly thrown into the air and I was falling.... falling....

I awoke, bathed in sweat and with Lann standing in the doorway, dawn's early light forming a corona around him. "Warlord? Did you call?"

I sat up and smiled. It was Wyddfa and it was a dream. "No Lann. I was just dreaming. Fetch me some water and my armour."

I could not face food and I lead Hogan and the equites along with Mungo to the bridge. We pulled ourselves across and it took longer than it normally did. That was good for it enabled me to scan the shore and see what was amiss. Our standard still flew at Pasgen's fort and the wall appeared unbreached. I could see, to the south the masts of two ships which I presumed to be The Wolf and The Dragon. What I could not see was the band of men who should have been there at the bridge."Take the bridge back and go with them Mungo. Until we know that all is well I will not risk you too. We can swim the horses back if the fort has fallen."

The man from Strathclyde reluctantly agreed. We mounted and rode towards the southern wall. Our weapons were unsheathed and we were on high alert. "Spread out. Lann and Pol stay behind me." There was a strange silence broken only by the lapping of the sea on the shore. I knew that we had at least a thousand paces to go to reach the wall but I had expected that we would have seen men ere now.

Suddenly I saw warriors on the southern rampart and they looked to be a mixture of archers and Calum's warriors. Of course they could have been Iago's men in dead men's clothes but I did not think so. I kicked Scout on and we began to trot. As we neared the wall I heard a thin cheer which spread along the whole wall. And I heard the chant of "Warlord! Warlord!" Unless this was a really elaborate ruse then the fort was still ours but it begged the question, where was the garrison?

As I reached the wall Walch, the archer came to greet me. His leg was heavily bandaged and he limped. “Warlord, we wondered why you had not come.”

“I will explain later but where are Prince Pasgen and Captain Calum?”

He pointed to the south. “They left yesterday afternoon to pursue King Iago as he fled. We defeated them at the walls.” I could just see the tops of the masts and he gestured to them. “The two ships broke up their shield wall and then Prince Pasgen charged them when they were still disorganised and we poured arrows on them like water from a fall. They broke and Captain Calum joined the pursuit.”

“Good. You have done well. Has someone looked at your leg?”

“Aye my lord we have healers.”

“Hogan, take the equites and find Prince Pasgen. He may need your assistance.”

Walch laughed, “I think the mood those two are in they will take on the world.”

I finally smiled. We were safe and we had beaten our two closest enemies. I was Dux Britannica still.

Part 4
Saxon Blood

Chapter 17

It was harder than I thought it would be, saying goodbye to Pol and Hogan. It had taken a month to arrange the voyage; any longer and it would have risked the autumn storms. We sent five scholars in the end. Miach sent his son, Daffydd ap Miach, Brother Oswald sent Brother John and Bishop Stephen requested that we send Brother Matthew from the monastery. I did not mind for Andronikos had not specified a number and the more who went the more knowledge we would have. They would be away until the spring. The captain of their transport told us of the time it would take and I was sad. Myfanwy also shed tears. She was very fond not only of Hogan but Pol both of whom were like sons to her.

As we watched the ship from the cliffs slowly disappear south, it seemed a final act to what had been an eventful year. King Iago had escaped Prince Pasgen despite his best efforts but his army had been hacked to a shadow of its former self. The king would do well to hang on to what he had and would pose no threat to us. The Hibernians had sent a peace envoy who swore loyalty to us and begged to be our ally. My message back was that we would think about it and finally we began to get droves of volunteers who wished to serve the Dux Britannica. Some came from as far afield as Gaul and Italia while others came from Northumbria, Strathclyde and even the Saxon kingdoms. The men we had lost would soon be made up in numbers if not quality. Garth, Tuanthal and Miach spent every waking hour training them to their usual high standards. We had received the first of the payments for the wheat and they came in the form of a set of armour and helmets for twenty equites. It was a small number but it was a start. We now had stone walls around our settlements and not wooden walls. Our near disaster of the autumn had been a lesson well learned. We would improve our defences to keep our families safe. The New Year promised much, especially as Myfanwy was with child again and my family would become larger but no less precious.

Before that we had a Yule celebration and, with Hogan missing, I made sure that Raibeart and Aelle brought their whole families to cement the bonds of blood.

The trade with the Empire had resulted in some luxury goods being available. Andronikos had sent Myfanwy a present of some exotic spices and the food that Yule was particularly exciting. Gareth had also traded for some amphorae of wine which enriched and enlivened the celebrations. Aelle's and Raibeart's children were now grown and they enjoyed playing and spoiling their new cousin. Lann Aelle also looked more confident as he showed his cousins and siblings around the castle he now called home. He knew every nook and cranny. He even took his father and uncle on a tour of the military side of the castle and they were impressed with the improvements we had made since the attack.

Myrddyn and Brother Oswald had built towers which protruded from the wall to allow archers to pick off men trying to climb the walls. As with the forts at the Narrows the ditches were made steep on one side, ankle breakers Myrddyn called them, and gentle on the other. We could not divert a stream here but we would use jagged pieces of rock to be permanent traps which would not need replacing after every attack. The watch towers, not only at the castle, but also across the island were improved and increased. We only needed them to be made from wood which meant that we could build them quicker and taller.

After the feast while the younger people danced and sang I retired with my brothers, Garth, Tuanthal, Miach, Ridwyn and Myrddyn to my solar. It was dark and there was no view but it was a place that Myrddyn and I used when we wanted to mull something over. It was natural that the men should gather there with our beakers of unwatered wine and reflect on the year that had gone and the year that was to come.

"Your new towers should aid us brother."

"They will Raibeart but the Hibernians showed us how vulnerable we are to coastal attacks. I intend to use the two ships to patrol our waters, in opposite directions. They can be out at sea and give us early warning of any attacker. I know that their captains will need to trade but they can alternate. Gwynfor's shipwrights are already building two smaller boats with just two bolt throwers on board to help them."

"And what of the new men? I hear there are many."

I chuckled. "I did not think that my new title would attract so many but it has. How many men have we now Myrddyn? I saw you and Brother Oswald with the lists the other day."

"There have been three hundred men who volunteered. We have not begun to speak with them properly yet, we have merely put them in the warrior hall which is a little overcrowded."

"You are telling me. Some of my equites wish to sleep in the stables. It is warmer and less crowded."

"Aye well they have come from all over. There are four from Gaul, three from the Rhenus, three from Italia and the rest from Britannia. There are many from Gwyr and they are doughty warriors who hate Iago."

"I hear there are some Saxons too?"

Myrddyn nodded at Aelle's question. "Not full Saxons but much as you Lord Aelle, they have a Roman or Celtic mother and a Saxon father. It seems they heard the story of the brother of the Warlord and feel that if he could make the change then so could they."

Aelle looked at me with his most serious expression, "If I can help with the training of those half Saxons I would be pleased. I think that I would understand them more than some others."

Miach snorted, "Meaning gruff old buggers like me might upset them."

Aelle smiled, "I would never dream of saying that."

"But you are probably right. I have the habit of calling a spade a shovel!"

Miach's bluntness was legendary. "I am sure that will prove useful once we have assessed each warrior and made sure that their intentions are the right ones."

"What do you mean?"

"I mean, Raibeart that it would be the perfect opportunity for an enemy to slip some of their men into our ranks as spies. Myrddyn here did just that once before."

"Yes my lord and it is not just Saxons who are joining us but men from Gwynedd and Hibernia. Many will be genuine but it is up to us to weed out the rest."

"That is a large number to train. How will it be done?"

"The equites will be taken by Tuanthal and they can stay here. Half of the warriors will remain here with Garth and I was going to divide the others between you, my brothers for some of the warriors can serve as your garrison. Miach will train the archers."

"And what of slingers?"

I smiled, Aelle had been the leader of the slingers and they had been a potent force. "They will come from our people anyway and you can train those if you have a mind."

"I would. Raibeart and I became aware that we needed to pull our weight more. You have to save us all the time and that is not right."

"No Aelle, my job is to protect all of the people."

"Then we can share the burden for we are your brothers."

I spread my arms around the solar. "You are all my brothers, my brothers in arms!"

In the cold, crisp days of the midwinter we spent many days speaking with the volunteers. Ten of them were patently not suitable and were brigands and thieves looking for plunder. Aedh and his scouts escorted them to the Narrows and sent them on their way. The others were divided into the three groups based upon their size and their skills. My captains could train them to become more skilled in weapons but it was an attitude we were looking for. The fewest were the equites for we tended to get those from the young scouts who grew up in the saddle. It was hard training a grown man to be an equite. Many of the scouts acted as squires to family members who were equites and they became the best of warriors. The warriors, who had the most strength of arm, were selected for the archers but they were fewer than the warriors for they needed skill as well as brute strength.

They were hardened up and fed well. In the early spring they were sent throughout the island to help the farmers to plant crops and build walls. It made them work as a team as well as building up their strength and when that work was done they were assigned to their trainer. I enjoyed a couple of months with Nanna and my wife. For the first time with one of my children I had the chance to watch them change each day as they grew and acquired those quirks which made them individuals. Nanna was also lucky in that both Myrddyn and Oswald took a keen interest in her and she would be well educated as she grew. Andronikos had told me of the powerful eastern women who controlled and ruled countries. I wanted the same for my daughter. She would be her own woman and not dependent upon a man taking her for a wife.

Hogan and the others would be back from Constantinople at the end of summer and I took the opportunity of riding with Lann and an escort of Aedh's scouts to visit with the settlements on the island. By the time I returned I would only have a month to wait to see my son. I had missed him; more than I thought I would. The trip would take my mind off the empty space in my heart. As we were about to leave, Myrddyn, decided that he would come. I was surprised but he said, "I have a mind to visit Wyddfa on midsummer's eve. It is a special place at that time of year." He grinned at me, "When you are Dux Britannica and have conquered the entire province we will visit the ancient stone circle in the south of Britain."

I shook my head. Myrddyn liked to tease me. He was the only one save Myfanwy who would have dared to do so and I did not mind. "Let us just make this island strong enough to withstand another invasion and I will be happy."

Raibeart was happy with his new warriors and wanted to retain all of them. "The men from Gaul are ferocious warriors. They look a little terrifying but they would make a solid shield wall."

"You may retain twenty for your garrison but we need a bigger army if I am to reconquer the province for the Emperor. Are there are whom you mark out as potential leaders?"

"Aye, Bellatrix is a natural leader."

"Good then I need him for Garth and Ridwyn need good subordinates." I could tell that Raibeart had planned on keeping him for himself.

I laughed, "You are too honest for your own good brother."

When we reached the Narrows I visited Mungo first. "I am glad that you have come, Warlord for I was going to send a message to you."

I was intrigued. "Why?"

He smiled enigmatically, which was a little disconcerting for he had teeth missing which made it like looking into a graveyard. "I will let Prince Pasgen tell you. It was he who requested you." He noticed Lann besides me. "And when do our boys get back from the east?"

I liked the way that all of my officers regarded my family as an extension of their own. "At the end of the summer; it seems a long time since they left."

"But it will be good to learn what the new Romans know." He patted the bolt thrower on the wall. "These make all the difference. I have my men making new bolts in their quiet time and they are happy to do so. That shows you how effective they are."

As we crossed on the pontoon bridge I was intrigued by Mungo's comments. What was the surprise to be? Myrddyn did his mind reading act again. "Wondering what the surprise is will not give you the answer. We have a short time to wait for look, there is Prince Pasgen himself."

We rode from the bridge and he greeted me. He smiled, "I can see from your expression that Mungo has told you that I wished to see you?"

"Aye and he has me intrigued as do you."

"Indulge me Warlord, until we reach my castle. You will see why when we reach it." He spread his arm at the burgeoning site. "We have made many improvements since Iago's last attempt to destroy us."

"I can see and I have some news for you. We have many new volunteers. I am thinking of building another fort at the head of the monastery valley. It will give advance warning to us of an attack and afford some protection for Bishop Stephen."

He shook his head. "With respect, my lord, there is a better site a few miles along the coast from us here which is even better than this site. The mountain comes down to the sea and the gap is the same as the size of Castle Perilous, a Roman fort. I had thought of this myself but I lacked the men."

"You must show me and you shall have the men by Yule."

We passed through the gates and I saw that the bases had been strengthened and the drawbridge and bridge were now studded with iron bolts. Axes would not destroy them the next time they were attacked. The whole castle now had a more permanent feel about it. The wall which had been created by the land slide had been tidied so that it looked as though it was made by man and not nature. While Aedh saw to our horses Pasgen led Lann, Myrddyn and me to his quarters.

We sat in his comfortable chairs and sipped his excellent wine. "Come on Prince Pasgen. You cannot keep me in suspense."

"Just a little while longer. While we wait perhaps I can give a little preamble. As you know we have received many volunteers and Mungo and I have sent on all the ones we thought suitable."

"And they have been excellent. Is this about another volunteer?"

"Sort of…" Just then there was a discreet knock and then the door opened. "May I present Prince Cadfan of Gwynedd."

My mouth must have dropped open for both Pasgen and Myrddyn burst out laughing. The prince smiled and gave a slight bow, "I am pleased to see you again, Warlord."

"And I you, but I am at a loss to know the reason. Do you wish to fight for me?"

"Yes but I also seek sanctuary. Let me explain."

"Pray sit, Prince Cadfan."

"Thank you Prince Pasgen. My father remarried some years ago and his new wife has borne him a son. She is little older than I am and she hates me." He shrugged. "I spurned her advances once and women never forget. Anyway she has gradually turned my father against me. When the prince defeated us last year I was blamed."

"Why?"

"My warriors did not fight to the death when surrounded, they fled."

"A natural thing to do and understandable."

"But it was the excuse my step mother wanted and she poisoned my father's ear. I was imprisoned in a cell. Luckily, I still have some friends and four of them broke me out. Three died during the escape and I arrived here with Dai, the last of my friends." He paused and looked me directly in the eye. "Will you give me sanctuary and let me serve you?"

One of the qualities men like about me is the ability to sum a man up quickly. I was the one who first saw the flaws in Morcant Bulc, Ywain and Bladud. I was the one who identified Miach, Riderch and Tuanthal as great leaders. I closed my eyes and listened to my voices. There was silence and then a small voice told me to trust him. I opened my eyes and saw that all but Myrddyn were staring at me. "I will, Prince Cadfan, for I feel obligated to you. I rescued you once and it seems that the gods or wyrd wish me to continue to watch over you. Will you swear loyalty to me, become an oathsworn?"

He knelt on one knee and said, "I so swear. Lann Warlord of Rheged and Dux Britannica."

We left for Aelle's Burgh the next day. Myrddyn left us to visit the mountain but he told me, in a quiet moment, that he agreed with my decision. I know that if he did not he would have told me and so it meant a great deal. Dai was about the same age as the prince and seemed to be a quiet affable youth. He and Lann got on well as we rode north. I rode next to the prince to ask more of him and his father while Lann and Dai exchanged stories of their own lives.

"I think another reason he has turned against me is because I told him that the Saxons were our enemies and not our neighbours. I think the fact that our army drove them away from yours made him believe that we were better. Before then he had been a little afraid of your warriors and now, having been defeated twice he blames you for those defeats as though you instigated the war. I did not like the way he hired the Irish to attack you. They are nothing more than pirates and brigands and they have enslaved many of our people before now."

So he had paid the Hibernians, that, in itself, was interesting. I wondered where the money was now? If Felan was wise, and he was certainly cunning, then he would have left it at home and he could now hire another army for there were always Irishmen for hire. Already I had gleaned much from him.

Aelle's Burgh had the same busy feel as Raibeart's and the people looked happy while the men being trained looked industrious. Like me Aelle was intrigued at the presence of the prince but he made the youth feel welcome. That evening while Lann and the two youths strolled around the burgh I spoke with Aelle.

"Are any of these warriors going to be wanted by you for your garrison? And are there any would be potential leaders?"

He grinned, "I would say all of them if I did not know that you wanted a large number yourself. There are some twenty or so, a mixture of archers and warriors who would make a good garrison." He drew me close. "But there are some interesting warriors who I think will make good leaders but, two of them are Saxon, or like me, half breeds."

"Do not denigrate yourself. Your Saxon blood does not stop you being a Roman does it?" Since the visit of Andronikos we had thought of ourselves more as Romans than as Britons.

He shrugged. "It does no bother me but I know there are others who sneer. Not to my face and certainly not to yours but they are out there."

That annoyed me. I would have to discover who they were and let them now what I thought of that. "So, these leaders, can I meet them tomorrow before I leave?"

"Of course. I will show you the men training and you can judge for yourself. I will not identify the leaders and we will see if we agree."

The next day Aelle brought out his forty would be warriors and divided them into two teams; one slightly larger than the other. He would act as referee and decide when some one was dead or incapacitated. They were using the wooden swords the Romans had used to avoid serious injury but having used one myself I could attest to the fact that a blow from one of those was not easily forgotten. He gave the smaller team the task of holding a small dune. This was one of those times that others would say I could read men's minds or do as Myrddyn did and see into the future but that was not so. I just knew my brother. I knew that the potential leaders were in the smaller group who had the harder task of defending when outnumbered.

Lann was quite excited to be watching while I think that Cadfan and Dai were bemused. As the two teams planned their strategy he sidled over to me. "Warlord, do many of your warriors practise like this?"

"All of them. We have done so since we were in Rheged. It is the Roman way."

He looked puzzled. "But does it work?"

"Oh yes Prince Cadfan. The warriors can find out how their comrades perform in almost battle conditions and they can try things out which may work or may not." I wondered if I ought to go on, this was a potential spy but that little voice in my head was still there. "Do you remember in the battle I fought against your father when we came upon you suddenly and had to retreat?"

"I remember. My father thought that he had you."

"But we escaped because we could turn and move swiftly. That does not come accidentally. We had practised that in games such as this. What do your warriors do when they are not fighting?"

"They fight against each other in practice bouts."

"With real weapons?" He nodded. "And they get injured?" Again he nodded and then smiled; he was beginning to understand it. "A battle is not fought man against man, it is men against men. You can have the finest warrior in a battle but unless he has good warriors around him then he will lose. We win more times than we lose because we fight together and we know each other." I turned to Lann. "Look at Lann here; he stands behind me in the shield wall and I know that he will, with my other warriors protect my back. Lann here has slain warriors who were about to strike me and has saved my life. Is that not so squire?"

Swelling with pride my nephew said, "I am oathsworn. It is my duty."

"Ah, I will watch this combat with new eyes. Thank you for explaining it to me Warlord. This is the first real lesson in war I have had."

The combat was about to begin and I saw that both groups had been trained well and knew how to use the shield wall but the ones standing on the dune were directed by two blond haired warriors who organised their men into two ranks. Even though this meant they could be outflanked I knew why they did it. I knew, just by watching them, which were the two potential leaders. One placed himself in the front rank and the other stood behind the second.

The larger group were using their superior numbers to outflank the enemy. Suddenly the sand dune band charged down the dune. They struck the middle of the larger group and knocked them from their feet, striking down with their wooden swords as they did so. Then they turned to make two lines back to back and attacked the two flanks of the enemy which they outnumbered. It was all over in less than a heartbeat. The group on the dunes had two casualties and all of the rest were eliminated. My three companions clapped enthusiastically. "That was well done was it not, Warlord?"

"It was indeed Prince Cadfan. Those two blond boys have fought before."

We wandered over to speak with the warriors. Those who had been struck were nursing bruises, grazes and even cuts. The blond boys were retelling the story to each other. I had experienced that myself. When you won you could not wait to tell others, even if they were there at the same battle, what had happened. Aelle gave me a sly look as he approached me. "Well?"

"I confess that I knew who they were before the battle began but they are impressive leaders. That was as comprehensive a victory as I have ever seen. Introduce me please."

As soon as we approached they all stood and bowed their heads. They had seen me when they joined and were a little in awe of me. "The Warlord would like to speak with you."

"I like the way that you fought, even those who lost." I saw rueful smiles. "We cannot win every battle."

One of Aelle's bodyguards who was close by blurted out, "You do Warlord!"

Aelle silenced him with a nudge and my three companions all laughed. "Even when you lose you should fight as hard as you can for there will always be another battle. I look forward to the time you join my shield wall and go to war with me and my warriors, my Wolf Warriors!"

They all began banging their wooden swords against their shields and roaring. Aelle held his hand up for silence. "You may go with Tadgh here for more training but Aelfraed and Aethelgirth, can you stay behind to speak with the Warlord."

"When we were alone I said. "You led well there. What is your story? Where have you come from? I can see that you have fought before."

The one called Aelfraed spoke. "I am half Saxon. My father took a woman from Elmet when they defeated the king. I was treated badly by him and he beat my mother. When I became strong enough I killed him and fled with my mother but they sent dogs after us and tore her to pieces. I hate them."

I nodded. I could understand his hate. "And you Aethelgirth?"

"I too am half Saxon but my mother came from the land of Deira by the river the Romans called the Dunum. I too was badly treated by my father and my mother and I fled. We lived in the land of the lakes for a while and then the fever took my mother. I did not want to be alone and I heard of the Warlord of Rheged who had a brother who was half Saxon and thought that I could find a home here."

"And you both have. When my brother has finished with your training you two will be joining me at my castle and Captain Garth will train you to become leaders of men."

Chapter 18

Prince Cadfan fitted in well at the castle. He was polite and Myfanwy adored him. Garth and Ridwyn were a little suspicious of him at first and I sat with them and Myrddyn to discuss the issue. "Let us suppose that he is a spy. What can he tell his father?"

"Well, Warlord, he knows the defences of Prince Pasgen's castle and this one."

"Excellent Ridwyn. What does that tell him that Iago would not have seen by looking?"

Ridwyn looked perplexed. Myrddyn enjoyed the Northumbrian's discomfort. He remembered the sea voyage when Ridwyn had enjoyed the discomfort of his passengers. "If the prince suddenly leaves and goes home then we will know that he was a spy and we can expect an attack. While he is here we are safe."

Ridwyn blushed, "It is good that I am just a warrior and others make the important decisions. Sorry Warlord."

"No it is good that you question me for the answers make everything clear."

The prince and Dai enjoyed the training and Lann was able to show them around and share with them the experience of being a training warrior in the land of the Romans. I was busy with my newly born son, Urien. We named him after the man I thought was the greatest leader the island had ever seen and I hoped that this son would do as well. When he was born it made me think of Hogan even more. I was just counting the days until he and the others returned.

Their ship arrived after the first fierce storms of autumn and both Myfanwy and I were worried that he would not return. Myrddyn had that annoying self satisfied look of someone who has seen the future. I suppose I should have trusted him when he said that they would return safely. We had just launched our two smaller boats, The Eagle and The Hawk. Both were fast little ships and it was they who brought the news that an imperial ship was approaching from the south. It meant that we were all there to greet our family when they arrived. Bishop Stephen could not make it in time but I knew that he, too, would be keen to find out about the world of Constantinople.

After our four small ships the huge cargo ship seemed to dwarf even the port. I looked desperately along the rail to look for my son and his colleagues but all I saw was a row of darkly tanned sailors. I leaned down to speak to Myfanwy, "Perhaps Hogan is below decks."

She laughed, "You goose! He is there on the deck, waving at you!"

"But where is his beard?"

She shrugged, "He has shaved and a good thing too. He looks much more handsome and I bet easier to kiss than a hairy warrior who rarely bathes!"

Hogan was one of the darkly tanned sailors. I had not recognised my own son! I waved back. It may not have looked authoritative but at that moment I was just any other father welcoming his son home. It seemed to take an age to tie up and I saw the passengers disappear, to get their belongings I presumed. Once the gangplank was down the five of them almost ran from the ship. Hogan threw his arms around Myfanwy and his new brother. "What is it a boy or a girl?"

"Why you have a little brother. Can you not tell?"

He kissed Myfanwy and I could she that she was pleased. He shrugged, "All babies look alike to me!" He turned to embrace me. I have missed home, father, and it looks even better than it did."

"You look different."

He pointed to his face, "You mean the tan? It is hot and sunny all the time. You cannot believe the times I was desperate for a little cold or some rain."

He grabbed Myrddyn's hand as I turned to greet Pol. "And you too have changed my standard bearer. Perhaps you will want to be a strategos now."

He pointed to his chest, "In here, Warlord, I have not changed and I am happy to carry the Wolf Banner unless young Lann has now claimed it?"

"No but he too has changed. Come, all of you, we have a feast planned and you can tell all of us your adventures and what you have learned."

Myrddyn said, "I will stay here and bring the goods sent by Andronikos."

The feast was a joyous occasion. It was as much a celebration of my son's birth as a welcome for our travellers. I watched Prince Cadfan look enviously at the obvious love between Hogan and his step mother. No doubt he was reflecting on the different relationship he had with his own. I sat between Pol and Hogan and Hogan between me and Myfanwy. Myrddyn sat on the other side of Pol. I found myself totally fascinated by their experiences. Miach sat with his son and, blunt as ever, asked the question which had been on all our lips. "Why do you smell like a woman and where is your beard?" he then added, unnecessarily I thought, "You haven't started liking boys have you?"

Hogan showed great maturity when he answered for Daffydd. "No Miach, in the east they bathe more frequently than once a year and they feel that smelling sweet is better than smelling like a horse."

Miach looked offend and sniffed his own arm pits, "You could be right Lord Hogan. I may try this bathing eh?"

I asked Hogan, "What made you shave?"

He blushed although with his tan it was hard to tell. Pol laughed, "It seems the Greeks think that beards are for Persians and barbarians. Hogan spilled a little Greek blood before Andronikos explained that. Once we had all shaved, Hogan's knuckles healed!"

Pol had been deeply affected by all that he saw. "They have many cities which would swallow Civitas whole and Constantinople is so big that it takes more than a day to walk across it! And the peoples who are there Warlord! I saw brown people, black people, and even yellow people! I did not know so many varieties existed. And the food; you have never tasted some of the things that they have. They have a cream which is sweet and as cold as snow! There are more spices than they have sent us before. I brought some back for I like the taste."

He finally stopped and drank some wine. He pulled a face. "And the wine tastes much better than this." He suddenly realised what he had said, "I am sorry Warlord, I did not mean to offend."

"No offence taken but, "I lowered my voice, "Some of the others may get a little sick of hearing how wonderful it was and how bad it is here. If you could mention it to the others?"

"Yes Warlord. You are right and I will do so."

"Now what did you learn of war and weapons?"

"That you are a military genius Warlord."

"Pol, you know I hate flatterers."

"No, my lord. That is what Andronikos said of you. He said, to the Emperor, that you were a genius who had implemented one of your own ideas that they used in the east. He said it showed that you had a natural ability for war. The heavily armoured equities, the reinforced shields, the tactics we use all of them are commonplace in the east but everyone uses them. I now know why we are unbeaten and with the knowledge that Hogan and I have brought back we will be even better in the future."

Later when Pol and the others were telling their tales, I sat with Myrddyn, my wife and babes having retired and spoke of what we had heard.

"You were right to send them Warlord. They have brought back valuable information. The two monks have some interesting ideas about buildings and how to make them stronger. Daffydd has plans for his father to make better bows, and better machines of war. I just pray that we have time to put things in place."

There was something in his voice which made me suspicious. I looked at him and had a sudden clarity of thought. He had dreamed in the cave. "Tell me, wizard, what was the dream about this time."

"You are getting the second sight. I was warned about vipers in the nest and dragon ships."

"Saxons and spies."

"That was my thinking."

"And we have many newcomers too from the Gauls through the Saxons to Prince Cadfan."

"My thoughts too."

"And have you a picture of who the spy might be?"

"Not yet and it would take a dream but you are missing the point Warlord. You said it yourself about Cadfan. A spy has to get his information back to his master. If anyone deserts or leaves then they are the spy. And what could a spy tell them? Now that the world knows of the Greek Fire, we have no secrets and if we think it is the Saxons then we know they will come by sea. We have four ships now, let us use them. Let us use the new volunteers to man signal stations around the coast. With Hogan back we have more equites for Tuanthal to use and we can patrol twice the area."

"I still do not like the idea of spies in my land."

"Nor do I and I will try to sniff them out."

As all of my commanders were in the castle, as well as Aelle and Raibeart I held a meeting. Part of the meeting was given over to Hogan and Pol who told us of what they had learned. Then I spoke of the possibility of spies. Aelle bridled a little and took offence.

"Are you saying that we must have no warrior who is not from Rheged? If so we will have a mighty small army." Raibeart patted his arm to calm him down but I was not angry.

"No brother. We need warriors from anywhere and Pol and Hogan have already said that the Emperor uses his enemies in his army. What I am saying is that we should be watchful. If there are spies then when there work is done they will disappear. That will be an indicator that something is about to happen but I can tell you that I believe that there are spies in our ranks." They all gasped and I held up my hand. "And I am not worried. It is how we deal with the results of the spying which is more relevant. I want you to use your volunteers to build additional signal towers along the coast and to man them in rotation. It will help to make them feel part of our defence. I want our four ships constantly on the look out for the Saxons."

"Saxons!"

"Yes Aelle. I have information that the Saxons are planning something and I want us to be ready. Tomorrow I will escort Bishop Stephen's monk home and Hogan and I will visit with Pasgen. He is close to Iago and it will be good to get his opinion about this." I paused and looked at each man in turn, finally stopping at Aelle. "I am not accusing anyone of spying. I will not be suspicious of any one man over another but, until we know who the spies are, then every warrior who is not in this room is a potential spy."

"So you trust us brother?"

"I always have and I always will. The day that I cannot trust those in this room is my last day as Warlord!"

The next day as we headed east, the ninety equites rode with me. Pol and Hogan had been given full Cataphractoi armour and I saw every other equite looking enviously at them. Hogan laughed, "Do not worry boys. I have the plans for making the helmets and I have given them to Ralph. Once he has made the steel you will all look as handsome as me and Pol."

I gestured for Tuanthal and Hogan to join me. "I intend to have two groups of equites. You will be in overall command Tuanthal, with Hogan in command of the lancers. I want the two of you to patrol the island. If you have officers you can trust and rely upon then you can subdivide but I want you able to get to any part of the island within two hours. If we do have another sneak attack I want a quicker reaction. I am also increasing the scouts. You will both have ten scouts attached to you so that you can cover a wider area. Finally, now that Daffydd Ap Miach has brought back the horse bow we will train ten archers to be part of each command. You will both be self-sufficient. I am hoping that the shield wall will only be used as a last resource in the future."

"You know father, that they have a strange view of us in Constantinople. They see this island as a smaller version of their city with white walls, turrets and nobles riding around the land fighting barbarians."

"Truly?" I was amazed at the misconception.

"Truly. I think that part of it is fostered by the Emperor and those in power for they have built a legend and myth about Rome surviving in a desert when all else withers."

"What is a desert?"

He laughed, "A place of sand without water and filled with heat and sun."

"But Andronikos knows better."

"Of course but there is so much intrigue in the city that one must watch what one says for there are spies everywhere."

"Did you think I did right with our potential spies?"

"One of those who was speaking to us and teaching us how to win wars told us to keep our friends close but our enemies closer still. I think that it is sensible."

As we were going close to the land of Iago we had left Cadfan at the castle. "And Prince Cadfan, what do you make of his situation?"

"I feel sorry for him. When I look at Myfanwy and you then I feel lucky. It must be hard to be rejected by a father."

"He could be lying; we only have his word for it."

He shook his head, "No, I do not believe it. I have looked in his eyes and seen only truth. Besides you and Myrddyn are the ones who look in men's souls and know the truth. You do not believe he is a spy. You believe and trust him."

I looked at him askance, "It seems this second sight may be hereditary!"

Prince Pasgen wanted Hogan's new armour. I could see his eyes light up as he examined every individual piece of mail. He looked towards me with a pleading expression. "Warlord, we must have these for our equites! We would be invincible!"

"Ralph and the smiths are making them but they will not be ready until after Yule."

"I envy you Hogan and Pol. You have visited the centre of the world and seen wonders we can only dream of."

"And yet, Prince Pasgen, I am happier to be home. How do you feel Pol?"

"The same; it was an experience I would not exchange for the earth but this land is my world and is far more precious and dear to me because we have earned the right to be here and we cling on despite our enemies!"

When we reached the monastery Bishop Stephen was pleased to see his monk safely returned and to see us. "We heard how close you came to disaster and the lord watched over you. We prayed hard." I liked the bishop and I kept my mouth shut but it had been iron and wood which had saved the island not prayers. "And I hear that Prince Cadfan is with you?"

"Yes. What do you hear of that?"

"The story which reached us was that the new bride of the king resented the prince and poisoned the king's mind. He was imprisoned by his father." He shook his head. "I am a celibate man who will never father a child but I cannot understand a man who treats his own offspring in such a way."

Hogan looked at me, "It is strange to me too bishop."

We were treated with great hospitality and I felt the same about Bishop Stephen as I had about Bishop Asaph; he was a good friend and a sympathetic ear. "Bishop we intend to build a fort along the coast from here where it narrows to the mountain. I mention this because should you need a refuge, from any invader or enemy, then it is there for you."

"That is kind, Warlord, but we hear that King Aethelfrith is considering Christianity as the religion of his people."

I knew the Saxons. If they chose Christianity then it would be a political act. The religion of peace and turning the other cheek was not the Saxon way but I said nothing and merely smiled. "The offer remains no matter what the future holds."

He laughed, "Then Myrddyn is still the fortune teller eh?"

Once we were back in my castle we worked even harder to produce new weapons and armour and train men while we had this brief respite from war. The news from the bishop had done nothing to calm my fears; if anything, it heightened them. If Aethelfrith was making overtures to the church then it meant he was planning something and we would be ready. Prince Pasgen and Calum worked hard and quickly to build a fort on the coast. They would use wood in the first instance and then, in the spring they would use stone. The new warriors were sent to build and man the new towers as part of their training and Brother Oswald made a map showing the new towers and identifying the warriors who would be guarding them. We now had ten priests and clerics who worked for Oswald. I knew that Brother Oswald used them to convert the pagans amongst us but I did not mind. So long as a man obeyed me first then he could worship any god he liked. I had the better of the bargain for I had immaculately kept records of men and arms and I knew to the last sword what we possessed. When it came to war I would know what we were capable of.

After the new warriors had helped to collect the harvest in, another successful one, according to Oswald, then they began their watch keeping duties. Our ships still patrolled the waters and I was disturbed to hear of sails on the horizon which disappeared when approached by our own ships. Someone was watching us and I liked it not.

As the weather turned cold Hogan, Pol and Brother John came to me to ask if they could try to build a hypocaust and a bath house. They had their plans drawn and before I could mention the need for industry on military matters they came up with a system which would use the clerics and warriors who were not needed for training. As Pol said, "It will build up their fitness my lord, and help them to work as a team."

I could not argue with them for I had missed the comfort I had had at Civitas and Castle Perilous. It was during the building that we had our first inkling of danger. Aelle and his bodyguards rode in one afternoon when the skies were threatening another autumnal storm. His face was filled with joy but the news he brought me was grave. "The Irish landed a raiding party last night."

I became alarmed, "Why did you not light the beacon?"

"Because the problem was solved by Aelfraed and Aethelgirth. They spied them from the tower and, after raising the other warriors from the nearby towers ambushed the raiders and slaughtered them. And they captured their ship! Now what do you say of Saxon blood!"

"I say what I have always said, a man's blood does not bother me but his heart does. I told you I trusted your judgement and I am pleased that Aelfraed and Aethelgirth have proved so resourceful. How would you feel if I stole them from you to base them here and train them as officers?"

"I would be delighted for I have the others who came with them and they show the same promise." He grasped my arm, "Thank you brother."

"What for? It was your eye and your judgement that picked out the warriors. I should be thanking you."

The two young warriors arrived at the end of the week. Garth took one and Ridwyn the other. They had shown their prowess in the shield wall and it would have been foolish not to use their skills and talent. Both of my captains were pleased with them. Garth and I were walking along the cliffs looking at the stormy skies to the south and he discussed them both. "They have both fought before Warlord. In fact I can see that they have both led men in battle."

"Aelle used them as leaders when training."

"No, Warlord, these men have led and fought in wars. We are lucky to have them. I can see them being commander of ten soon and then commander of fifty. Eventually they could replace Ridwyn and me."

"Now you are being foolish Garth."

"No, Warlord, none of us are young men anymore."

"And that includes me I suppose."

He smiled, "All men grow old and the grey flecks in your hairs are not the salt spray are they Warlord?"

I laughed, "You are right. Give me progress reports on our new warriors."

We had a festival for the harvest. It was one of those times when pagan and Christian could celebrate together for while we worshipped the Mother, they thanked their White Christ for the harvest. Aelle and Raibeart left a skeletal force watching the towers and brought the rest to the hall. We now had more rooms for, with the arrival of my new family, Hogan needed his own rooms and he and Pol shared a chamber adjacent to that of my family.

It was a joyous celebration and it was only then that I noticed that the other equites had copied Pol and Hogan and were now clean shaven. It marked them as different from the warriors of the shield wall for they were all bearded, some of them, like Aelfraed and Aethelgirth, with braided moustaches. It was the first time I realised the power and effect of my son. He was becoming my heir and I was happy that he would be the next Warlord. I had also noticed a change in the way he conducted himself. The headstrong Hogan of yesteryear had been replaced by a Hogan who was calmer and less reckless. Both those qualities would stand him in good stead when he became leader.

I sat and spoke with him and Pol while the others became drunker and drunker. It pleased me that the two new officers, Aelfraed and Aethelgirth also seemed to handle their intake better and they smiled at me with a slight bow as they withdrew to bed. They would make good officers. Myrddyn came to join us. He, like me, never seemed to drink too much.

"A good celebration Warlord."

"Aye, they deserve it. We have had a good year and it is right to thank the Mother for her bounty and reward our people for their hard work."

I looked at Pol who was now a man grown. He had been my squire and then trained Hogan. He had never asked for anything and was as loyal a warrior as one could wish. "Pol I have a mind to find another warrior to carry the Wolf Standard."

His face looked as though I had slapped it. "Warlord! Have I offended you?"

I held up my hand, "Please Pol, hear me out. You and Hogan were sent to the east to learn to become better warriors. You have both shown that you have learned much. It would be a waste to have you merely guard my back. I would have you as Hogan, a leader of equites." I looked to Hogan for help.

"He is right my friend. You are a leader. The men have always looked to you. I looked to you when I was growing up. The two men I wanted to be were my father and Pol."

Myrddyn nodded his assent. "But we have two leaders already."

"Aye but Pasgen now has more warriors and the only other officer I could give to him would be Aedh who is a fine horseman but he is a scout and he leads my scouts well. The only warrior who can lead as well as Prince Pasgen is you. Will you become a leader of my equites? I would have four companies of a hundred men each. We are short of that number but we are growing and the new mares have produced fine offspring. What say you Pol?"

"I would be honoured Warlord."

He took my arm, "Good and now I too will retire for my days of carousing until dawn are long gone." I headed for my bed and the arms of Myfanwy who would I knew be waiting for me. She had had that twinkle in her eye and I knew what it foretold. When I opened the door to the bedchamber she was sitting up in bed.

"The children are with the servants tonight. I thought that we could celebrate the harvest too."

Chapter 19

I was not asleep when I heard the birds on the nearby cliffs already waking. Myfanwy was asleep in the crook of my arm and I was loath to move her. She had a contented expression on her face. Suddenly I heard the clash of arms outside the door and the noise of violence. I jumped, naked from the bed and grabbed Saxon Slayer. I flung open the chamber door and saw Pol and Hogan with bloodied weapons in their hands. At their feet lay Aelfraed and Aethelgirth. Aelfraed still lived although for how long I knew not as the wound in his chest was bleeding and pouring blood over the wooden floors.

"We heard a noise and when we came out of our chamber the guard at the end was dead and these two were approaching your door."

Aelfraed gave a coughing laugh and blood seeped from the corner of his mouth. "*Wyrd*! We would have had you and my uncle would have had his revenge, Roman!"

"So you are not the son of a daughter of Elmet then?"

"No! And I have fought against you ere now! Would that I had succeeded. You will not hold on to this island for long Roman and it will become Saxon soon enough!" He coughed again and more blood came up. He looked at Hogan with hatred in his dying eyes. "I will see you in the Otherworld Roman and we will finish this." And then he died.

"Quickly wake Garth, Raibeart, Myrddyn and Aelle and bring them here. I will get dressed. We have little time to lose." I could see the questions in their eyes but they obeyed me. When I returned to the chamber my wife was awake. "Assassins came to kill us but they are dead. I must dress. We are all in danger!"

She helped me to dress and she kissed me tenderly. "So long as you are our leader the danger will soon be over."

My brothers and my advisers arrived quickly and without dressing. Aelle paled when he saw the bodies and he looked at me. "I am sorry brother!"

I waved my arm in irritation. "This is no time for recriminations. Tell me Aelle, did any other of the Saxons who came with Aelfraed to join attend them here?"

He looked relieved, "No they all volunteered to stay on duty at two of the signal stations."

He looked perplexed at my suddenly serious face. "It is as I feared. The Saxons will invade tonight."

"How can you be sure father?"

"Remember his dying words. Soon he said. As soon as Aelle said that the rest had remained behind I knew that they would attack. The two stations will be close together which means they can attack and the people will have no warning. Add to that the fact that most of the garrison is here and…" I suddenly became angry. "I have no time to argue here! Just obey my orders. I want the equites ready to ride. Aelle you will come with us for you know where these signal stations are. Raibeart return home and light your beacons. I need Miach and the archers with me. Garth you can retain one hundred warriors, the ones who are suffering the most for the defence of the castle. Leave them with Ridwyn and then bring the rest to Aelle's Burgh. That is where they will attack. Myrddyn, take charge here. It will need a calm head and a quick mind."

"Yes Warlord!"

Lann Aelle had heard the commotion and he had my armour ready as soon as I had finished. "Well done Lann."

"Did my father do wrong Warlord?"

"No Lann. He trusted someone and they let him down. It can happen to any man. It is just that when you are a leader the consequences are more damaging for your people."

We rode from the castle with Aedh and his scouts ahead of us. I knew that there would be spies in Aelle's Burgh and I needed to destroy the ones at the towers first and then take out the other traitors. We had over a hundred and fifty men with us and I knew that would be enough to deal with the spies but I was not sure that they would be able to deal with the invasion.

"Aedh, I want you to ride to Mungo. Explain what has occurred. I want all of Pasgen's equites and half of his warriors to meet with me at Aelle's Burgh." He threw me a questioning look and I snapped irritably, "He needs to be told by someone he knows and trusts. Get back as soon as you can!" He grinned as he galloped off. "Prince Cadfan, please take charge of the scouts until Aedh returns."

He looked shocked. "You trust me still?"

"I told you all before that I trust every man until he lets me down and when he does he had better flee to the ends of the earth for my reach is long!"

He nodded and kicked his horse on as he and Dai led the scouts in a semi circle ahead of us. I did not think that the Saxons would have launched their attack yet. They would need to secure the towers first.

Aelle rode next to me. He was subdued. "The first is just a mile over there."

"Cadfan!"

The prince was next to me quickly. He had been listening for the order. "Take the scouts and ride in a loop to the beach. Stop any of the Saxons escaping and warning the ships."

"Tuanthal, take Pol and half of the men and go to the tower to the east. We will take the tower to the west. One prisoner is all we need but I do not want to risk any more lives. Hide the bodies of the dead."

"Yes Warlord."

"Hogan, these are your equites you know how to use them. You give the orders."

"Thank you, Warlord." He turned and passed on his instructions to the men nearest him.

"Aelle, take Miach and go to your burgh. Have your men seize the spies and find out the details of this plan."

"I will not let you down again. My Saxon blood will not betray me more."

"You have not let me down. It was just *wyrd*! Now go."

I drew Saxon Slayer. He would soon be drinking deeply once more. We rode quickly towards the tower which was clearly visible, rising high above the stumpy wind blown trees. We knew they had seen us when the arrows flew at us to smack harmlessly off our armour. They must have known it was a hopeless situation they were in and would die but they were brave. They rushed to the bottom of the tower just in time to be speared by Hogan and his equites. Hogan had heard my words and his spear lanced into the thigh of a warrior. He quickly dismounted and disarmed the man. I reined in next to him. We crouched close to the man who was badly wounded. "How many ships are coming?"

"Enough to kill all of you Romans. You are too late. You will all die." He pulled a dagger and lunged at me. The blade almost struck my armour but Hogan's mace smashed into the Saxon's skull making it unrecognisable.

"Thank you, son. When you have finished off the rest get Tuanthal and meet me at Aelle's Burgh. Hide the bodies, I want their leader to think they have gone to the fort." I turned to Lann Aelle who held Scout's reins. "Let us find the prince."

There were two dead Saxons near to the twenty scouts. Prince Cadfan pointed out to sea. "There are ten ships, at least, out there."

"Come with me. We have work to do."

We headed towards Aelle's Burgh some two miles away. I hoped that we were in time and that the traitors had not had time to capture the settlement. When I saw the bodies at the open gate my heart almost stopped. Had I sent my brother into a trap? I was relieved when he and Miach greeted me. "We were just in time. These traitors had killed the night guards and were about to slaughter the rest of the garrison when we arrived."

"We have no time now to feel smug, there are ten ships out there. Get the garrison roused and seed the ditches with caltrops. Load the bolt throwers. This is where Myrddyn's Greek Fire would have come in useful." I know there was no point in wishing for what we did not have but it annoyed me that we had a superior weapon and could not use it. "We must hold on until Garth can reach us."

Soon the ramparts were filled. We alternated archers and slingers with warriors. "We will leave the gate open and hide below the ramparts. I want them to think their spies have done their work." I heard the galloping of hooves and went down to the gate to meet the horsemen. I waved to Hogan, Tuanthal and Cadfan. "I intend to tempt the Saxons into attacking. We will leave the bodies of the guards here. There is a ridge a mile away to the south. Take the horsemen there and await my signal. When you see the Wolf Standard raised then charge them. I hope by then that they will be occupied with us. If Garth has arrived by then he can attack on your left flank. Remember when we fought the Hibernians, it was small charges which weakened them. Repeat that tactic now. Miach's archers and Aelle's slingers will harass them but it is you, my equites, who will defeat them. Now go!"

"We will not let you down. You can count on us!"

They rode away and I suddenly felt alone. Lann and I walked slowly back into the fort. "For today, you shall raise the standard but you must wait until I say."

Aelle strode over to meet with us. "Everything is in place."

"Good. I want your ten best warriors here ready to slam shut the gate on my command. I want the Saxons committed to the charge before we launch our horses."

Aelle looked doubtful. "It is a risk brother."

"Life is a risk but we are trusting Tuanthal and Hogan and I believe they will not let us down. The Saxons have not met us with our lances and maces yet. They will get a shock."

Aelle shook his head. "I still cannot understand how this has happened. The recruits never left the island."

"They did not need to. The date was the key. We hold the festival at the same time each year. Aelfraed and his confederates would have been ordered to eliminate the guards. They would not have known about the towers; that was Aelfraed being clever. The Saxons would have known that many of the guards would be drunk on this night. They have planned this carefully but, with the help of the Allfather, we will prevail."

Dawn was not far away when I saw a shadow moving from the east. I knew that it was the Saxons. I hissed a warning. "It is the Saxons. Await my signal before you show yourselves." They moved quickly and it was strange to see the sun begin to peep over Wyddfa and show the enemy, almost as though the mountain was now on our side. I took it as a good omen. There looked to be well over five hundred, perhaps even a thousand warriors who came across the rolling land quite quickly. There was no order to them. They thought that the Burgh was theirs for they could see the gaping gate. "Lann Aelle, take off your helmet, stand and wave them on."

Lann had blond hair and might be taken for Aelfraed. Certainly it would encourage them. He played the part well and I saw a wave in return.

"Steady!" I waited until they were forty paces from the gate and I roared, "Now!" The gates slammed shut and then the eighty slingers and archers stood and began to thin out the Saxon lines. The two bolt throwers cracked and whooshed into action cutting swathes of men down. I would not summon the horses until whoever led them had committed them all to the attack. Once the equites had begun the charge then we would not be able to use the bolt throwers. The slingers, archers and bolt thrower crews were already lathered in sweat as they sent missile after missile at the enemy. They had now reached the ditch and I heard the screams as they found our traps. The men on the walls now began to hurl down the huge rocks we had readied and they killed any who survived the arrows, stones and caltrops.

Aelle rushed over to me. "They have surrounded us on three sides and the ships are approaching the fourth."

"Then shift the crews of these bolt throwers to the ones on the seaward side. We will launch the cavalry soon. You take charge of the seaward side brother. Destroy their ships!"

"With pleasure! The sea shall run red with Saxon blood."

I turned to Lann Aelle. "Ready nephew?" He nodded eagerly. "Unfurl the banner but keep it hidden until I tell you and then wave it from side to side until you see Hogan."

I drew Saxon Slayer. I wanted the enemy to know who they fought and to focus on the banner and me. I did not want them to see the line of horsemen who would be hurtling towards them. I could see that there had been about a thousand Saxons but it was now less than eight hundred and I decided that the time was right. "Now Lann!" As he stood I roared over the ramparts. "Saxons flee or die! I am your nemesis, I am the Warlord of Rheged." I thrust my blade into the air. "I am Saxon Slayer!"

It was like Myrddyn's Greek Fire. The Saxons seemed to erupt like a volcano in an attempt to get at me. Miach, who was next to me, said, without taking his eyes from his target. "Let's hope your son gets here before they tear the walls down!"

It was then that I both saw and heard the equites as the silver line galloped towards the unsuspecting Saxons. The dragon wail attracted their attention first but by the time they had turned Tuanthal and his horsemen were less that fifty paces away. Hogan and his lancers were at the centre, leaning forwards and the leading Saxons seemed to be transfixed with terror. "My lord!"

I looked to Lann who was pointing at the warrior being hoisted over the ramparts by his comrades. I swung Saxon Slayer which took his head in one blow. It rose in the air to crash down on the men near to the gate. I heard the crunch as the line of horses, spears and lances struck the Saxon line. It disappeared and they were into the heart of the Saxons. I saw a silver mace rise and fall and knew that it was my son. I leaned over the wall to stab at the neck of the next warrior who was climbing. One of them threw his spear and suddenly Aelle's buckler deflected it harmlessly off to the side. "Thank you Lann! That was well done."

A young slinger ran to me. "My, lord the ships are landing more men!"

"Miach take half of your archers and support the north wall."

My equites had to finish these Saxons quickly; we could not fight on two fronts without Garth's men. I quickly looked to the west but could see no sign of them and then I heard a wail from the east and, in the distance, I saw Prince Pasgen leading his equites with Aedh whipping his horse to reach us. "Help is at hand! Fight for your lives. On equites! On!"

Lann jabbed the banner like a spear and pushed a warrior who was pulling himself up to crash on to the warriors below. The equites of Tuanthal were now withdrawing ready to charge again. I could see that their horses were tired but the Saxons looked even more exhausted. Then I saw the welcome sight of two hundred mailed warriors trotting along behind Garth, my shield wall had arrived. I ran along the ramparts to the corner nearest them. Garth began to form them into a wedge. I cupped my hands and yelled. "Attack the men on the beach." To emphasise the point I gestured to my right and Garth nodded. He took his lethal weapon off around the side of the fort. They cut through the Saxons who stood in their way. They simply walked over them. Tuanthal led his men in another charge. There were fewer of them but they were still a formidable sight. I saw Prince Cadfan with his sword held before him and his shield, with the red dragon upon it, to the right of my son. They made a noble picture; the dragon and the wolf! At the same time Prince Pasgen had formed his men into a line and they charged too.

"Lann come with me." I led Lann around to the north wall. I could see that this warband was not as big but there were no ditches on the seaward side. Aelle and Miach were struggling to hold them and they were already clambering over the walls. The warriors at the corner were looking to the centre and had not seen me as I ran at them. I held my sword before me and made no attempt to swing it. I struck the six of them putting my entire weight behind my shield. My sword pierced the side of one of them and three of them fell to their deaths in the yard below. Lann stabbed with his seax into the neck of the Saxon who lay on his back while I struck the edge of my shield down on the throat of the last one. He died quickly. I looked down the line. The Saxons were climbing on shields to clamber up the walls but Garth and his men came like an arrow between the sea and the fort. Once they struck then the sting would be gone from the attack. I looked out to sea. Three of the boats had either been sunk or damaged by the bolt throwers and I saw our own four ships sailing from the east and from the west. They would be trapped between our forces soon.

As I scanned the lines of Saxons I realised that I could not see their king. After his defeat by King Iago he must have decided to become more cautious. As Garth and his men sliced into the side of the Saxons they began to stream west. Miach and his archers now had easier targets and then Prince Pasgen and his men appeared at the eastern end of the line and completely encircled the Saxons. There was nowhere left for them to go. We had slaughtered the Hibernians who had been forced to swim out to their ships. Here the ships were too far away and under attack themselves, they could not help the stranded Saxons who were dying on the beach. I could see the golden sand become darker as it was dyed with the red Saxon Blood. My warriors were in no mood for leniency and we opened the gates to allow those who had fought on the ramparts to finish off the foe. They were brave warriors and none asked for clemency. They formed small shield walls and were killed by warriors who had better armour, better shields and better weapons. They were also led by warriors who fought alongside them and that made a difference.

I had not seen anyone making the decisions and I wondered if Aelfraed, the nephew of the king had been their leader. If so they had made a major error of judgement. The leader should lead the men. I had seen Aelfraed lead and fight. He could have inspired his warriors but he now lay dead in my castle. *Wyrd*! By noon the tide was taking the bodies out to sea and the gulls were feasting on the body parts. We had won. Many of our men and horses lay dead but the Saxon threat was gone, at least for the time being.

As the day drew to a close I could be happy in the knowledge that, despite the losses we had suffered, we had beaten all three of our enemies and we were, at least for the time being safe from threat and safe from attack. When the spring came we would be even stronger and we could begin to reclaim the land of Britannia. I now felt like the Dux Britannica. Hogan, Cadfan and Pasgen all joined me on the beach along with Tuanthal, Aelle, Miach and Garth. Their bloodied armour showed that they had all fought hard and had survived.

"This day we have shown that we are an army which is worthy of the name Roman. The Saxons use it as a term of insult but to me it is a term of honour. Today you have all shown that you are great leaders. Look at our enemies and know that they died not because they were poor warriors or because of their blood but because they were badly led. We will not lose because we do not have bad leaders and, no matter where we were born we are all Wolf Warriors!"

Tired though they were, they all, men and leaders alike, began banging their shields and chanting, "Wolf Warrior!"

The End

Glossary

Characters in italics are fictional

Name-Explanation

Aedh-Despatch rider and scout
Aelfere-Northallerton
Aelfraed-Saxon volunteer
Aella-King of Deira
Aelle-Monca's son and Lann's step brother
Aethelfrith-King of Bernicia and Aethelric's overlord
Aethelgirth-Saxon volunteer
Aethelric-King of Deira (The land to the south of the Tees)
Aidan-Priest from Metcauld
Alavna-Maryport
Ambrosius-Headman at Brocavum
Artorius-King Arthur
Banna-Birdoswald
Belatu-Cadros-God of war
Beli ap Rhun-King of Gwynedd until 599
Bellatrix-Gallic Warrior
Bhru-Bernician warrior
Bladud-King Urien's standard bearer
Blatobulgium-Birrens (Scotland)
Bremetennacum-Ribchester
Brocavum -Brougham
Caedwalestate-Cadishead near Salford
Caergybi-Holyhead
Civitas Carvetiorum-Carlisle
Cynfarch Oer-Descendant of Coel Hen (King Cole)
Dai ap Gruffyd-Prince Cadfan's squire
Delbchaem Lann-Lann's daughter
Din Guardi-Bamburgh Castle
Dunum-River Tees
Dux Britannica-The Roman British leader after the Romans left (King Arthur)

Erecura-Goddess of the earth
Fanum Cocidii-Bewcastle
Felan-Irish pirate
Freja-Saxon captive and Aelle's wife
Gareth-Harbour master Caergybi
Garth-Lann's lieutenant
Gildas-Urien's nephew
Glanibanta-Ambleside
Gwynfor-Headman Caergybi
Gwyr-The land close to Swansea
Halvelyn-Helvellyn
Haordine-Hawarden Cheshire
Hen Ogledd-Northern England and Southern Scotland
Hogan-Father of Lann and Raibeart
Hogan Lann-Lann's son
Iago ap Beli-King of Gwynedd 599-613
Icaunus-River god
King Gwalliog-King of Elmet
King Ywain Rheged-Eldest son of King Urien
Lann-A young Brythonic warrior (Lann means sword in Celtic)
Llofan Llaf Difo-Bernician warrior-King Urien's killer
Loge-God of trickery
Loidis-Leeds
Maiwen-The daughter of the King of Elmet
Metcauld-Lindisfarne
Miach-Leader of Lann's archers
Monca-An escaped Briton and mother of Aelle
Morcant Bulc-King of Bryneich (Northumberland)
Mungo-Leader of the men of Strathclyde
Myrddyn-Welsh wizard fighting for Rheged
Niamh-Queen of Rheged
Nithing-A man without honour
Nodens-God of hunting
Osric-Irish priest
Oswald-Priest at Castle Perilous
Pol-Equite and Lann's standard bearer
Prestune-Preston Lancashire
Prince Cadfan Ap Iago-Heir to the Gwynedd throne
Prince Pasgen-Youngest son of Urien

Radha-Mother of Lann and Raibeart
Raibeart-Lann's brother
Rhydderch Hael-The King of Strathclyde
Ridwyn-Bernician warrior fighting for Rheged
Roman Bridge-Piercebridge (Durham)
Solar-West facing room in a castle
Sucellos-God of love and time
The Narrows-The Menaii Straits
Tuanthal-Leader of Lann's horse warriors
Urien Lann-Son of Lann
Urien Rheged-King of Rheged
Vindonnus-God of hunting
Wachanglen-Wakefield
wapentake-Muster of an army
Wide Water-Windermere
Wyddfa-Snowdon
Wyrd-Fate

Maps

Courtesy of Wikipaedia

Britain in the late 6th Century

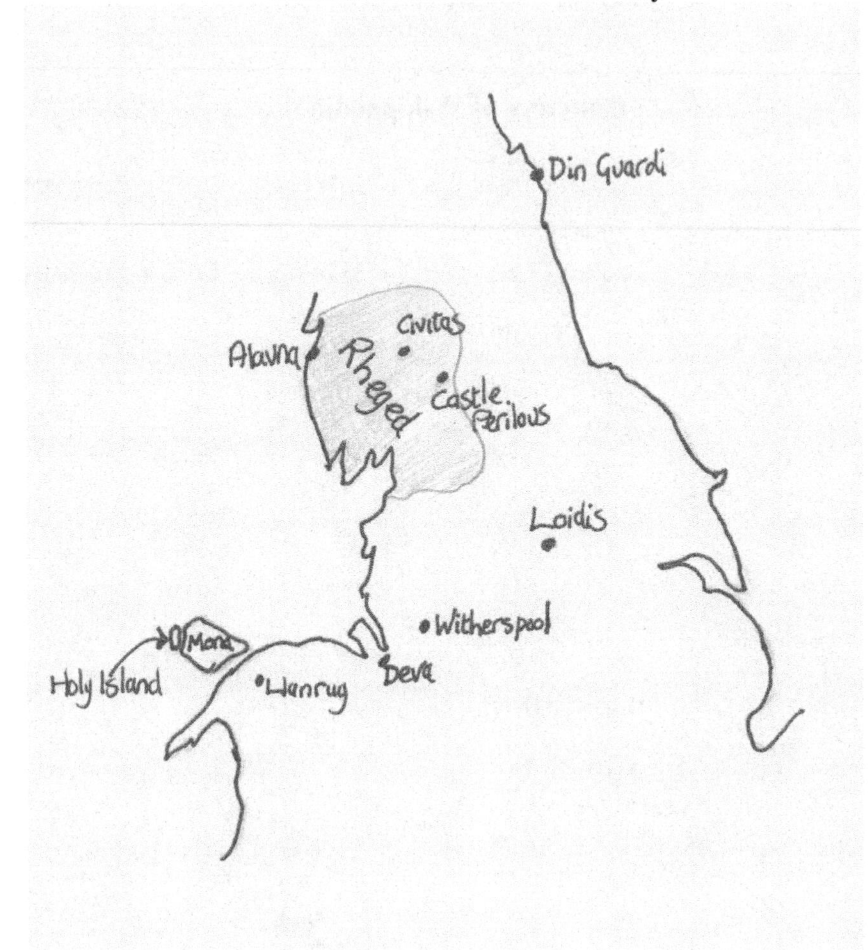

Map by the author

Holy Island (Mona)

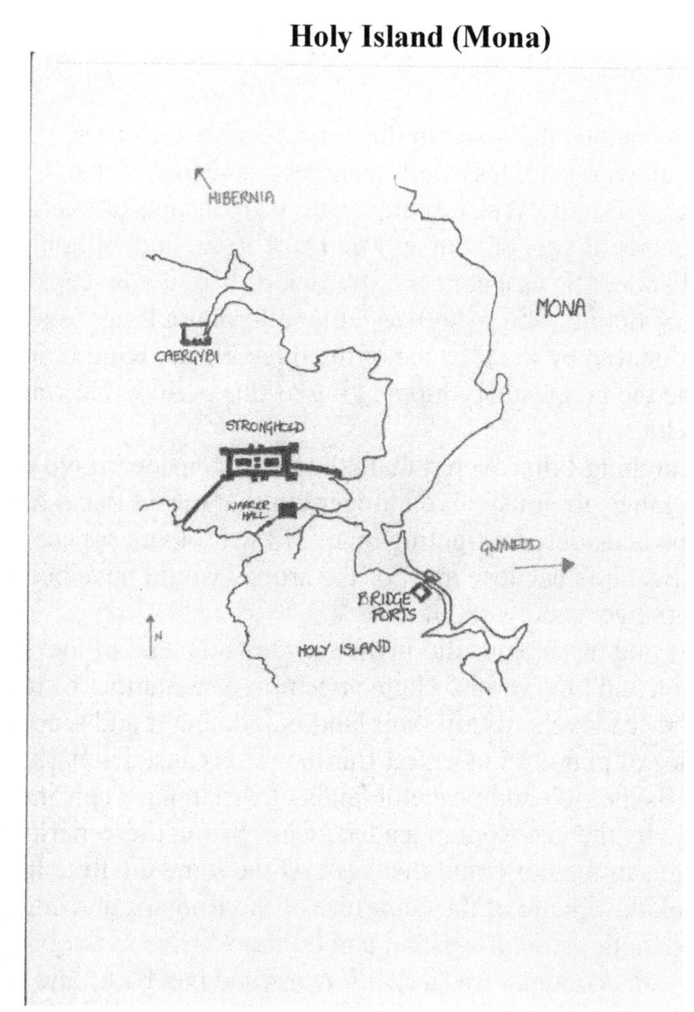

Map by the author

Historical Note

All the kings named and used in this book were real figures, although the actual events are less well documented. Most of the information comes from the Welsh writers who were also used to create the Arthurian legends. It was of course, ***The Dark Ages***, and, although historians now dispute this as a concept, the lack of hard evidence is a boon to a writer of fiction. Ida, who was either a lord or a king, was ousted from Lindisfarne by the alliance of the three kings. King Urien was deemed to be the greatest Brythionic king of this period. He was succeeded by Aella.

While researching I discovered that 30-35 was considered old age in this period. The kings obviously lived longer but that meant that a fifteen-year-old would be considered a fighting man. If the brothers appear young then I suspect it is because most of the armies would have been made up of the younger men without ties.

The Angles and the Saxons did invade towards the end of the Roman occupation and afterwards. There appear to be a number of reasons for this: firstly the sea levels rose in their land inundating it and secondly there were a series of plagues in Central Europe. This caused a mass movement towards the rich and peaceful lands of Britannia. Their invasion was also prefaced by the last Roman leaders using Saxon mercenaries to fight the barbarians to the north and the west. At the same the time Irish and the Scots took advantage of the departure of the Romans and engaged in slave raids and cattle raids. It was not a good time to live in the borders.

Carlisle, by all accounts, was a rich fortress and had baths and fine buildings. The strong room in the Praetorium is a fact. There is an excellent one at Corbridge, which is what gave me the idea. There are steps down and it could accommodate ten men; three would have not posed a problem. Carlisle exceeded York at this period as a major centre. Rheged stretched all the way from Strathclyde down to what is now northern Lancashire. Northumbria did not exist but it grew from two British kingdoms which became Saxon, Bernicia and Deira. This eventually became the most powerful kingdom in Britain until the rise of Alfred's Wessex. Who knows what might have happened had Rheged survived?

Morcant Bulc was king of Bernicia and he was jealous of King Urien who was considered the last hope of Romano-Britain. All of the writings we have from this period come from Wales which is the distance from Rheged and perhaps they were jaundiced opinions. In the years at the end of the Sixth century the kingdoms all fell one by one. Rheged was one of the last to fall.

I do not subscribe to Brian Sykes' theory that the Saxons merely assimilated into the existing people. One only has to look at the place names and listen to the language of the north and north western part of England. You can still hear anomalies. Perhaps that is because I come from the north but all of my reading leads me to believe that the Anglo-Saxons were intent upon conquest. The Norse invaders were different and they did assimilate but the Saxons were fighting for their lives and it did not pay to be kind. The people of Rheged were the last survivors of Roman Britain and I have given them all of the characteristics they would have had. This period was also the time when the old ways changed and Britain became Christian but I have not used this as a source of conflict but rather growth.

There was a battle of Chester, when the Saxons finally claimed the whole of England but this was fifteen years after my story. Beli ap Rhun was king of Gwynedd at the end of the sixth century. Asaph was the bishop at the monastery of St. Kentigern (Aka St. Mungo) and they named the town after him. Julius Agricola swam horses and men across the straits between Wales and Anglesey four hundred years earlier and I thought that Lann could do the same. There is no evidence that Ywain succumbed to the Saxons but Prince Pasgen did rule, briefly in Rheged. The Bishop of the monastery of St Kentigern was called Asaph and he did become a saint. Bishop Asaph was the second bishop at the monastery and town which now bears his name. He did die at the end of the sixth century as did King Beli who was slain by Saxons. His monastery did survive quite well against raids by Saxons and the Irish. I have used Lord Lann as the protector of the monastery; it seemed as plausible a story as any.

King Iago did succeed King Beli and his son was Cadfan. I did not learn much about them when I researched other than when they died. I have given them their attributes as they fitted in with my story line. For all that I know King Iago was a good king but I couldn't resist casting him as the baddie! King Aethelfrith did capture Chester in 613 and King Iago died in the same year; the writings of the time say he was killed in battle.

Phocas did become Emperor at the end of the Sixth Century and he was an officer. He was very unpopular and like many military leaders a tyrant but it suited by story to have him making overtures to Lord Lann.

I mainly used two books to research the material. The first was the excellent Michael Wood's book "***In Search of the Dark Ages***" and the second was "***The Middle Ages***" Edited by Robert Fossier. I also used Brian Sykes book, "***Blood of the Isles***" for reference. In addition, I searched on line for more obscure information. All the place names are accurate, as far as I know and I have researched the names of the characters. My apologies if I have made a mistake.

Griff Hosker August 2013

Other books

by

Griff Hosker

If you enjoyed reading this book, then why not read another one by the author?

Ancient History

The Sword of Cartimandua Series (Germania and Britannia 50A.D. – 130 A.D.)

Ulpius Felix- Roman Warrior (prequel)
Book 1 The Sword of Cartimandua
Book 2 The Horse Warriors
Book 3 Invasion Caledonia
Book 4 Roman Retreat
Book 5 Revolt of the Red Witch
Book 6 Druid's Gold
Book 7 Trajan's Hunters
Book 8 The Last Frontier
Book 9 Hero of Rome
Book 10 Roman Hawk
Book 11 Roman Treachery
Book 12 Roman Wall
Book 13 Roman Courage

The Aelfraed Series (Britain and Byzantium 1050 A.D. - 1085 A.D.

Book 1 Housecarl
Book 2 Outlaw
Book 3 Varangian

The Wolf Warrior series (Britain in the late 6th Century)

Book 1 Saxon Dawn
Book 2 Saxon Revenge
Book 3 Saxon England
Book 4 Saxon Blood
Book 5 Saxon Slayer
Book 6 Saxon Slaughter
Book 7 Saxon Bane
Book 8 Saxon Fall: Rise of the Warlord

Book 9 Saxon Throne

The Dragon Heart Series
Book 1 Viking Slave
Book 2 Viking Warrior
Book 3 Viking Jarl
Book 4 Viking Kingdom
Book 5 Viking Wolf
Book 6 Viking War
Book 7 Viking Sword
Book 8 Viking Wrath
Book 9 Viking Raid
Book 10 Viking Legend
Book 11 Viking Vengeance
Book 12 Viking Dragon
Book 13 Viking Treasure
Book 14 Viking Enemy
Book 15 Viking Witch
Bool 16 Viking Blood
Book 17 Viking Weregeld
Book 18 Viking Storm
Book 19 Viking Warband
Book 20 Viking Shadow

The Norman Genesis Series
Rolf
Horseman
The Battle for a Home
Revenge of the Franks
The Land of the Northmen
Ragnvald Hrolfsson
Brothers in Blood
Lord of Rouen
Drekar in the Seine

The Anarchy Series England 1120-1180
English Knight
Knight of the Empress
Northern Knight
Baron of the North
Earl
King Henry's Champion
The King is Dead

Warlord of the North
Enemy at the Gate
Warlord's War
Kingmaker
Henry II
Crusader
The Welsh Marches
Irish War
Poisonous Plots
Prince's Revolt

Border Knight 1190-1300
Sword for Hire
Return of the Knight
Baron's War
Magna Carta

Modern History
The Napoleonic Horseman Series
Book 1 Chasseur a Cheval
Book 2 Napoleon's Guard
Book 3 British Light Dragoon
Book 4 Soldier Spy
Book 5 1808: The Road to Corunna
Waterloo

The Lucky Jack American Civil War series
Rebel Raiders
Confederate Rangers
The Road to Gettysburg

The British Ace Series
1914
1915 Fokker Scourge
1916 Angels over the Somme
1917 Eagles Fall
1918 We will remember them
From Arctic Snow to Desert Sand
Wings over Persia

Combined Operations series 1940-1945
Commando
Raider

Behind Enemy Lines
Dieppe
Toehold in Europe
Sword Beach
Breakout
The Battle for Antwerp
King Tiger
Beyond the Rhine

Other Books
Carnage at Cannes (a thriller)
Great Granny's Ghost (Aimed at 9-14-year-old young people)
Adventure at 63-Backpacking to Istanbul

For more information on all of the books then please visit the author's web site at http://www.griffhosker.com where there is a link to contact him.